Another
Woman's
Child

BOOKS BY KERRY FISHER

The Island Escape
After the Lie
The Silent Wife
The Secret Child
The Woman I Was Before
The Mother I Could Have Been

KERRY
FISHER

Another Woman's Child

Bookouture

Published by Bookouture in 2020

An imprint of Storyfire Ltd.
Carmelite House
50 Victoria Embankment
London EC4Y 0DZ

www.bookouture.com

ISBN: 978-1-83888-847-3
eBook ISBN: 978-1-83888-846-6

To my dad, who taught me about being a good friend.

PROLOGUE

Ginny

I'd never admitted to anyone what happened that night. And I'm a woman who processes her stuff by telling *everyone*. The woman on the supermarket checkout probably knows as much about me as my mum did. It might have confirmed what they all thought of me anyway. The party girl, the good-time girl, the no-surprises-there girl.

I was nearly thirty and long-term love didn't look like it was going to happen for me. And I really wanted kids. So it wasn't what I imagined, nothing like that fairy tale I think we all have in us right from the word go, that there's one unique man out there who, somehow, through a miracle of timing, serendipity, God's will or whatever, will stumble across us, realise we're the one and be desperate to combine the best bits of himself with the best bits of ourselves. Preferably when we're financially stable with a good idea which direction life is heading in.

No. I can categorically say that little fairy tale disappeared quicker than the trail of Hansel and Gretel's breadcrumbs. But once I knew I was pregnant – and it took me a bit of time, helloooo, Ginny, wake up girl! – I kind of made peace with the fact that what happened that night was a secret I'd have to take to my grave. That no one could ever know.

Ironic really that I've been saved from decades of secret holding by dropping dead at forty-seven (unless I learn to walk on water) rather than at the ninety-five I'd hoped for. But, of course, that's a double-edged sword. I'm the only one who can tell Victor the facts about his dad. But should I? Will it help him? Will he want to know?

It's funny the thoughts I'm having. I'm even sort of glad Mum died early so she hasn't had to live through me dying too. She'd probably have added that to the list of things I'd done to let the family down. She'd already had to bear the disappointment that I didn't become a lawyer. 'I'm still writing about the truth, Mum. Journalists do investigate things, just in a different way.' I'd nearly curled up and died when Mum had rushed out to buy five copies of the first magazine I'd worked for, only to discover that my contribution was interviewing women about their favourite sex toys. 'You are a disgrace to this family.' Nonetheless, she told all her friends I was 'a very important writer'.

Her disappointment about Victor still hurt me though. 'A baby? With a white man?' As though skin colour was the thing that mattered above whether the father had been a kind and decent person with good morals passing down his DNA. I'd phoned her from Canada, warming her up with the excellent news of my promotion to publishing editor of two prestigious women's magazines. It didn't quite have the effect I was hoping for, as her response was: 'Why couldn't you get a job at the BBC?' It had been so tempting to bang the phone down and not tell her my other bit of 'news'. I couldn't back away from it though. It was one of those now-or-never conversations. Delaying wouldn't change the outcome of my mother's reaction and I needed the grey cloud of doom hanging over me to dissipate, so that my baby didn't absorb disappointment into his bones before he'd even left the womb.

I'd been hanging onto the fact that as she'd been asking me since the day after I graduated when I was going to get married – 'I don't want to be too old for grandchildren!' – that she might overlook the lack of wedding ring and celebrate the baby. But she'd done a whole dramatic wail down the phone. 'You have finished me. You want to kill me.'

I'd ended the conversation promptly. The evening ahead, the pinnacle of my career so far, should have been a grand excuse for champagne celebrations. Instead, I sat huddled up, drinking green tea in my armchair, imagining Mum and Dad's faces, struggling to adjust to welcoming my white husband into the family. For the time being, it was better than imagining the disbelief that would follow as they adjusted to not welcoming any husband at all into the family.

When I finally confessed months later that there was no Mister in the picture, Mum sniffed and said, 'Let's hope the baby don't turn out too white.'

In the event, my beautiful boy had skin several shades lighter than mine and the bluest of eyes, but, to my mother's relief, was 'still more black than white'. When I admitted defeat and came back from Canada when he was two months old, Mum couldn't resist him. I needed family to help me. By the time he was six months old, my mother had put herself in charge of two very important roles: making sure he ate pounded yam and egusi soup and never missed church.

The best thing of all as far as she was concerned was that for the rest of her days, she could blame any bad behaviour on his whiteness. When he refused to latch on, fussed and fretted until Mum and I had practically worn out her hall carpet pacing up and down, regurgitated his milk all over her sofa, her only comment was, 'It's the Canadian blood in him.' She never asked me about his dad directly. For all I know, she convinced herself that Victor was the ultimate proof that the Virgin Mary wasn't just a fluke.

Thank God my brother, Gabriel, provided her with the big wedding she'd hankered after, though with the peachiest, creamiest, most English-looking blonde you could conjure up, rather than the Nigerian daughter-in-law she'd been rooting for. 'What is it with you two?'

Gabe had emigrated to Australia shortly afterwards, but at least he had the good grace to qualify as an engineer – a fact she would bring out every time she got on the bus. 'You got a lot of smoke coming out that exhaust. My son could sort that. He's an engineer.' I never witnessed this statement leading to any respect from the Cardiff bus drivers, who were more interested in hurrying her through the relentless counting out of her twenty pences, but you had to hand it to her, it didn't stop her trying. Again. And again.

Dad asked me about Victor's father once, when I knew the cancer had spread. I nearly buckled. It wasn't the sort of question my dad threw out indiscriminately, unlike my mum, who had flung out queries like background noise – 'So what did that Canadian say? What excuse did he give for not marrying you?' – without seeming to require a response. No. Dad really wanted to know. He had braced himself for the answer. For how bad it might be.

But I couldn't allow anything to taint Victor. I'd looked him in the eye with a supreme effort of will. 'I don't think knowing that is going to help you, Dad.'

His insistence that this was a good time to come clean wobbled me. Not least because although I'd come to terms with the fact that I was going to die, if Dad was asking me, it meant he had admitted it too. And the tiny little glimmer of hope I'd held in my heart faded. If Dad with his supreme belief in God and his power to come up with a miracle cure had given up on me, then I really had to accept my time had come.

It didn't stop me wanting to control what I left behind though. What people thought of me. How they viewed my memory. But maybe I had to admit defeat and let people judge the way they wanted to. Victor never asked who his dad was any more. No one did. But he probably had a right to know, even if the answer wasn't what anyone wanted.

CHAPTER ONE

Twenty-five years of Ginny as a best friend and I was still late for her funeral. My husband, Patrick, and I tried to creep into the little church near Cardiff Bay without disturbing the service. My sixteen-year-old daughter, Phoebe – never knowingly under-entranced – banged the door shut with such a clatter, one of the candles at the back of the church blew out.

Ginny's father, Tayo, glanced round. It took me a moment to recognise him. He'd been such a big man, a robust engine of noise and merriment, now huddled, frail and grey in a wheelchair. I didn't make eye contact, didn't raise a hand in apology. I wanted to hide, to pretend I wasn't with Phoebe, that I hadn't brought up a child who would behave like this, today of all days. But, most of all, I didn't want to see his pain.

Despite our friend, Cory, gesticulating discreetly that he'd saved us seats at the front, we shuffled into a pew at the back. I couldn't face clacking down the aisle, past the rainbow of people who'd followed Ginny's orders to wear something colourful. Patrick had the brightest neon-pink tie; I'd dug out one of my maxi dresses, the closest I got to bright, in grey and turquoise, more fitting for a day at the beach than a funeral.

Despite my protestations that it was bad manners and plain wrong to ignore the wishes of the deceased, Phoebe had gone full Hollywood grieving widow, the black lacy dress and pillbox hat complete with endless posing and primping until Ginny's funeral felt less like a tragedy and more like an eBay shopping opportunity. I'd suggested a bright top and a knee-length skirt she'd worn for work experience. 'Mum, I can't wear that. I'm a sixteen-year-old girl, not a forty-five-year-old granny auditioning for a part as a nun.' And suddenly, time was marching on, and we had to leave. And as always, Phoebe got her own way.

The cool wood did nothing to soothe the heat emanating from my body. I breathed deeply, trying to concentrate on the vicar's words that would never – could never – calm my rage that Ginny had died so young. And more quickly than we'd bargained for. In fact, we'd discovered we didn't have any bargaining power at all. Neither did Ginny, despite her resilience and determination and her endless waving away of our concern. 'You were always such a pessimist, Jo. I'm not going anywhere yet.'

But even the mighty will of Ginny, and along with it, the big bark of her laugh, had dwindled to a whimper during April and May. The call we hadn't expected for at least another couple of months dragged us from our sleep around five-thirty; Victor's Welsh accent more pronounced with the emotion of delivering the news in the early hours of that June morning. The sky was already light and disrespectful in the climb towards summer, with all its promise of long evenings and conversations under a balmy sky. It felt so much more obscene than slipping away on a grey January day when the sun struggled to make it over the treeline.

I lost the first ten minutes of the service to overcoming my embarrassment at our entrance. It wasn't until Victor walked to the front that I was able to focus on the words rather than the disapproval of everyone around me that Phoebe's push-up bra was visible through the lace of her dress. She might as well have broadcast to the world that she'd been caught on video up to no good outside the chemistry labs at school with Ryan Baker. I had no intention of introducing her to Ginny's dad.

Patrick sighed beside me as Victor took a moment to steady himself and began to speak, quietly at first, then with greater conviction as though he thought Ginny could hear him.

My heart squeezed with sadness, with anger, that this seventeen-year-old boy would never be carefree again. Never have that naïve certainty that whatever happened, whatever went wrong, there would always be a solution. Sometimes there just wasn't and the good guys lost out.

There was something so gentle in his words. He wasn't speaking to impress us or out of duty. He'd gathered up all that love Ginny had poured into him over the years and held it in his heart to give him strength to pay tribute to her. He looked handsome, even in his distress, his white shirt standing out against his dark skin, his body held with the same poise and elegance Ginny had possessed.

Next to me, in perfect contrast, was Phoebe, slouching away, her face set as though she was locked in a battle with her hands to resist pulling out her phone and checking her Instagram likes. Nothing about her suggested she understood the magnitude of losing a parent. If anything, she looked like she was weighing up the bonus of missing a day of school against the inconvenience of having to be around me when I was crying so hard I kept making little squeaks of grief. I waited for a flicker of sympathy, some sign that in extreme circumstances she could see beyond herself, recognition that losing my best friend deserved a suspension of hostility for the time it took to bury Ginny and scoff down a couple of cheese straws. But my wait was in vain.

Three more months and Ginny would have made Victor's eighteenth birthday at the end of September. She'd been determined, wouldn't countenance the idea she wouldn't be here, refused point blank to discuss moving to a hospice at any stage. The last time I'd seen her, five days before she died, she'd been propped up on the sofa, relishing the sun streaming in through the French windows. Her fading strength was a contrast to the vigour of her garden, to the warmth, the dazzle and the promise of these days. Just a few metres away, her garden was vibrant with fat roses, the marigolds spangled their orange bursts in the borders. And the lavender. She loved her lavender; it spilled out of the terracotta pots and flopped over the path. 'You see, Joanna, got myself a piece of Provence right here in Cardiff.' I still thought we had more time, that we'd be able to take up the promise of fragrant evenings where we might even be able to sit with a glass of champagne – 'It's wasted on me, I've got a cheap palate,' Ginny would say. But it wasn't wasted on her. She was worth every bubble.

My heart ached for how much more there'd still been to say, to give each other. I'd had confidence, that rare faith, the sort that comes along once or twice in a lifetime, that Ginny always had my back. Not in a 'when it's convenient for me' sort of way, but in the most important way of all – 'when it's not convenient for me'. I could tell her my most undignified, humiliating or petty thoughts and know she'd never hold them against me. Gloriously, she would defend me against any detractors when – especially when – I was wrong.

I felt the familiar swill of guilt, that I'd dithered when it was my turn to be a warrior on her behalf. I hadn't squeezed her hand and said, 'Of course, Victor can come and live with us. Don't even think about it.' When she'd needed me most, I'd allowed Patrick to derail me.

When I'd first broached the subject, he'd thought I was joking. 'You're not serious, are you? We can't even keep Phoebe on the right track, let alone a kid who's missed a great big chunk of school and recently lost his mum. Not to mention the fact that we're both flat out at work. It's just not practical to spread ourselves even more thinly.'

'But who would be better placed to help Victor? We've got a long history with Ginny. We both know her really well, we'll have some idea what she would think was right for him.'

'Did she make an attempt to track down his dad?'

I'd blown up at him, something that had taken me years to have the courage to do. 'You'd rather see him shipped off to a "dad" he knows nothing about in Canada, someone who, as far as I can make out, was the "real thing this time" until he turned out to be married? How is that going to help Victor, bursting in on a family with a wife who probably has no idea he even exists? He's only going to be living with us for two years, then he'll be off to university.'

Patrick kept shaking his head, the argument coming as it did on the end of several months of Phoebe's plummeting grades and far too many humiliating meetings with the headmistress that had not gone unnoticed by the other parents in our little village with kids at the same school. 'What about her brother? Her dad?'

'Her brother lives in Australia! Victor's probably met him twice in his life. Ginny said he's hardly been in touch at all, so I don't think he's rushing to guarantee Victor's future. And her dad lives in a sitting room converted into a bedroom because he can't get up the stairs. Victor would end up being his carer – and he's done enough of that already.'

'Surely there's someone better than us. We're not exactly best placed to make sure he keeps his culture and traditions. We never go to church and I know you're a good cook but you're not going to make the same stuff as Ginny.'

He knew as well as I did that was a low blow. Of course there were things we'd do differently but I was pretty sure that would be the same with any family Victor ended up with. Yes, Ginny loved going back to her parents' on a Sunday for obe ata, Jollof rice and plantain. And we all begged her to make suya chicken skewers with her secret recipe of spices, despite Cory teasing her that she was just fobbing us off with 'Nigerian KFC'. But alongside her traditional dishes, she was also a great fan of pesto pasta and Greek salad. And we had a church practically next door to us, so I couldn't see how that aspect of Victor's life would be so difficult to manage. But nothing I said seemed to convince Patrick.

Throughout spring, Ginny pressed me for an answer, then, as she got weaker and weaker, seemed to take it for granted that I'd agreed. Meanwhile, Patrick and I batted the same arguments backwards and forwards without reaching a conclusion, old hurts resurrected and aggravated.

'You were prepared to spend a fortune on IVF trying to have a sibling for Phoebe and now you won't accept one that's ready-made and, in case you hadn't noticed, an orphan. It might be good for our daughter to have another child in the house. She might behave a bit better if all of our attention isn't on her.'

He'd looked at me. 'Jo, there was no obvious reason why you couldn't get pregnant again, I thought it was worth a try. Anyway, a baby of our own or an almost adult from a completely different family, and bereaved to boot, are two entirely separate things.'

And when I tried to discuss the idea with Phoebe, she just dismissed it as one of my crazy notions, a passing whim, before standing back in horror when she realised I was serious. 'Have him live here full-time and go to my school? That would be so embarrassing.'

But when Ginny died more quickly than we expected, I'd put my foot down. 'He's coming here. We can't let him down.' Reluctantly and with an attitude of 'on your head be it', Patrick agreed, as long as I promised to review the arrangement after six months. Phoebe greeted the news with a sulky 'don't expect me to entertain him' and slammed out of the room every time I tried to reassure her that I'd do whatever I could to make it as easy for her as possible. It took me all my strength not to yell that it wasn't what I wanted either, that, shamefully, I wished there was someone else who could step in. The fact remained though that I couldn't live with myself if I let a boy who'd already lost so much forgo the best chance he had of being happy.

It was the right thing. It had to be. We were past the point of no return now.

I pulled my attention back to Victor, standing there at the front, his face contorting with the effort of not crying. I was willing him – *willing* him – to say what he'd planned to say. That she'd been everything to him, that he'd never missed having a dad because his mum had so much personality that he only had to close his eyes to hear her great big booming laugh.

Ginika Yaro would not be going gently into that good night. I tried to imagine her bursting through the gates of heaven, a swirl of magenta and turquoise scarves: 'Here comes the main event,' scooping up the shy and the reticent. Just as she had when she'd burst onto the graduate journalism programme at the magazine where I worked as the editor's PA nearly three decades ago. She'd only been there five minutes, in contrast to my three years, but she was always scooting me down the stairs at lunchtime, introducing me to people, bounding through life as though she expected everyone to love her.

But right now, I couldn't fill my mind with those images. I could only see her, gripping my hand, her big brown eyes pleading, 'Take Victor for me, Joanna. He's not even eighteen yet. He needs someone to rely on.'

I steadied myself on the back of the pew, my eyes flickering from the emerald shawls to the bright orange shirts dotting the congregation as my misgivings swirled in and out. I still couldn't see what else I could have done. He deserved a chance, this boy, whose voice was thick with tears but still strong, still audible, still all those things that Ginny had instilled in him – never thinking that the world owed him, a grafter like her, proud to be who he was.

If Ginny hadn't had the bad luck to die of breast cancer, I would have been properly jealous of her relationship with Victor. I didn't know where I'd gone wrong, because on paper I felt like I'd done everything right: stayed at home when Phoebe was little, still married to her dad. We weren't rushing off to Michelin-starred restaurants every weekend, but Phoebe hadn't had to get a job in a supermarket two evenings a week like some of her friends. Anything other than a robotic delivering of food, clean clothes and cash seemed to irk her. All that giving and providing, the listening and loving and, latterly, the *negotiating every damn thing* hadn't delivered up the great big pay-off I'd expected when the midwife had wrapped her up and placed her into my arms all those years ago.

At a loud sob from me, Patrick put his hand on my arm. He wasn't crying, but his mouth kept twitching. That was probably as much emotion as a bloke who'd been brought up by a mother whose catchphrase was 'Chin up, no one likes a crybaby' could manage. He'd loved Ginny. Like me, she'd made him less serious, more spontaneous. When we'd all worked together in publishing and ended up sharing a flat in Stoke Newington along with Cory, Ginny had been at the heart of it, the planner of parties, the provider of cauldrons of food at short notice.

As Victor's eulogy drew to a close with the words, 'I didn't keep her for long enough, but how lucky I was she was my mum,' I felt pride sitting behind my grief. Pride that I hadn't taken the easy way out, that, in the end, I hadn't let Ginny down. I'd stood up to Patrick and Phoebe and pointed out that given how fortunate we were, we could afford to be a bit generous to Ginny's son.

Victor stumbled down the steps of the platform and I slipped out to meet him and led him back to his pew.

'Well done, love. Your mum would be so proud of you.'

He bowed his head, tears coursing down his face. There was no way I could have packed this poor boy off to Sydney.

I tried to push away the fear that in helping Ginny's family, I'd end up destroying my own.

CHAPTER TWO

Five weeks later, at the end of the summer term, Patrick and I drove to Cardiff to pick up Victor from his granddad's house. I tried to be upbeat as we made slow progress along the motorway, but everything Patrick said, from 'We would have to choose the hottest day of the year to start lugging cases about' to 'Let's not hang about once we've packed everything,' made me feel as though he was just going through the motions of supporting me. I suspected it wouldn't be much of a leap if it all went wrong for the words, 'You were the one who wanted to do this' to rumble through the house.

I failed to hold in the 'I'm sorry Ginny didn't die at a more convenient time of year,' though just managed not to yell, 'Oh for God's sake, just forget it. Turn the car round and we'll let Ginny's eighty-four-year-old dad who needs a carer himself pick up the pieces' in case he took me at my word.

I'd always loved the fact that Patrick weighed up the pros and cons of any decision, not least because he did all the boring legwork on pensions and mortgages. I'd been secretly smug when the mums at school moaned about their husbands gambling on the horses, booking ski holidays they couldn't afford or changing jobs on a whim and it all ending in disaster. But today, I would have loved a reckless husband, who said, 'Don't worry, it'll be an adventure.' A man who embraced a bit of chaos, who didn't do an involuntary frown when Phoebe and her friends were shrieking away in the sitting room when he got home from work. Who could just hold my hand and at least pretend we were in this together.

And I didn't feel any more confident when Victor opened the door. He was trying so hard to be polite, to act grateful that we were offering him a home, but there was anger in his movements, the way he slammed his cases down by the car, shoved his assortment of holdalls and carrier bags onto the back seat as though he couldn't care less what he left behind.

As we staggered up and down the garden path laden with lamps, coats and boxes of books, Ginny's dad, Tayo, sat in his wheelchair by the front door, repeating, 'He'll be so much better off with you, with other young people around him.'

But his old eyes were rheumy with emotion, his proud face working every last muscle to produce a smile whenever Victor said, 'You'll be all right, won't you? You'll remember how to FaceTime me?'

Tayo swatted him away, 'You won't be wanting to waste your time with me. You've got all that life to live, son.'

Several times during the packing and unpacking of the boot in order to get everything in, Patrick muttered, 'God knows where we're going to fit all this when we get home.'

Eventually I couldn't resist retaliating by saying, 'Well, now's probably a good time for you to have a clear-out of your shed. Perhaps we could store some of it in there,' before tipping him over the edge by appearing with three rugby balls and two sets of dumbbells.

When we'd crammed the last pair of trainers into the car, I went to say goodbye to Tayo. His hands were bony and cold, but there was no disguising the strength of emotion as he grasped my forearms. 'Keep him safe. Keep him looking forwards. Not backwards.'

I could only nod and hug. I left Patrick to guide Victor back into the house to say goodbye to his granddad, ashamed of falling at the first hurdle by not containing my own grief, let alone helping him manage his.

As I sat in the car waiting for them to reappear, I thought about Ginny, the way she'd fling herself onto her dad whenever I came back home with her, a joyous and noisy entrance, so alien to the way I'd pause outside my mother's front door, braced for an observation about how I'd put on a bit of weight/looked tired/didn't suit my beige coat/yellow dress or needed a fringe.

I cried a bit harder, mourning the loss of her vivaciousness in the world, that energy she had that rubbed off on everyone around her, that made me buy into her philosophy that sleep was for the dead and we really did need another bottle of rosé. If she could see me now bawling my eyes out and searching desperately in the glove compartment for anything that could be used as a tissue, she would have laughed at me. 'God, you'd cry at the crushing of a crisp.'

Then Patrick was shaking Tayo's hand and gently moving Victor down the garden path, past the hydrangeas with their big mop heads and the roses, those flowers that Victor had probably never taken any notice of but would make him think of his granddad every time he came across them.

I did a huge sniff before they reached the car and jumped out to open the door for him. 'Come on, love. We'll bring you back to see your granddad just as soon as you're settled with us.'

Victor sank down into the tiny space in the back, hemmed in by shoes, duvets and a sleeping bag. For all Patrick's moaning, I was pretty sure Phoebe would have had twice as much. Half-finished pots of shampoo, body lotion and fake tan alone would have needed their own suitcase.

I patted his shoulder. 'It's okay to be sad, it's normal,' I said, dissolving into a fresh flood of tears myself.

Patrick gave me a little smile of encouragement. 'Come on, let's get going.'

The journey home was punctuated with both of us scratching about for conversation. Patrick came up with 'Which radio station do you listen to?' He tolerated Victor's choice for about twenty minutes before saying, 'Shall we just have a bit of quiet for a moment?' I defaulted to chat about Phoebe's school where Victor would be joining the sixth form. He answered us, but not in a way that encouraged further discussion. By the time we arrived home, I wanted to lie down and sleep for a week.

By the third week, when Victor had yet to initiate any conversation himself beyond 'Could I have another towel?' I'd begun to dread mealtimes. I felt under pressure to show Victor that he'd come to live with a jolly family, who, alongside our passionate eating of broccoli, avocado and cabbage, engaged in lively debates about the environment, the various merits of politicians and the possibility of an election later on in the year. Instead, Phoebe – while picking the peas out of the shepherd's pie – announced that she was never going to vote because all politicians were idiots. Both Patrick and I waded in with how hard women fought for the right to vote. But rather than convincing Phoebe of her civic responsibility, it just exposed her lack of historical knowledge surrounding the Suffragettes. I might have laughed in an exasperated way before Victor's arrival, but now I felt she was deliberately showing us up. Ginny probably had all sorts of fascinating and intellectually stimulating exchanges with Victor.

When I moaned to Patrick about Phoebe's apparent disinterest in the world, he shrugged. 'You just need to relax and stop trying so hard.'

'Well, who would be trying if I wasn't? We'd all be sitting staring at our plates and counting the grains of rice, for all the effort you and Phoebe make.'

Patrick stared at me. 'Honestly, the boy's just getting used to being here. He's probably way more concerned about how long it will be before he can escape back to his Xbox than he is about any election or Emmeline Pankhurst, for that matter. We shouldn't have to pretend to be anything other than who we are. This is our family, take it or leave it.'

'That's easy for you to say. You're not a seventeen-year-old with nowhere else to go. We do have to adjust a little bit. I don't mean talking politics, but finding ways to include him.' I couldn't escape the sensation that both Patrick and Phoebe were waiting for me to realise that I'd made a bad decision and somehow reverse it.

As he did so often these days, instead of replying, Patrick buried himself in his laptop as though he had fifty-five urgent emails to deal with.

I was desperate to get Victor feeling comfortable at home before he had to run the gauntlet at school in September. I begged Phoebe to include him on trips into town with her friends. 'What's he going to do when we're all trying on stuff in Topshop?'

'Could you, I don't know, go bowling or something?'

She rolled her eyes like I'd suggested a session with Play-Doh. But after much frantic stabbing at her phone and endless video calls, they went, with me throwing ridiculous amounts of money at them for snacks and drinks out of the pure joy of having a few hours without worrying about whether Victor was bored.

Patrick kept saying, 'He's just got to get on with it. We can't be planning events to keep him entertained. We've got to live our lives too.'

Which was great in theory, but really difficult to stick to when I imagined him lying on his bed upstairs, studying the cracks in the ceiling and wishing he could go back to his old life with Ginny, that none of this had ever happened. Worse still was when I overheard him FaceTiming Tayo, with both of them trying to be brave.

Surprisingly, Phoebe provided the watershed. 'We need to paint Victor's room.'

Patrick immediately leapt in with, 'But we only had the decorators in about two years ago.'

Phoebe's head dropped. 'Yes, but, Dad, it's beige. Boring.'

I was so keen to say yes to anything that either Phoebe or Victor showed enthusiasm for, I said, 'What were you thinking?'

Phoebe nodded towards Victor, who looked as though he wished he was somewhere else. 'Well, you're always on about how Victor needs to feel at home, so we thought we'd paint it the colours of the Welsh flag.'

'What, red and green?' Patrick asked, failing to disguise his irritation at the suggestion.

Phoebe clapped her hands together. 'Yes. We'll paint it ourselves. And Niamh said she could paint a dragon on the wall.'

Patrick's forehead wrinkled at the mention of Phoebe's friend, Niamh, as though he was hearing her name for the first time, despite her coming to our house at least twenty times in the past year.

I baulked at the colour scheme. 'Don't you think red and green might be a bit… overpowering? It's not a very big space.'

'I knew you wouldn't let us.' She turned to Victor. 'I told you Mum would spoil it.'

I pushed away the rage that I was getting the blame for saying no, when I was pretty sure Patrick wouldn't agree either. So, in a moment of impulse, I said, 'Why not? If it makes Victor feel at home, then I'm all for it.'

Patrick glared at me. 'Really?'

I nodded with more confidence than I felt and before I could change my mind, they were off on the bus to Homebase, with me shouting, 'Nothing too bright…' after them.

They both came back giggling, with several cans of bright green and red gloss. Patrick took one look and started to tell them that there was no way they were using gloss paint.

However, it was the first time I'd seen any real energy about Victor. His eyes were bright, his face mischievous, as though just for a few minutes he'd forgotten about Ginny.

'Come on, we can paint over it if it's terrible.' I directed myself to Victor, 'Great idea to bring a bit of Wales to our corner of England. Let me just find some old sheets to put down.'

I wanted to show Victor I could be devil-may-care like Ginny. She'd had the knack of suggesting something no one else wanted to do and convincing everyone to join in. She'd dash straight into the sea while we were all debating whether it was warm enough. Insist on a barbecue on a day when the weather looked uncertain and I'd already decided it would be much easier to cook in the oven. But we'd all go along with it and end up having a great time.

And, just once, I wanted Phoebe – and Victor – to think I was that wild mum, completely cool with them transforming his bedroom into a cross between a postbox and a leprechaun lair.

Patrick followed me out. 'You're not going to let those two loose with those disgusting colours, are you? It's going to look like a bloody graffiti crack den.'

I hissed back. 'What have you done to get Victor interested in anything? Anyone can sit on the sidelines carping about what they don't want to happen.'

'Sorry for having an opinion. I'd forgotten that what I want doesn't count for anything these days.'

In that moment, the injustice of that statement transformed itself into a little fantasy about divorce papers landing on the mat, out of the blue, with Patrick standing there saying, 'What? Why?' as I tossed a couple of cases and an airline ticket into the back of a car.

Over the three days that Phoebe and Victor were decorating, Patrick huffed and puffed about 'everyone still needing some boundaries' and 'not being able to give him special dispensation indefinitely'. I veered between wanting to check that the old sheet was covering the carpet right up to the skirting board and feeling like the most liberal mother on the block when Phoebe's friend, Georgia, gasped as she walked in, 'Your mum let you do this? That's so cool!'

The summer wore on in an odd one step forwards, two steps backwards rhythm. Occasionally there'd be a moment that ticked all of my happy family boxes, when, unbidden, Phoebe dug out the Swingball from the garage and, over several days, had a super-competitive tournament with Victor, which even Patrick joined in. But far more often I'd fret about Victor spending too much time in his bedroom – even a bedroom complete with a Welsh dragon that looked like a winged pug. And just when I was beginning to hope Phoebe was forming some kind of bond with Victor, she'd moan about him taking over the TV or being in the way when she wanted to talk to her friends. I also couldn't help wondering if Phoebe's escalating rudeness was the result of having less attention from me.

And simmering through the months was the sense that Patrick was tolerating rather than participating in our expanded family. 'Why don't you ask him to go jogging with you? Exercise is a great way for him to work out his feelings.'

Patrick would wrinkle his nose. 'I just want a bit of time in my own head after being at work all day,' he'd say, which made the line between love and hate feel perilously thin.

On the days when Victor felt like part of the furniture, volunteering to take out the bins, or carrying in the shopping or I'd hear him laughing with Phoebe over a YouTube video, I'd tell myself we'd done the right thing, that we'd all learn from this and come out better people for it. But far more frequently than I could admit even to myself, I felt overwhelmed, ashamed of my irritation at his trainers discarded in the hallway and the toast crumbs all over the work surfaces and increasingly feeling I was failing on more fronts than I'd known existed.

By the end of August, the start of school couldn't come soon enough for me. I couldn't wait to be in an empty house without anyone needing me. I wanted to go to my office, without checking where Victor was, annoying him – though he was too polite to say so – by asking if he wanted any breakfast/lunch/to change his bed/ another blanket. I longed to walk out of the bathroom in my bra, not feel embarrassed about my pants hanging on the washing line, spend half an hour on the phone with Faye, my best friend in the village, telling her – and maybe laughing about – all my shortcomings as a guardian without being overheard. I wanted to be able to miss Ginny and allow myself to be really sad without feeling an obligation to Victor to be cheery and upbeat at all times, instead of infecting him with my grief when he already had so much of his own to bear.

And after a summer of snappy exchanges every time we had to accommodate Victor's needs instead of just thinking about our own, I couldn't deny that I was looking forward to being able to have a long-overdue row with Patrick without worrying about attracting an audience.

CHAPTER THREE

Two and a half months after Ginny's funeral, I lay in bed when the alarm went off, feeling nowhere near old enough to face today: the start of term for Phoebe and Victor. I'd counted down the days to establishing a routine that didn't depend on me as the family master of ceremonies. But now it was here, the task of getting them to school on time without a huge drama – either belligerence from Phoebe or plain broken-hearted reluctance to start afresh from Victor – made me want to stay in bed, eat toast and read my Kindle for the rest of my life.

Seventeen months separated Phoebe and Victor, but they looked years apart. Tall with broad shoulders, Victor was already a man, moving about in the calm, deliberate way that came with adulthood, in contrast to Phoebe's scattering around the house, charging up the stairs with theatrical urgency to a background of shrieks and giggles emanating from her iPhone. I hoped Victor wouldn't find her and her friends horrendously immature now he'd be with them all the time. Especially given he was staying down a year after missing so much education while Ginny was ill.

I counted to three and swung my legs out of bed. I went downstairs and made tea for everyone except Phoebe, who would just launch into a diatribe about how I'd forgotten she was 'intolerant' of cow's milk, or maybe this week soya milk irritated her stomach lining, or almond milk didn't agree with her, followed by an impatient shake of the head. 'I told you!'

Carrying a mug back upstairs, I knocked lightly on Victor's door. 'Tea outside the door.' I didn't dare go in. I had no idea whether he slept naked or not. Probably did if he was anything like Ginny when Patrick, Cory and I lived with her. I'd just about lost the habit of putting my dressing gown on before I went into the kitchen after two years sharing a flat with them all, but I never felt comfortable when the boys were eating toast in just their boxers or Ginny was clutching her coffee in a T-shirt that barely covered her knickers.

A deep baritone rumbled back. 'Thank you.'

'Would you like scrambled eggs for breakfast?'

'Yes please.'

'Come down when you're ready.' At least Victor was more grateful than Phoebe for clean clothes and a cooked dinner.

Patrick wandered out in his boxers.

'Put your dressing gown on,' I hissed for at least the fiftieth time in ten weeks.

He rolled his eyes. It was all over his face – why should I live any differently?

'I don't want Victor to feel any more awkward than he already does. He hasn't grown up with any blokes in the house.'

Patrick shook his head. 'Newsflash. Seventeen-year-old boys don't give a shit what old men wear at the breakfast table.'

But our conversation was cut short by Phoebe bursting onto the landing. 'Where's my iPhone charger?'

I'd set myself the goal of being extra kind to her, to remember that if Patrick and I had found adjusting to our new circumstances hard, it wasn't surprising that we'd had a few outbursts from Phoebe. 'I don't want him hanging around me and my friends all the time!' It was not a goal I always attained.

But this morning I was determined to start off on the right foot. I forced myself to be helpful rather than snap, 'Where did you put it?'

'Have you looked in the kitchen, love? Or maybe by the telly? Try not to be late though, because I've got to take Victor in and introduce him to his teachers.'

Phoebe scowled. 'He's not a toddler. Why does he need introducing? Can't he just go into school on his own? That's so cringe to be taken in by you.'

I hoped Victor couldn't hear her. I ignored her and went downstairs. She wasn't going to help me out on this occasion.

As I made Victor's breakfast, the sadness that Ginny wasn't around to reassure her son as he stepped up to yet another new challenge sat heavily in me. I stirred the eggs, offering some to Patrick as he wandered in with the newspaper. 'I don't think Phoebe is going to smooth Victor's entrance into the world of school.'

Patrick sighed, as if he didn't have the energy to expend on worrying about that particular dynamic.

And with that, Phoebe flounced in, not wearing the expensive suit that she'd persuaded us she had to have for sixth form – 'Everyone is getting a suit and *no one* is getting it from Marks and Spencer' – but a barely-there skirt and a blouse with buttons that gaped.

'Aren't you wearing your new suit?'

'Not today.'

I was becoming a coward. I couldn't face another great big row where we'd end up being late for school. Not on the first day. But I'd really looked forward to joining in with all the other mums, taking photos of the girls starting sixth form. But there was no way I was having her stand next to all of her friends in their posh suits, looking like she'd just escaped from the local pole dancing club. I had hoped today would signal the start of a new era after – contrary to everyone's expectations – she'd done okay in her GCSEs.

The beat of time where she waited to see which way this morning was going to go was broken by Victor coming in, super-smart in a dark suit and pale blue shirt. I smiled at him.

'You look great. Are you nervous?'

He nodded – 'A bit' – and scanned the kitchen table as though looking for confirmation of where he should sit.

I pointed to the place opposite Patrick and put down his breakfast. I willed Patrick to offer up something that might make him feel better about starting a new school, which was daunting for anyone but especially if your mum had been dead less than three months and you were still grappling with the etiquette of whether or not to flush the loo if you got up in the middle of the night in your new home.

Patrick did at least glance up and say, 'I think a routine is good for everyone,' spoilt by the little twitch of irritation that he had to pull *The Times* towards him to make room for Victor's plate.

When Victor finished eating, he went to put his dirty crockery in the dishwasher, but I took it from him. Phoebe raised an eyebrow. If only she understood that I'd feel more inclined to do things for her if she volunteered to help without being nagged into it.

At the last minute, Phoebe decided she couldn't possibly wear the new shoes I'd bought because they were rubbing her heels and 'You forgot to buy any blister plasters.' As the time ticked away, I ran upstairs to find her digging in her wardrobe like a dog on the scent of a long-lost bone for her old shoes that she'd been adamant that she couldn't wear any more because they didn't stay on.

I pushed down the frustration pulsing around my body, embarrassed that Victor was standing by the front door, everything ready. He must wonder what bloody madhouse he'd ended up in. No doubt he'd already be planning to apply to universities in Aberdeen or Plymouth.

'Come on, love. We're going to be late and it's not fair to Victor.'

'What do you suggest? Shall I go barefoot? Or shall I stay at home because I haven't got any shoes to wear?'

The impatience drained out of me, replaced by something cold and steely.

'I'm going to get in the car with Victor. If you're not there in two minutes, you can walk to school. Or not go at all. Or fail your A levels completely and work in Woolworths for the rest of your life.'

'Woolworths? What century do you live in?'

Trust me to choose a shop that had closed down over a decade ago.

I didn't answer, just made my way to the front door, reassuring Victor with 'Phoebe's having a wardrobe crisis. You know what teenage girls are like.' I ushered him out to the car and was backing out of the drive when she came flailing along, barefoot, with a pair of trainers in one hand and an armful of folders in the other. It was so tempting to pretend I hadn't seen her, to savour a quiet moment with Victor when I could put Smooth Radio on without a barrage of criticism about how I must have been born 'in the 1900s' to like this sort of music.

In she scrambled. I fumbled about for some conversation. Anything I could say to Victor about an exciting new beginning seemed hollow and insulting in the face of his loss. I drove to school in a self-conscious babble of 'the nights will start drawing in soon/bet they'll be glad to have you on the rugby team/Phoebe's favourite teacher is Mr Earnshaw, who'll probably be taking you for Chemistry.'

Phoebe was surprisingly compliant. 'Yeah, he brings chocolate biscuits to lessons. He's all right.'

Who knew a chocolate biscuit could make the difference?

When we got to school, Phoebe scuttled off, mumbling, 'Have a good day' to Victor and, yet again, I felt a flash of shame that she couldn't be kinder, put herself out a tiny bit.

I also wished I had some of Ginny's natural affinity with people. 'Jo, honestly, if you ask someone loads of questions and let them talk about themselves till their fingers get cramp around the microphone, they'll think you're the most interesting person they've ever met.'

I'd learnt from her over the time we'd lived together in London, but I still didn't have that innate self-assurance, that certainty that whatever situation came my way, I'd find the right words to handle it. That was painfully obvious now with Victor walking along beside me. I couldn't think of a single thing to help him, to give him courage.

I'd never really noticed how white the school was before as I waved to various acquaintances and friends. It must be so odd walking into an environment where he didn't know anyone and no one looked like him. It wasn't something I'd given much consideration to around Ginny because she'd always seemed so confident about her place in the world. But suddenly, seeing Victor – this seventeen-year-old boy whose certainty about life had already taken such a battering – walk into school with reluctance and resignation in every step made me want to ask him if he was aware of it too, but I didn't know how to phrase it in a way that didn't make me sound weird or racist.

Thank goodness for Mr Sanderson, Head of Sixth Form, coming our way, a smiley bald-headed man who held his hand out and said, 'Victor? Great to have you on board. Sorry you've had such a tough time of it. Come with me and I'll show you around.'

Victor's response nearly undid me. 'Thank you. It's very nice to meet you.' All the teachers would love him because he was so well-mannered. I quickly crushed the thought about them clucking out unfavourable comparisons with Phoebe – 'His real mum did a stunning job'.

Mr Sanderson carried on. 'Mrs Clark tells me you're a great rugby player. That's going to make you very popular. Rugby season starts this Saturday, so we'll have to get you down for a game.'

And with that, they launched into a conversation about which position he played, a rundown on the school's arch rivals, and it was time to take my leave. I wandered back to the car, my heart aching. I had such a clear memory of picking Ginny up from the airport when she moved back from Canada with two-month-old Victor, a few weeks before our wedding. I'd expected her to be knackered. But she glowed, as though she'd been flopping about searching for a purpose in life and dropped right into the bull's eye.

And Victor was much bonnier than I'd envisaged. At nearly two months premature, I'd expected a scrawny, sickly scrap. Instead, he seemed contented and robust.

Ginny had laughed. 'I knew my great big bosoms would be good for something. I'm like a Jersey cow with my super-rich milk. He's piled on the weight.' And she'd nuzzled her face into Victor's little cheek with a relaxed confidence that made me want to applaud her.

As I reached my car, I bumped into Andrea, who had a daughter, Helaina, in Phoebe's class – 'Not Hel-ena. Hel-AINA'. I always felt as though my eyebrows needed plucking whenever she was around.

'How was your summer?' I asked, not because I actually cared if she'd spent it in a tent in the back garden, but because I knew she thought Phoebe was a troublemaker and I wanted to show her that it wasn't my fault, that I was a decent, sensible person with, inexplicably, a difficult child. As soon as the words left my mouth, I knew I was setting myself up for twenty minutes of hearing about her brilliant holiday waterskiing in Croatia, cycling in Provence or whatever other activity her perfect daughter had leapt out of bed to do at seven-thirty every morning. No doubt *Helaina* also repeated, 'Wow, Mum, this is a great holiday, I'm loving every minute', rather than refusing to come in the pool because it made her skin break out.

Actually, it was worse than I'd imagined: Helaina had done a cookery course in Tuscany and now had a glittering certificate that meant she wouldn't have to volunteer in the Rabbit Rescue charity shop to fulfil her Sixth Form Enrichment targets.

Andrea finally paused in the roll call of filial achievements, to say, 'Did you have a good summer?'

I toyed with the idea of saying, 'No, it was entirely shit, my best friend died,' but decided I might either burst into tears and confirm her view that Phoebe's behaviour was her unhinged mother's fault or risk her telling me to download an app 'because meditation is the answer, honestly, you'll feel so much better.'

I shrugged and said, 'Not bad, nice not to be tied to the school run.'

I pointed the fob at my car in a signal that I'd used up the crumb of interest I never had in talking to her in the first place, but she grabbed my arm conspiratorially and said, 'I hear you've added to the family?'

I barely blinked at the fact that Andrea was already party to our news – gossip was the beating heart of our village. 'I've got my best friend's son living with me at the moment.' I didn't want to elaborate, but I wasn't going to escape the town enquirer and font of all community knowledge that easily.

'How long for? Is it permanent?'

'Well, his mum died at the end of June, so…' My voice trailed off, the doubt about whether we could make it work underpinning my words.

'I'm sorry to hear that. Crikey. That's a big change for all of you.'

'It certainly is.' I tried to sound upbeat, as though we were only doing what any normal person would do, but my beat was struggling to find the up after all these weeks of Victor emerging from his room, puffy-eyed but rejecting any entreaty to talk. I was exhausted by the 'family dinners' when Phoebe was openly scornful of my attempts to find common ground. And Patrick was equally annoying, having switched from 'It's early days' to the far more irritating, 'I don't know what you expected.'

Standing in front of someone who knew all about Phoebe's suspension last term for her shenanigans by the chemistry lab did nothing for my self-esteem. I felt obliged to put into words what I was pretty sure Andrea was thinking. 'We're not the obvious choice as foster parents, but there wasn't really any family that he could go to.'

Instead of doing what any normal person would do and waving my comment away with 'He's very lucky to have you', Andrea did a funny little nod of agreement. Although I'd made the joke against myself, I felt the sting of insult as though she'd said, 'You can't bring up your own child, let alone anyone else's.'

'It must be quite an adjustment for Phoebe, being an only child?'

I didn't want to discuss Phoebe with her. I felt guilty enough that I'd forced this upheaval on my daughter, I didn't want Andrea's opinions inserting themselves under the thin carapace of my sanity, like leaflets under the door from charismatic politicians you knew were lying but were almost tempted to vote for. But with half the school community whispering about Phoebe being a wrong 'un, I was determined to put the shiniest spin on our lives.

'She's doing brilliantly, though obviously it's tricky for any teenager. I think she likes having someone closer to her own age around.' Maybe if I peddled this image of our family out loud, it might somehow become reality.

Andrea nodded, but she failed to look entirely convinced. 'What an incredible thing to do. How lovely of you to give him a home.'

'I'm sure you'd do the same,' I said, even though I knew Andrea ran her life on a 'What's in it for me?' basis.

She pulled a face. 'I don't think Rod would go along with it. Patrick's very generous to open his house to another child.'

It was all I could do not to blurt out that last week he'd sulked for a large part of Sunday morning because Victor had used up all the milk making some disgusting pea protein shake to build himself up for the rugby season.

I dug deep for my wifely loyalty. 'He was very friendly with Victor's mum as well. We all rented a flat together in our twenties.'

Andrea raised her eyebrows. 'It's still a big thing to do. We're just not as liberal as you and Patrick.'

She articulated the word 'liberal' as though we were in the habit of naked orgies in a back garden hot tub or spent our evenings canvassing door-to-door for people to sign up to SussexSwingers. com. Andrea was the sort who confused a preference for a lentil salad with a political statement.

I resisted the urge to say, 'I think by "liberal" you just mean kind.' I had the sense of being wrong-footed, criticised for taking in a boy who'd lost his mother, as though I'd made a bold and controversial statement about how everyone should live their lives. Yet again it was a conundrum why I even cared what Andrea thought. At forty-eight, it was a disappointment to me that I still wanted people to like me, even the ones I couldn't stand myself. Ginny had always teased me mercilessly about what she called my 'smiling at people you'd like to spit on'.

She finished the conversation with her usual charade, the one that had been going on for the last five years since our daughters started at senior school. 'Let me know when you're free for coffee. Would be great to catch up.'

I nodded, in full-on TV, film or play mode. 'Very busy at work at the moment, but as soon as it eases, I'll let you know.'

I was just grumping off to my car when another mother, Jasmine, wandered up, a trail of little children behind her in a kaleidoscope of hand-knitted sweaters. I never knew which were hers and which were the offspring of her older kids, now in their twenties. But she never looked stressed, despite always having about six children in tow. Not even now, when at least three of the kids were going to be late for school.

As she chatted to me, breaking off every now and again to instruct a child not to poke a snail with a stick, I felt an overwhelming urge to cut the conversation short and take responsibility for her kids not getting a late mark. Eventually, she waved them off, 'Have a gorgeous day!' to an answering chorus of grunts and one twinkly little 'See you later, love you!'

In the pre-rebellious-Phoebe era, I would have joined in with all the others twittering their disapproval over Jasmine's refusal to conform, homing in on the easy targets of the way she dressed, her country accent, her free-range children. Her refusal to meet everyone's expectations of a school mum at a high-performing grammar that prided itself on getting the vast majority of kids to university. But now, I wanted to grab her by her tie-dye scarf and say, 'Well done you for never caring what people think.'

I saw my best friend, Faye, getting out of her Range Rover and had a surge of discomfort about chatting to Jasmine. I knew Faye would make fun of her – 'She been sharing her pattern for knitting your own knickers?' – and I didn't want to join in.

I tried to tie up my talk with Jasmine. 'Well, back to the grindstone now. Better get to work while I've got an empty house.'

'Before you go, I just wanted to say how kind you are taking in your friend's boy, Victor, isn't it?'

'Thank you. He's a lovely lad.'

'Phoebe's great too. She really helped Kai with his French GCSE. He's not the best at languages.'

'She has her moments, thank you.' I wanted to throw my arms around her and burst into grateful sobs that someone, somewhere in the school universe, didn't just see me and Phoebe and think rubbish mother/problem child.

Jasmine smiled. She must have picked up on my uncertainty. 'Remind me to tell you the scrapes my older two got into back in the day.' She patted me on the arm. 'I see a dodgy video and I raise you a whole load of things you'll never even have thought of. It all comes out in the wash. They turn out okay in the end because we've put all that goodness in them from the beginning. It would be a boring old world if everyone toed the line all the time.'

And off she went with her colourful crocodile of little ones, splashing in puddles and singing a song I'd never heard before, but that appeared to have 'motherfucker' as the chorus, tinkling out of the mouths of her innocent babes.

I felt strangely uplifted and waved to Faye, who was cutting across the car park. 'Jo!'

I walked towards her. We hugged, my heart lifting with the simple pleasure of being with someone I could just be myself with.

'See Old Mother Jasmine cornered you. How many kids has she got now?'

'Some of them are her grandchildren, I think. She's quite nice really.'

'Careful. She'll have you joining her on a sit-in about the proposed runway at Gatwick.'

I didn't want to slag off Jasmine, so I diverted Faye: 'Our girls in the sixth form! Where did that time go? Seems yesterday that Phoebe snatched the Jesus from Georgia in the Reception nativity!'

I'd loved Faye for how she'd hooted over that. It was the start of an irreverent friendship that had seen me through many a competitive cake bake. She'd also been pretty vocal in her support when things had started to go downhill with Phoebe over the last year – 'Honestly, all teenagers do this stuff. If I'd had access to a smartphone at fifteen, who knows what trouble I could have got into?' She'd made a point of standing with me at the final assembly before they went on study leave for their GCSEs and whispering comments about the amount of Botox present in the room.

I filled her in now on Andrea's nosiness about how we were getting on with Victor.

'She probably doesn't realise that beyond her dinner parties and stuffed quails' eggs, there's a whole universe of people doing unselfish things for the good of mankind. Don't worry about the likes of her and her little band of evils.' She winked at me. 'I think you're doing brilliantly. It's bound to be hard – teenagers are testing at the best of times. Can you sneak out for lunch one day soon? Gonna need a bit of a sanity check with Georgia getting on the Oxbridge treadmill. Not going to need my telescope to spot the competitive parents there.'

'I'm sure I can squeeze in a lunch. Are you going to watch Jordan play rugby on Saturday?' I asked.

'Yes, why? Are you going?'

'Apparently so. Mr Sanderson's just invited Victor to join the team on Saturday. Not quite sure if he'll actually get to play much, but it's good that he's getting involved.'

'Woo! Brilliant! Look forward to some female company among all the dads who think they're bloody Tuilagi. See you there then. Jordan's captain this year, so I'll give him the nod to make sure Victor gets a bit of a turn and that all the boys give him a proper welcome into the team.'

I thanked her, waving her off, feeling a bit less furious with myself for not telling Andrea the truth, that I asked myself every day if we'd made a huge mistake. Thank God for Faye, helping me put silly gossiping mums into perspective.

When I got home, as a penance for allowing myself to wish Victor wasn't complicating our lives, I decided to change the sheets on his bed. I made Phoebe do her own and told myself off for encouraging Victor to think that boring household drudgery was beneath a man, but I just wanted him to feel welcome. I hovered at the door of his room, wondering whether he'd mind me poking about when he wasn't there. In the end, I decided that I couldn't bring back Ginny but I could offer the momentary joy of climbing into a bed with fresh linen.

I smiled at the mural they'd painted on the wall, the wonky Wales lettering above the dragon-pug. I brushed away the twinge of nostalgia for my classy cream guest room and studied the photos on the desk. Victor at the Millennium Stadium with his friends, with their red and green hats, all waving their flags. He must find our Sussex backwater so different from city life. The photo of Ginny and Victor clinking glasses down at Cardiff Bay on her last birthday winded me. We still hoped.

As I stripped the bed, I knocked into the bookcase at the foot of it, dislodging a shoebox on the top shelf. The contents scattered over the floor. Ginny's memory box for him. A yellow card commemorating his first haircut, with a dark curl taped to it. A photo of Ginny and Victor when he was a baby. The identity bracelet from the hospital. I ran my finger around the plastic ring, reading: Victor Yaro. 3.62kg. 25 September 2001. I imagined Ginny, giving birth to a baby almost two months premature in a hospital in Vancouver.

She must have been so lonely and frightened. But nowhere near as desperate as she must have felt putting all these little pieces of her life with Victor into a box, knowing that there would be a cut-off point, a finite end to the memories she could store for him.

I popped everything back in, his school reports, his baby shoes, the Mother's Day card with the tatty tissue paper daffodil. I'd intruded on something sacred. I'd have to tell him and hope he'd forgive me. I lay the little hospital bracelet on top. 3.62kg. I frowned. Wasn't a kilo 2.2lbs? That made him well over 7lbs. Probably nearer eight. Which was a good-sized baby.

Ginny had always joked that she'd squeezed out five packs of mince. 'Two and a half kilos of Waitrose organic, mind you, none of that value stuff. Thank God he came early. God knows how huge he'd have been if I'd got to full term.'

She'd teased me when Phoebe was born, weighing 6lb 3oz. 'Victor was only eleven ounces lighter than her and he was seven weeks early!'

Given that I'd needed stitches after my supposedly 'tiny' baby, we'd giggled about how lucky she'd been not to give birth to a 10lb bruiser, how she'd got off lightly with 5lb 8oz.

That little bracelet must have been from another hospital admission before she came back to the UK. Poor Ginny. It struck me how much she must have kept to herself, the reality of dealing with a premature baby and trips backwards and forwards to the hospital. Typical Ginny to just get on with it and not worry me. I felt a rush of shame that while she'd been adjusting to a new baby in fragile health, I'd been so caught up in my wedding preparations that I'd barely paid attention.

I put the box back on the shelf and took time smoothing the duvet. I hoped I wouldn't let her boy down.

CHAPTER FOUR

The lead-up to Victor's eighteenth birthday nearly overwhelmed me with the need to make it a joyful occasion. In reality, the thought of waking him up on the morning he became an adult made me feel as though I'd be shining a megawatt torch right into the hole Ginny had left behind. I couldn't get away from the fact that even singing 'Happy Birthday' felt like a taunt.

I spent hours trawling through grief and loss websites trying to understand the best approach. I wished that Ginny and Victor had lived closer when Victor was growing up, so that we had more of a connection to work from, a better insight into what was normal for him. He was so quiet. I remembered him as a livewire when the kids were young and we got them together nearly every school holiday, before they started having their own plans and refusing to come.

Patrick was far more pragmatic. 'Of course he'll miss Ginny, but I still think he'll want presents and a cake and a bit of a fuss making of him. I mean, he does have days when he seems to forget about her.'

'Do you think so?' I asked, immediately wondering if we were doing enough to keep her memory alive.

Patrick tutted with irritation. 'Not forgets, but you know what I mean. He just gets on with normal life, doing what Phoebe does – films, stuff on YouTube. Why don't we ask him what he'd like to do?'

'Can you do that? I'm afraid I might burst into tears.'

Patrick ruffled my hair. 'Yes of course, I'll be big and brave,' he said.

My shoulders relaxed at the thought of Patrick taking some of the burden, rather than relying on me to hold it all together. At least he hadn't put the ball back into my court with his customary, 'I don't know, love. What do you think Ginny would want?'

On the actual day, I turned to Patrick in bed and asked, 'When shall I give him the photo albums Ginny left for him? Before school or after?'

'After. He'd have to be made of steel not to cry when he looks through those. I think he needs a bit of privacy. He might not even want to see them now. Might be too soon.'

When I got up, I put the albums to one side. I'd offer them to him later, though God knows what the proper etiquette was for 'Here, on your big birthday, are all the pictures of you and the mum you'll never see again'.

I never understood how Ginny had had the strength to put that album together. She'd started on it as soon as she'd found out her cancer was terminal, the year before she died. How could she bear to look back at that sweet toddler splashing about at Penarth Beach, the boy with the big gap in his front teeth, the teenager with his first rugby cup? What special torturous pain must it have brought to her heart that she wouldn't be part of the university success, the wedding, the grandchildren that she probably assumed would be her payback for the tedious afternoons spent playing shops and colouring in? Her answer was always the same. 'It's not about me, Jo. I've let him down by dying before he didn't need me any more. But I'm going to make sure he knows how much I love him. I've got some letters too for him. You know, for the high days and holidays.'

Her eyes had filled then. I'd been useless. I'd cried with her and then we'd laughed. And I still hadn't dared say that the thought of being responsible for Victor scared the shit out of me. I kept telling her what Phoebe had got up to in the fifth year in the hope that she'd realise packing Victor off to Australia with her brother would be a far better option. In the end though, I wouldn't have hesitated if it had been solely my decision. I didn't know how to explain that marriage made being a good friend so much more difficult because I couldn't just do what I wanted. I wasn't sure Ginny would understand: she'd never had to answer to any man, and even if she had, compromise wasn't her most notable quality. Right up to when she died, I just didn't know whether I had the confidence to take such a life-changing decision on my own.

But here we were. I passed a little pile of presents to Victor. Oddly, free rein to order stuff on the internet for his birthday had led to Phoebe undertaking a secret mission to find out what he wanted, the most engaged she'd been in the whole time he'd been staying with us. 'Here's a few things from us.' He said thank you but hesitated to open them. I panicked in case he didn't like what we'd bought, in case he cried, in case he displayed one of a million possible reactions that I didn't know how to deal with and that would have Patrick flapping the pages of his newspaper and Phoebe gawking but not helping.

'You can unwrap them when you get back from school if you want to. I've got some things from your mum that you might want to open then.'

He gathered them up and said, 'Thank you. Something to look forward to this evening.' As he went upstairs to put them in his room, I had no idea whether that was a genuine response or something I should be trying to talk to him about because school was so hard to get through or any of the other fifty things I should be doing to ease his transition into adulthood.

Before we got to the enjoyable part of the day, I had to break the news to Patrick that my mother had invited herself out with us for the curry that Victor had chosen as his birthday celebration at the weekend. He dropped his head in an exaggerated expression of despair. 'So Victor's low-key meal now has your mother centre stage?'

'She phoned and asked what we were doing because she didn't want to sit in on her own again. Does it matter? It was only us anyway.' I hadn't wanted her to come either but contrarily, I hoped Patrick would embrace the idea.

'Come on, Jo, the evening was supposed to be about Victor and our memories of Ginny. Your mum will make it all about her.'

'What was I supposed to say?'

Patrick frowned. 'We're already busy but come for a cup of tea on Monday?'

As always, as soon as I tried to make it right for one person, I made it wrong for someone else. Patrick missed his parents, but he did have the luxury of having the upper hand because he was also automatically saved from finding out quite how badly they would have behaved in any given situation.

'Shall I see if Cory can come? I could ask him to bring his photo albums of us when we all shared the flat? Give us a joyful way of talking about Ginny while taking the spotlight off Mum?'

'Christ, what a dream evening for the man about town.' Patrick flicked his hands in resignation. 'If he's free and up for it, why not?'

I rang Cory to ask. I imagined him in his bachelor pad in London overlooking the river, feet on his pale grey sofa, rubbing his beard. 'See, who knew back then that the twenty-three-year-old advertising exec addicted to Pot Noodles would be the elder statesman you turn to in a crisis?'

I had to grin at that.

He carried on. 'Fortunately for you, I had planned to cook dinner for my new girlfriend, but we will both come over. I suppose she had to meet Patrick at some point.'

Cory was in the elite band of people who were allowed to criticise my husband. As soon as they got together, Cory would start teasing him about his idiosyncrasies. 'Jo, don't tell me he still does that thing of leaving a millimetre of milk in the carton so he can claim "there was still some left"?' 'How's his sportsmanship at Monopoly these days?' – a nod to a marathon game we'd played over an Easter bank holiday – at least twenty years ago – when Patrick had gone to bed in a huff after landing on Cory's Mayfair hotels.

Patrick, in return, would throw his arms out, gesturing to our cottage, me and Phoebe and say, 'Yeah, but I don't have to go to champagne bars and fancy restaurants to find my entertainment. Look where my competitive spirit got me, eh, Cor?'

And Cory was too kind to say, 'A fairly average wife, with dirty blonde hair and teeth that would have benefitted from a brace.'

To be honest, I don't think Cory even 'saw' me any more. We'd been friends for so long, since we all worked at the magazine back in the nineties. In the same way, to me, he was just Cory, good-looking – though the years of client entertaining and international conferences were starting to pad him out – but I never gave it much thought until a new girlfriend came along, making every excuse to touch him, straighten his tie and, like many before her, hoping to be the first woman to get him up the aisle.

'Looking forward to seeing you and Lulu on Saturday. Come here first and have a glass of champagne with Victor. Will Lulu mind if you bring the photo albums? I don't want her to think we're deliberately excluding her, but it would be nice for Victor to see some photos of his mum in her younger days.'

Cory's voice was serious. 'Victor needs this. Don't suppose it will endear me to Lulu from a feeling part of the gang point of view, but it's not like Ginny and I were lovers. Though I think I tried it on a few times when I'd been at the Smirnoff Ice.'

It was ridiculous after all these years to have a twinge that Ginny had always been a man magnet. When we all lived together, I always had a tingle of unease that, behind my back, the boys were lusting after Ginny and saying, 'Yeah, I mean, Jo, she's a lovely girl and all that, but, you know, you wouldn't, would you?'

I pulled my focus back to arrangements for the weekend. 'I owe you big time, Cory. Thank you. Oh, and one thing I forgot to mention was that my mum will be with us.'

Cory let out a big hoot of merriment. 'Now you tell me. No worries, I'll be thrilled to see Gwen, treat her to a bit of the Cory charm… she'll be the perfect baptism of fire for Lulu.'

I wanted to be sarcastic, to tell him off for thinking he was God's gift to women, but I was so relieved that Patrick would have someone to talk to, and I was pretty sure Victor would enjoy getting to know him better, that I just gushed out a thank you.

By the time Saturday chunked around, I couldn't have been more grateful that Cory was coming to the rescue. I'd given Victor the letter Ginny had instructed me to hand over. He'd been quite moody since his birthday, more monosyllabic than ever, as though turning eighteen without Ginny had truly cemented in his mind that she really had gone. I tried to let him know that I was there for him but just succeeded in making us both more self-conscious with my 'I know it's such an odd time for you, Victor, losing your mum and coming to live with us, as well as starting a new school. But I'm always here for you to talk to, if there's something bothering you.' I immediately wanted to snatch those words back in. 'Bothering' didn't seem big enough for what he was going through. He was probably asking himself at that very minute how his super-smart dynamic mother had landed a dullard like me as a best friend. I suspected he'd rather implode with grief than speak to me.

I nearly suggested the school counsellor that I'd tried to get Phoebe to see – 'Mum. No. Only "special" people go to the counsellor. I'm just not doing it.' – but I didn't know how to broach it without making Victor so awkward he'd never come out of his room again.

Just before Cory arrived, I mentioned my concerns to Patrick.

'What did you think would happen? The boy's lost his mother, moved away from everyone he knows, at a school where multiracial means there are a couple of Asian kids whose parents are medics, and that's without everyone taking the piss out of him for sounding like Tom Jones.'

'I shouldn't think anyone their age knows who Tom Jones is.'

Patrick sighed. 'You know what I mean. I don't know, Alun Wyn Jones, then. Poor lad stands out like a sore thumb among all of us southerners. I hope he makes some friends before the Six Nations, otherwise he'll be stuck here watching it with me.' Patrick managed to bring rugby into everything. He brightened for a moment. 'Maybe he'd like to come to a match with me if I can get tickets?'

Given it was one of the few times Patrick had shown any real initiative in organising anything for Victor, I didn't do my usual 'How much would that cost?' The mere thought that Patrick might participate in topping up everyone's happiness quotient made me want to shower money at anything he suggested. 'Yes, why don't you look into tickets?'

'Don't need telling twice.'

And then Cory and Lulu arrived, and we'd barely done the introductions when Mum turned up fifteen minutes early, 'Didn't want to keep you waiting,' as though we'd all been peering out of the window in breathless anticipation of her arrival.

I shuffled them all into the sitting room, aware of Lulu's gaze flitting around. If she'd been hoping that Cory's friends had a great big country mansion in keeping with his fancy flat in Battersea overlooking the river, she was going to be disappointed.

'This is very cosy,' she said.

I was so busy making sure my mother didn't corner Cory before I'd even had the chance to take his coat, I hadn't tuned in my 'judgement of Cory's new girlfriend' antenna sufficiently to know whether she was being genuine or not. Most of his girlfriends were pleasant enough – 'innocuous', as Patrick frequently described them – but often seemed a strange choice for a man who, when we'd lived with him, loved engaging in debates, loved the challenge of sharpening his very smart brain against an equal match. He could never sit still or bear a moment's silence, which made him entertaining or infuriating depending on the mood. If silence threatened, he'd launch into one of his list games, which we'd all shout down but end up getting dragged into. It was thanks to Cory and his interminable lists – 'Give me all the countries in Europe.' 'Name twenty Olympic sports' – that I had any general knowledge at all. It certainly wasn't because my parents had rushed me off to any museums or art galleries while I was growing up. Unlike Phoebe, who'd only had to say, 'When did the Titanic sink?' and we'd find an exhibition about it, which she'd drag herself around asking if we could go to H&M on the way home.

I hoped we wouldn't have to rely on Cory and his lists tonight. My mother was always good for lots of rambling stories, though of late they were a bit arthritis- and funeral-dominated.

I shouted up the stairs for Victor and Phoebe. Victor came down immediately. He paused on the bottom stair as though steeling himself to face us all, to gather in his grief so the rest of us wouldn't feel embarrassed. My heart ached for him. When he was little, he'd been so boisterous, racing about everywhere, high-spirited and adventurous. Ginny had been full of stories about him playing pranks on teachers, who still seemed to like him despite his tendency to be the class clown. But now he looked as though life had sucked the mischief out of him, replacing it with the burden of loss.

I held out a glass of champagne to him. 'In you come.'

Cory took charge, giving Victor a bear hug. 'How are you doing, big man? This is Lulu.'

Lulu shook Victor's hand. They'd barely finished saying hello before my mum rushed over with big lobstery arms. 'Let's have a look at the birthday boy! A proper man now. Aren't you getting tall?'

Victor submitted to Mum's embrace, while I tried to ignore the thumping noise from upstairs that signified Phoebe doing a ridiculous amount of sit-ups to counteract going out for dinner. I decided not to allow myself to snag that particular guilt tripwire tonight – I couldn't worry about her as well as making sure Victor had at least a few good memories about his coming-of-age celebrations.

'Anyway, my love, did you have a lovely birthday? What do you think of Phoebe's school? Nice, isn't it?'

It was one of the few occasions in my life when I found myself wishing I was more like my mother, trotting out whatever came into my head without tying myself in knots overthinking things.

While Victor was responding with more enthusiasm than I'd seen for some time, Phoebe appeared wearing the skimpiest piece of cloth that could loosely be termed a dress. A sneeze could easily send her boobs flying out of the top. Patrick's eyebrows shot up and, for once, I decided to leave being the bad guy to him. I simply couldn't have another conversation about 'You have to make a decision about whether you want to be remembered for the smart, funny girl you are or the one who can show the largest amount of flesh.' Which always resulted in a vote for letting her butt cheeks hang out below her skirt rather than a decision to dazzle the world with the knowledge she had about English literature.

Before Patrick could speak, my mother threw her hands up. 'Good God, Phoebe, what on earth are you wearing?' She looked at me. 'Surely you're not letting her go out like that?'

Phoebe immediately folded her arms in a gesture I recognised as 'taking a stand'.

'She'll be wearing a coat. Anyway, we'd better go, otherwise we'll be late for our table.'

We hustled out of the door, with Mum twittering on about Phoebe catching a cold, which was the least of my worries, and me hissing at Patrick, 'Feel free to step in any time.'

He was pouting as though semi-naked daughters were entirely my department. He went ahead with Cory, who had engaged Victor in a conversation about school in such an easy way I had a treacherous thought that I wished Ginny had asked Cory to take him in. In the meantime, I trailed along, my arm linked in Mum's to avoid adding 'pensioner stumbling off the kerb and breaking an ankle' to the evening's entertainment, though frankly I would have liked to stomp on ahead and down a couple of G&Ts just to take the edge off my grump.

Phoebe was a few paces behind, the light on her phone a giveaway glow, signalling walking and texting at the same time.

Mum was acting as though Phoebe lived in another town, rather than within hearing distance. 'Do all the young girls go out like that? Good job your father isn't alive to see it. You'd have been grounded till kingdom come.'

'Mum, it's the fashion. Much better to get it out of her system now than be running around like that when she's forty.' I could feel Phoebe's eyes on me. 'She's got a lovely figure, and if you can't get away with something like that now, when can you?' I knew I was shooting myself in the foot for next time Phoebe went to a party, but Mum's disapproval now would have nothing on what lay ahead if Phoebe spiralled into a full-on tantrum, when we'd all be ducking the F-bombs.

For once, I just wanted to have a nice time. I wasn't sufficiently deluded to think that Phoebe would demand a selfie with me that she'd then post with the caption: 'Best Mum in the World!!' provoking a plethora of 'Gorgeous, hun!' responses, but I was hoping for an evening of five-minute bursts without anyone sulking, which, on current performance, still seemed a lot to ask.

As we all crowded into the curry house in the village, I hung back with Phoebe. 'I'm sorry about Nan. She's a bit set in her ways. Who do you want to sit next to?'

Phoebe puffed out a breath of air, as though the people assembled were a collection of the biggest dullards on the planet.

'Cory? At least he's funny.'

As we were shown to the table, I semaphored to Cory with my eyes… 'So, if Phoebe sits next to Cory, and Victor between Cory and Patrick…' I took one for the team by sitting next to Mum and let Lulu take the hit on the other side on the grounds that, a) Cory would probably dump her before she ever came again, and b) she wouldn't have heard Mum's top five stories before.

Usually getting impatient for the drinks was Patrick's department, but I'd already knocked back two glasses of wine before the beers for the lads had materialised. I tried to ignore Mum, who, in between clutching her orange juice, was watching every sip I took like a golden retriever following a fillet steak. 'Did you see that piece in the paper about alcohol causing breast cancer?'

'No I didn't, must have missed it.'

I turned my shoulders towards Lulu, the familiar feeling of not living up to Mum's expectations washing over me. I concentrated on Lulu, asking her about how she met Cory and how long they'd been seeing each other. Mum listened for a minute, before she felt obliged to burst into Lulu's story about working in fashion PR in Hampstead with an anecdote about being a secretary in Willesden Green years ago, the only common link being that both locations were in London. I attempted not to adopt the responsibility of reining Mum in and sat back eating poppadoms and trying to quell the rising unease.

At the end of the table, I saw Cory whisper something to Victor and then Victor caught my eye. I had a horrid feeling I was being talked about.

'No whispering at the table, Cory. You know better than that! Do share…' I tried to inject lightness in my voice, but there was a flash of irritation across Cory's face.

'Just having a quiet chat with Victor about Ginny…'

I blushed. 'Sorry. Carry on.'

But I'd ruined the moment.

Cory proposed a toast to Victor, who, despite smiling and clinking his glass, frowned as though he was still thinking about what Cory had been saying. The gesture was so brief, I almost missed it. Cory touched his finger to his lips in an 'our secret' gesture and Victor nodded in reply.

In between Patrick's clumsy attempts to engage a reluctant Phoebe in a conversation about where she might like to go to university ('St Andrews? Maybe Edinburgh? I've heard Scottish universities have a brilliant social life') and Victor dazzling us with actual courses he hoped to study rather than just which student unions sold the cheapest beer, I didn't get a chance to find out from Cory if there was something I should know about.

Slowly, as we ate our way through chicken tikka and even Phoebe thawed out enough to chat to Lulu about which brands were fashionable among girls her age, I felt some tension seep out of me. In fact, Phoebe sounded engaged and knowledgeable, and I smiled inwardly as she imitated Lulu's professional speak, bandying about phrases such as consumer psychology and brand awareness as though she really knew what she was talking about. Perhaps she did. She certainly knew more than me, but I daren't say Asos or Nike in case I pronounced them wrongly, so that wasn't a high bar.

Just as I was having a glimmer of pride, or at least of hope, that Phoebe would one day come out of her teenage rebellion and be a daughter I could confidently introduce to anyone and know she wouldn't let me down, Mum turned to me and said, 'Do you think Brexit means the people who own this curry house will have to leave?' just as one of the waiters started clearing the table.

'No, don't be silly.'

Mum carried on oblivious. 'I read in the paper that people were having to apply for citizenship even when they'd been here for years.'

'Mohammed and his wife were born here,' I hissed. 'I'll explain it to you later.'

Her eyes narrowed as she looked at Victor. She nudged me. 'Will he be allowed to stay?' she asked at a volume that couldn't be classed as a tactful aside.

'Of course! Don't be silly. Ginny was British, Mum, and so is Victor.'

I glanced over to see if Victor had heard but, thankfully, Phoebe had unfurled enough to get into a 'which teacher was the biggest dickhead' discussion with him. Every cloud in my life contained both a silver lining and a downpour.

I turned towards Lulu to see if she was listening, trying to read her face. I hoped she wasn't lumping me into the same ignorant category as my mother.

Cory came to the rescue before my mum put us even further on edge by tapping the waiter on the arm and asking whether he was about to be deported. 'Now, Victor, I bet your mum didn't tell you about my special talent for lists... part of your initiation ceremony to become an honorary member of the Square Bear Bunch – I know, stupid name, but the idea behind it was four of us playing the list game. So let's see what you teenagers know about the world, see if us oldies have a better general knowledge than the Instagram generation.'

Phoebe looked as though she'd just encountered a month-old coffee cup under her bed, but Victor had probably heard more than I hoped from my mother and was delighted with the distraction. He did that 'up for anything' grin that reminded me so much of Ginny.

Cory picked his specialist subject: country capitals.

'Right, easy one for you, Jo, Hungary,' he said, before regaling everyone with the fact that years ago, I'd thought Malta was the capital of Gibraltar. 'Mind you, you'd discovered mojitos that night so we'll let you off.'

The part of me that loved Cory for making me sound young and fun in front of Phoebe was balanced out by the squeaks of disapproval emanating from Mum. Not only did she think an advocaat at Christmas was the epitome of letting her hair down, but she fancied herself as an academic – 'If I'd had the chances you had, I would have definitely been university material.' My spell at secretarial college leading to top PA jobs in London and ultimately my career as a copywriter now had not fulfilled her maternal ambitions.

Cory kindly gave my mum France, ramped it up with Outer Mongolia for Patrick and then tested Phoebe with Somalia.

'I don't know.' I was aware her grumpy tone was covering her embarrassment at being thought stupid.

I wanted to rescue her but Cory was hellbent on getting an answer. 'Go on. It's where Mo Farah was born.'

Phoebe looked blank. 'I don't even know where Somalia is.'

My mother looked pained. 'What do they teach you at this school of yours? Somalia. Africa.' She swivelled in her chair. 'Victor, you tell her what the capital is.'

He shrugged his shoulders. 'I don't know either.'

Mum paused with a banana fritter halfway to her mouth. 'But you're from Africa! You don't even know the capital of your own country?'

Patrick growled from the other end of the table. 'For God's sake, Gwen. For a start, Africa is a continent, not a country. And Victor is Welsh. He's from bloody Cardiff! And anyway, Somalia is about four thousand miles from Nigeria – if that's the point you're trying to make – about the same distance as London from flaming Canada.'

A horrible wave of alarm rushed through me that we were skirting towards a place we wouldn't be able to row back from, one where we'd actually say what we thought.

Mum pleated up her napkin. 'Well, I just thought he'd be more *au fait* with his own culture,' she said, putting on a ridiculous French accent to deliver her 'au fait'.

Embarrassment rushed through me. Victor was looking apologetic, as though he'd let us down by not being the font of all knowledge for everything African. I wanted to rush over and hug him and tell him that I was sorry about the world he'd ended up in and that I hoped – really hoped – we'd be good enough to help him navigate losing his mum, especially in our little whitewashed community.

Cory saved the day by turning the spotlight on Mum. 'So, Gwen, because you were born in England, I insist you talk me through the rules of rugby.'

She flim-flammed about, torn between being the centre of attention and not being able to confound everyone's expectations by actually knowing them.

Patrick turned to Victor. 'I bet you know them. Starter for ten, three most important rules in rugby.'

And, good-naturedly, Victor gave us a rundown of the offside and scrum rules, which were in the category of things my brain welcomed in one door and wafted straight out of the other.

As Cory and Patrick split the bill and my mum patted Victor on the head and said, 'Your hair's much softer than I thought it would be,' I wondered if Ginny should have sent Victor to live with her brother after all. Then I chastised myself for falling into my own trap of thinking that as long as he was with someone black he'd fit in. I bundled Mum into her coat and marched her back to her bungalow before she could decide she wanted a nightcap.

CHAPTER FIVE

Faye phoned to ask if Georgia could stay at ours after a party in a couple of weekends' time because she wanted a night away with her husband for her twentieth wedding anniversary. 'Just up to London for the night, see a show. Pretend we've got a life.'

I'd agreed straightaway. 'I'm picking them up at midnight, though. I've told Phoebe she's not giving me the runaround – I've threatened to go in and cause social death if they're not out on time.' In reality, I hoped she'd pass the message onto Georgia to take charge of a prompt exit strategy as I knew that I'd never have the balls to march into a party and haul Phoebe off whichever boy was the recipient of her favours. Maybe that was a bit unfair, but the fumble behind the chemistry lab filmed from an upstairs window that made its way round school via Snapchat was etched in my mind forever.

Faye said, 'I'll warn her. Honestly, who knew that motherhood would be such a challenge?'

I rang off feeling a bit calmer. Georgia was a good influence on Phoebe, encouraging her to start visiting universities and thinking about possible courses. Because Patrick had gone to a red-brick university, he was a bit 'Bristol/Durham/Exeter or die' – a strategy guaranteed to make Phoebe decide that running off with the bloke from the amusement arcade in Bournemouth would be a much better idea. Clearly, in Phoebe's eyes at least, Georgia at seventeen knew way more than Patrick and me in our forties, but as long as she channelled her in the right direction, I was happy to wear the dunce's hat.

I judged my moment like a waiter snatching at a fly before it landed in the soup to ask Phoebe if she could wangle an invitation to the party for Victor. I softened her up by making 'healthy snacks' for her: gluten-free, dairy-free coconut cookies that were swimming in maple syrup and looked about as nutritious as a fried Mars Bar, splashed out on a shampoo especially for blonde hair, then took the plunge: 'Could you ask? I'm feeling bad about him staying in all the time.'

She didn't say no and, for the next week, I refrained from collaring her the second she came in from school to find out whether she'd remembered. Getting Phoebe to acquiesce to the smallest of favours was like attempting to make it across a river with only lily pads as stepping stones.

By Thursday, when I was desperate to have an evening in my own home without feeling as though I needed to put on a show for Victor, I crumbled.

She shrugged. 'Oh yeah, forgot to say. Matt said I could invite him.'

'Oh well done, love, thank you. Have you told him?'

She frowned. 'It's not that big a deal. I'll tell him later.'

We both went silent as Victor appeared in the doorway of the kitchen, pausing on the threshold as though he was scared of interrupting us.

'Come in, come in. Do you want a cup of tea?' I hoped one day that Victor would be able to exist in our house without me darting about like an over-enthusiastic waitress.

I looked meaningfully at Phoebe, who scowled but turned to Victor and said, 'You know Matt, the one who's the hooker in rugby, blonde hair? He says you can come to his party tomorrow if you want.'

'Are you sure?' He didn't have anything like Ginny's confidence. She had swirled into everywhere as though the evening's VIP had just glittered through the door, whereas Victor hovered, waiting for permission to enter. Maybe grief did that to you. Undid your certainty about life to such an extent that every social interaction felt precarious. Or maybe it was just damned hard to walk in when everyone knew that your mum was dead and your heart was shattered but there was still an odd expectation that you would shove your pain to one side so no one felt uncomfortable.

Of course, it could also be that nature had triumphed over nurture and Victor's Canadian dad didn't dash through life like a Labrador, convinced that every new person might be a potential friend. I wished I'd asked Ginny more questions about him now, but she had a knack of diverting me from topics she didn't want to discuss.

Phoebe put an end to my navel gazing with a monotone, 'Yeah, he said it was okay,' as she picked up her school bag and walked out.

Yet again, I wished that she could just be a bit more forthcoming. Everything about her was grudging, as though offering something up joyfully and generously somehow shaved a sliver off her own resources.

On the night of the party, Patrick shuffled Georgia and Phoebe out to the car. I was relieved to see that even headed-for-Oxbridge Georgia had her boobs hanging out like a couple of escaped breakfast bagels. They were both giggling and whispering in a way that suggested there had been a side order of vodka with the stick-on eyelashes. Victor followed, looking as though he wished he could stay at home. Despite his reticence, he was so handsome in jeans and a T-shirt that my eyes prickled at the small moments Ginny was missing. I wanted to hug him. He reminded me so much of myself at that age, apprehensive about events that other people looked forward to for weeks.

'Right, have a good time. Be sensible,' I said, trying and failing to get some acknowledgement that I'd spoken from Phoebe.

As soon as I shut the front door against the fog of sweet-smelling perfume, I sank down into the sofa, rejoicing in the silence. I put my head in my hands, massaging my eyebrows. I really wanted to go to bed and read my book, but given that Patrick and I had hardly talked about anything other than domestic logistics since Victor had arrived, I decided we should probably take the opportunity to catch up without Phoebe flapping in and having an opinion. I downloaded a box set, made up a cheeseboard and opened a bottle of wine, feeling quite the caricature of a date-night wife.

It worked. Patrick came back in and said, 'This looks nice.' He drew me into a hug. 'Thank God they've all gone out.'

We flopped onto the sofa. I squeezed his hand. 'I feel like I've barely spoken two words to you in the last couple of months.'

'I know. It is a bit like having a stranger in the house that you don't want to overhear your business, isn't it?'

Even though I agreed, guilt made me want to argue with him.

'But it would be a bit naïve to imagine that he was going to arrive and fit in as though he'd always been here. I think he's done pretty well. Phoebe could have been a bit more generous and welcoming.' I decided not to offer up my opinion that I felt that Patrick hadn't fallen over himself to include Victor either.

'It's hard for her though. I mean, she's used to being an only child and we did impose it on her. She didn't have much say in the matter.'

I hoped I was imagining the undertone of 'You just barrelled on and did what you wanted despite our objections.' I decided not to point out that Patrick was the first to dismiss Phoebe's views on anything except when they coincided with what he wanted.

I flicked on the TV before I soured the evening by setting off on a rant about how Phoebe's objections had mainly centred around the fact that we only had one bathroom and the Wi-Fi was already so slow 'without anyone else downloading films'. I'd been furious and got into a row about how she had everything she wanted and it wouldn't kill her to be a bit charitable to someone who'd just lost their mother. Patrick hadn't said a word to back me up, even though he was always moaning about her knowing the price of everything and the value of nothing. Tonight though, I shoved those familiar resentments back in the drawer, knowing with depressing certainty that there'd be other occasions for their moment in the spotlight.

I took a deep breath. 'I expect she'll get used to it. It's only for a couple of years.'

As the evening went on, we both relaxed, though by ten-thirty I was ready for bed and sending up a prayer to the teen party gods that this wouldn't be one of those nights when Phoebe and Georgia kept us up squealing and giggling until the early hours of the morning. As the credits rolled, my mobile went. I had a burst of hope that Phoebe was ready to come home and bedtime was closer than I'd thought.

It was a number I didn't recognise, which immediately made my heart speed up.

'Hello?'

A young voice on the other end introduced herself as the host's sister. She told me that Georgia wasn't very well.

'What sort of not very well?'

'She's a bit sick, but she wouldn't let me phone her mum and dad because she said it was their wedding anniversary.'

'I'll come and get her. I'll be about fifteen minutes.'

Patrick raised his eyebrows. 'Phoebe?'

'No, Georgia puking up. Gah. Should I phone Faye?'

'No. Let them have a night away. They're bound to have been drinking. Even in a cab, they couldn't get back from London for a couple of hours. Let's see how it looks when we get there. We can just stick her in bed with a bucket.'

I did love the royal 'we'. Patrick was a great one for coming over 'queasy' and disappearing in a puff of smoke the second any bodily functions were involved.

I grabbed a bucket from under the kitchen sink, an old towel and the remnants of my sense of humour and jumped in the car. Patrick came with me.

'I wonder why Phoebe didn't ring us?' he asked.

'I'll text her. I'm not coming back again to fetch her and Victor.'

We drew up outside the party to find Victor standing on the pavement with Georgia, who was retching into a bush. He was leaning forward holding her hair, trying to keep his feet out of the vomit.

I handed her the towel I'd brought with me. She was tear-streaked and dishevelled; nothing like the self-assured girl striding out in her high heels just a few hours ago.

'Oh dear. We'd better get you home.' I turned to Victor. 'Where's Phoebe?'

'I'm not sure.' However, his words had all the conviction of a cake that had failed to rise. 'Shall I go and look for her?'

I chivvied him along. 'Yes please. We need to get this one home.'

He scooted up the driveway.

Georgia was sobbing in that drunken way that accompanies way too much vodka. 'Sorry, Jo. Sorry. Don't tell my mum, will you? Don't ring her and spoil her evening. She was really lookin' forward to it.' I was more irritated by the dramatic wailing than by the prospect of a disturbed night while she purged herself of what was no doubt a glorious and ill-advised mixture of drinks.

Patrick was standing behind the bonnet of the car, far away from the sick splattering.

'Pass me that anorak out of the boot,' I said.

'That's mine!'

'I know. It can be washed. Or we can let a seventeen-year-old die of hypothermia. Your call.'

Reluctantly, he passed me the coat, turning his head away as the contents of Georgia's stomach made contact with the last of the marigolds refusing to recognise winter.

I opened the boot of our estate car and told Georgia to sit on the ledge. No sign of Victor and Phoebe. 'What have you been drinking to end up like this? Who gave it to you?' I asked.

She could barely string a sentence together. 'It was just there. At the party.'

I whispered to Patrick, or thought I had, 'You don't think she needs to go to hospital, do you?'

Just as Patrick was saying he thought she'd sleep it off, Georgia slithered off the ledge and started staggering away. 'No! I don't want to go to hospital.' She sank to her knees on the wet ground. Patrick and I hauled her back up again, my annoyance rising, along with my concern.

'You stay with her. I'm going to get Phoebe.'

I ground my boots into the gravel with each furious stride. A horrendous racket blared from the depths of the house as I rang the bell. I was amazed that the neighbours hadn't called the police. No one came to the door. I turned the handle and walked into a hallway of bodies in various stages of undress. I stepped over some legs and squeezed past a hand clamped over the buttock of Phoebe's form teacher's daughter. I bet half the parents had *no idea* what their kids were up to.

In the kitchen, the air was soupy with smoke, alcohol and that unmistakable smell of hormones, pouring out into the atmosphere. And some other smell that made me think of a seedy nightclub. A boy I recognised as a prefect was lying on his back on the table with a girl sitting astride him pouring a bottle of wine into his mouth.

My arrival had a dual effect: some kids scattered like the deer on our lawn when we switched our headlights on, some broke off from their snogging momentarily, then plunged in again, plugging back into their socket of teenage desire. I wondered if lust would ever have overcome my fear of parental disapproval at that age.

I slunk out of the kitchen, filled with self-loathing that I felt more judged by them than vice versa. There was something so hedonistic, so abandoned about them that, instead of outrage, I felt fat, sexless and shrivelled up. I peered up the stairs, wondering what I would never unsee if I ventured up there given that some spotty boy was snuffling for truffles down a girl's top about four inches from my face. At that moment, Victor emerged from the sitting room.

'Any luck?' I asked.

'Not yet, but I think I know where she might be.' His gaze flickered to the stairs. 'Give me a sec. You can go back to the car. I'll bring her out.'

I wished, wished so much in that moment, that I could ring Ginny and tell her that I flat out loved her son, that although she'd beaten herself up for him not having a father figure all these years, she'd done a brilliant job, produced a boy who was saving me from more conflict with Phoebe. 'Thank you.'

I didn't hang around and fled out of the front door to where Patrick was standing at a safe distance from Georgia. She was muttering about wanting to go to sleep.

Another car drew up next to us. I just managed to resist saying Georgia's name very loudly so the driver wouldn't think it was Phoebe and chalk another one up on the bad behaviour chart.

Jasmine got out as Georgia dry-retched and coughed.

'Ooh bless you, sweetheart. Eaten something that didn't agree with you, have you?' She winked at me. 'Staying with you, is she?'

I nodded.

'You've got a long night ahead. I can't tell you how many times my oldest boy came home in a state and threw up not just in his own bed but mine too. More than once I've ended up sleeping on the sofa and chucking out the mattresses.'

Even though on this occasion it wasn't my daughter, I bloody loved Jasmine for just being a bit normal, for admitting that kids did stupid things while they were experimenting on the path to doing sensible things. It was so refreshing to have someone say, so the whole world could hear, that their kids made mistakes and she wasn't going to turn her face to the wall in shame.

I giggled. 'I'll remember that at three o'clock.'

She gestured at Georgia. 'Faye's going to owe you one.'

I waved her off with a 'Have a good night yourself' as Victor appeared with Phoebe, who looked sweaty and smudged but didn't sound too plastered.

'Do you know what Georgia's been drinking?' I asked.

'Dunno. Vodka? Cider? Maybe she'd been doing Jägerbombs. She was worried about looking bloated in her dress so she didn't eat any pizza before we went out.'

As my dad used to say, 'I've seen more fat on a butcher's pencil.' Goodness knows what these girls saw when they looked in the mirror.

Phoebe was standing with her arms crossed, scowling as though Georgia heaving up was just one big inconvenience to her. The fact she was holding her head at a funny angle, tucked into her shoulder, registered in a distant part of my brain but failed to claim pole position in my immediate concerns.

'Right. Let's try and get her home.'

'I'm not coming now,' Phoebe said. 'Me and Victor are fine.'

'It's eleven-fifteen. By the time I get Georgia home, I'll be too late to come and get you at midnight. Let's go, it's only forty-five minutes.'

Victor was moving towards the car, but Phoebe started up the drive. 'I'll get an Uber or stay at someone's.'

I ran after her, just catching sight of the love bite on her neck as she turned away. 'Get in the car, now.'

'I'm not.'

'Yes, you are.'

'No, I'm not. I haven't done anything wrong. I don't have to leave early.'

With Georgia moaning like an extra in a zombie film and Victor no doubt wondering what kind of pathetically incompetent parent he'd landed as his guardian, I felt something snap. I grabbed her arm. 'If you don't want me to go in there and make a scene that the *whole* of the sixth form will still be talking about this time next year, you'll get in the car now.'

Phoebe glared at me, disgust all over her face. 'Oooh, you and whose army?' But it did the trick and we were soon on our way.

I started quizzing Phoebe as we drove home. 'How did she get so ill?'

As the 'Dunno, lightweight probably' came from the back of the car, in my rearview mirror, I intercepted her mouthing something to Victor, who was also signalling something I couldn't quite catch.

When we got home, I left Patrick and Victor hauling Georgia out of the car, while I bundled Phoebe towards the house.

As I unlocked the front door, I said, 'You'd better get straight upstairs before Dad sees your neck.'

'Oh big deal. It's just a hickey.'

'It is a big deal actually.'

It was only Victor staggering into the hallway with Georgia that stopped me blowing up completely. He ran to get her a glass of water, fetching the bucket out of the back of the car, while Patrick shrank back grimacing every time she made a noise, until I snapped, 'Just go to bed and let me sort her out.'

I helped Georgia into the shower, found her pyjamas, then Victor and I stuck her on a chair in the kitchen, where she seemed to sober up, managing to eat a piece of toast. We sat up until two. I told Victor that he didn't have to stay, but he seemed quite happy, watching *Divergent* and eating the best part of a baguette. Eventually, Georgia said she was well enough to go to sleep. I put her on a camp bed in Phoebe's room, with instructions to wake me up if she was ill again.

She looked so young as she snuggled down. It was difficult to believe those two pre-teen girls who used to practise their dance routines to 'Livin' La Vida Loca' in my sitting room were now going out and getting completely trashed at a party.

Her last words as I walked out were, 'Sorry, Jo. Please don't tell my mum.'

'Let's talk about it in the morning.'

Victor waved goodnight to me, batting away my 'Sorry about tonight.' He disappeared into his room and I couldn't help imagining him lying down, ticking off the days to when he could leave for university and live the way he wanted to, free from me flapping about, making sure he had his five-a-day and didn't stay on the Xbox until all hours.

I nipped downstairs to double-check the front door and to get some more bread out of the freezer. I couldn't believe how much Victor ate compared with Phoebe. The soundtrack to Ginny's life must have been the fridge door opening and closing. Whereas mine was Phoebe endlessly pinging waistbands and sighing about how fat she looked. I wished she could see how gorgeous she was now, rather than in hindsight when the multiple-way mirrors in a John Lewis changing room were not the middle-age friend.

I went into the bathroom to clean my teeth and picked up Georgia's microscopic skirt from the floor. A tiny plastic bag fell out with some green dried stuff in it. I stared at it, before my lumpy old brain joined the dots. I opened the package, sniffing it gingerly as though I might snort it up my nose and suddenly start cartwheeling down the landing. It had to be weed, though I'd actually never seen any in real life. No wonder she was sick. Now all those funny little eye flashes going on in the back of the car made sense – 'Don't let Mum know it was drugs.'

I took the bag with me and, feeling slightly guilty about disturbing Patrick's rasp of deep sleep, I shook him awake.

I thrust the packet under his nose. Blearily he frowned. 'I doubt that would be enough to get a sparrow off the ground.'

'What do you mean?'

'I should think she got it so she could show off to all her friends, but I doubt it would have much effect.'

'What do you know about weed?'

'Well, I did go to university.' Patrick lay back on the pillow and closed his eyes. 'We can't do anything about it now. Talk to them in the morning.'

I tried to follow his lead, but my mind was scratching round and round, wandering from whether Phoebe was taking drugs too, to what the hell I was going to say to Faye. For some reason, I thought about when Georgia had been round here with a couple of other girls when they were about twelve or thirteen. Phoebe had been a late developer and they'd teased her about looking like a boy until she cried. When I'd mentioned it to Faye, she'd frowned and said, 'Phoebe's always found it hard to take a joke.' I could quite imagine that she would come up with some excuse about Georgia not realising what it was or keeping it safe for someone else, unable to accept that on this occasion her destined-for-Oxford daughter had, just this once, behaved slightly worse than Phoebe.

And with that thought stuck on repeat in my mind, I tossed and turned until dawn, veering from phoning Faye first thing and prefacing the conversation with 'Don't shoot the messenger' to deciding that any messenger not carrying good news wouldn't be welcome and should therefore save himself – or in this case, herself – the aggro.

CHAPTER SIX

The next morning, I felt like I'd been on the wrong end of a spliff myself, whereas the three kids were downstairs, shouting and hooting away about some poor boy thinking his ship had come in because he'd 'got with' one of the sporty girls, not realising she'd done it for a bet.

Just listening to them made me wonder how anyone made it through their teenage years with the tiniest scrap of self-esteem intact. They all went quiet as soon as I walked in. Georgia avoided making eye contact with me, but I wasn't letting her off that easily.

'How's the head this morning?' I laughed, to show Phoebe that I was so cool, that I could handle a teenage crisis without making a big deal of it. She didn't acknowledge my attempt to join in, hunched over a bowl with a microscopic amount of yoghurt, while Victor ate a tower of toast.

Georgia said, 'I'm fine, thank you,' which was either designed to make me jealous that two glasses of wine left me jaded the next day or she was putting on a brave face.

I busied about making myself tea, but I was obviously the unwanted guest at their debrief party and they soon melted away, leaving crusts and smears of jam in their wake.

I dithered over whether to confront Phoebe and Georgia about the weed. I couldn't decide whether I was more likely to get the truth from Phoebe without the added barricade of her needing to appear cool in front of her friend.

As I poured my muesli into a bowl, Phoebe appeared at the kitchen door. 'Can you drop Georgia off now?'

'I haven't had a shower or any breakfast yet. Half an hour?'

'I've got loads of homework to do and she's got to do extra essays for Oxbridge. Faye said she needed to be home by 10.30.'

Honestly, an Uber driver got more respect than me.

She did, however, creep round and give me a hug. 'Thank you for not making a big fuss about last night.' My heart did a little swell of happiness that I'd won a bit of praise from her. I nurtured the hope that this might be a building block in establishing trust between us, pushing back the treacherous expectation that the hug was a precursor to a want, a need, an ask of some sort.

Surprisingly, none was forthcoming and I told myself off for my suspicious mind.

As we left the house, I handed Georgia her bag of sicky clothes. 'These might need a bit of a soak.'

Georgia took it from me without saying a word and I drove to her home, with both of them on their phones all the way, while I wondered whether to address the little bag of weed that was now sitting on my chest of drawers. Every time I formulated the question, my nerve deserted me and suddenly I was pulling up outside Georgia's house without having found a way to ask why drugs were dropping out of her clothes.

Georgia bolted out of the car with a quick thanks.

As I opened my door, Phoebe said, 'You don't need to get out.'

'I'm just going to make sure she gets in safely. I'm not dumping her on the doorstep.'

Phoebe grumbled. 'Don't start banging on to Faye if she's back. She doesn't need to know Georgia puked. She just didn't have enough to eat before we went out.'

'Well, she's got a bag of clothes covered in sick, so it's not going to be a big secret.'

I slammed the door and followed Georgia up the drive.

Faye appeared in the porch.

'You're back early,' I said. 'I thought you'd be having a long lazy brunch.'

She rolled her eyes. 'The fire alarm went off at six o'clock this morning and once Lee's awake he can't stay in bed. So we had an early breakfast and came back.'

'Did you have a good time, though?'

'Yeah, it was lovely, thank you.' She held out her arms to hug Georgia, then took a pace back. 'Good party? You look worn out.'

Georgia managed a wan smile, and again muttered, 'Thank you for having me' in my direction and disappeared inside.

I tried to ignore Phoebe's eyes boring into my back from the car.

'She had a bit too much to drink last night.'

'She wasn't sick, was she?'

'A little bit, but I stayed with her until she sobered up. You might want to get her clothes in the wash.'

Faye folded up with mortification. 'Oh God. I'm so sorry. You should have rung me.'

'What, and ruined your romantic night away? Don't be silly. They're just experimenting at this age, aren't they? We've all done it. It's just a learning curve.' I hoped she'd remember that I was kind and generous with Georgia next time Phoebe messed up.

'Well, as long as that's all they're experimenting with. You hear all sorts about what they get into at these parties.'

Phoebe shouted out of the window. 'Mum! I need to get on with my homework!'

I waved at her. 'I'm just coming!' I turned back to Faye. 'Now you mention it, there was a strong smell of dope where they were last night.'

Faye threw her head back. 'Really? Our two better not have been involved. Hopefully Georgia's got more sense than that.'

I noticed she didn't include Phoebe in the 'way too smart for that sort of nonsense' category.

'There's never been a problem with drugs at their parties before, has there?'

I shook my head. 'Not that I'm aware of.'

'How would they even get hold of drugs?'

I shrugged. 'Maybe someone from another school? Who knows? They're probably everywhere and we're bumbling about oblivious.'

I could feel the tension seeping out of me as I told Faye a half-truth. After all, I wasn't a hundred per cent sure Georgia had actually smoked the dope.

'There weren't any outsiders at the party, were there?' she asked.

'Not that I saw. I think it was just the usual crowd, but they all seem to take plus-ones these days, so it's hard to tell.'

'Some of the year above are eighteen now. They're probably going to clubs and pubs. I guess they can get drugs down at the Kahlua Club in town if they look hard enough. You'll have to keep an eye on Victor now he's had his birthday.'

I struggled not to feel irritated that Faye was immediately passing the problem to me to worry about, shifting the focus on to Victor when in fact, the issue lay with Georgia. 'I don't think he'll cause any trouble in that way. He's a good lad. As you know, Ginny was a really close friend of mine, I'd known her for nearly thirty years. She never did drugs and would have been super-strict about that with Victor.'

She nodded. 'You always said that she was a great mum. I suppose he might just be a bit more vulnerable if he hasn't dealt with his grief. Might feel like a good opportunity to blank everything out for a few hours. And he's used to living in a big city where drugs are so much more run-of-the-mill than they are here, so he might not find them quite as scary as our girls.'

I pushed back. 'He hardly goes out at the moment anyway. And when he does, he's always with Phoebe.'

Faye grimaced, as though Phoebe wasn't much of a barrier to disaster. 'I'm just saying you should be careful because you never know who might end up coming to the house. And it's a world we don't understand. The worst that we did at their age was gather in the park with a packet of Marlboro Lights. It all seems so much more dangerous now. And you don't want Phoebe being dragged into it.' Her tone suggested that I was ridiculously naïve.

All the while she was talking, I had to suppress the urge to shout, 'Take your blinkers off, look around you and ask yourself whether it's possible that your perfect daughter has decided to use a few of her brain cells up on cannabis that she has sourced herself? Maybe she's decided not to be a robot marching relentlessly towards Oxford so you can sit twitching on the edge of your seat in anticipation of someone asking where Georgia's gone to university.'

But I didn't say any of that. I nodded in the right places, despite it being on the tip of my tongue to wipe the smug look off her face by telling her what I'd found in Georgia's skirt.

Phoebe got out of the car, slamming the door. 'Mum! I need to get some work done!'

'I'd better go.'

Faye rolled her eyes. 'Thanks for having her again. Sorry it was all a bit wild.'

'No worries at all. Glad you had a good time.'

I waved cheerily as though her jumping to the conclusion that the boy living with us was likely to have issues with drugs was something every good friend did now and again.

'I'll probably see you at the match later. Bit weird being a rugby mum after all these years of watching netball,' I said.

'I might duck out and let Lee go on his own.'

'Oh, okay. Let's catch up for coffee, then, soon.'

She nodded but didn't suggest a day and I walked back to the car, hating myself for the note of feeble begging that had threaded through that conversation: the apologetic 'Don't hate me. Don't think badly of me' even though Faye was the one out of order.

All the way home, Faye's words played on a loop, her warnings about who might start coming to the house. If the flashes of anger and the low moods were anything to go by, Victor was a long way from 'getting over' his mum's death. But, honestly, what eighteen-year-old lost a parent and carried on as though nothing had happened within a few months? It didn't mean he was going to rush off to buy a stash of mind-altering substances at the first opportunity. But maybe I was so small-town Sussex that I didn't have the imagination to see the bigger picture. There had been such an insistent tone to Faye's words that she was making me doubt my own judgement.

I grumped in through the front door to hear Patrick and Victor watching some sports programme together, commenting and laughing. Nothing about Victor sitting there in the yellow and black jumper Ginny had said made him look like a bumblebee screamed 'boy likely to go and score drugs at the local nightclub' to me.

I pretended to myself that I had no idea why I didn't stand up for him, loudly and vociferously, instead of defending him with all the force of a damp firework left in the shed since last year. But deep down I knew why – I didn't want to risk falling out with Faye.

I followed Phoebe into the kitchen, where she was busy making a huge mug of hot chocolate and showing no hurry to get on with the pressing homework of twenty minutes ago.

I dug deep for my cheery, non-threatening, let's have a lovely heart-to-heart face.

'Are you all right, love?'

'Yep.'

'Can I ask you something?'

'Maybe.'

'Was it *just* drink that made Georgia ill?'

Her eyebrows shot up. 'Yeah, too much voddy. Can't hold the booze like me.' She was aiming for jovial, but I could hear that false note, the tone that was throwing lies over the truth.

I turned my back on her to make tea. 'You don't think she'd been smoking something, do you?' I asked, as if it was such a remote possibility it was hardly worth mentioning.

'Doubt it.'

I was going to have to be more direct. 'The thing is, when I picked up her skirt, a bag of something that looked like drugs fell out.'

I heard Phoebe slump behind me.

'It was probably only a bit of weed.'

The casual way she said 'only a bit of weed' confirmed it.

'So she had been smoking dope?'

'Dope? Christ, you sound like something out of the 1950s. Stop making it sound like she OD'd on heroin or something.'

'Okay, weed then. So where did that come from?'

'I dunno. Some boy from another school.'

Phoebe was like the little fish in the rock pools she used to love, darting away whenever you got near.

'What boy? What school?'

'I don't know, someone's friend. Or cousin.'

This discussion was making the debate over whether it was rude not to invite the whole class to a Build-a-bear party look like a piece of cake. At least then you knew every child by name and had their mum's phone number on a list.

Phoebe stood with her hands on her hips. 'You better not have said anything to Faye. What were you talking about with her?'

'I was just asking about her weekend. And I had to tell her that Georgia had been sick, it was all over her clothes.'

'You better not have mentioned the drugs!'

'I didn't because I didn't really think it was my place. That's a conversation Georgia needs to have with her own mum. We just talked generally about whether drugs are becoming a thing at parties now.'

Phoebe stared at me, her eyes hooded and disdainful.

How did other mothers do it? How did they have that relationship where their daughters just chatted about stuff, anything, in a normal backwards and forwards, you speak, I speak, we share our experiences way?

'So are drugs a normal "thing" at parties now? You're not doing drugs, are you?' I gave a little laugh as though I didn't believe for one moment she would be so stupid.

'I'm not getting into this conversation because whatever I say, you won't believe me. And you'll tell Faye and if she does find out Georgia was smoking weed, she'll immediately assume that's because I got her into it and, oooh big surprise, the blame will all fall on me.'

I registered that Phoebe hadn't actually answered my question but I pressed on, because I probably wouldn't get another shot at this topic. 'That's not what she said at all. In fact, she was more concerned about how easy it is for kids of your age to get hold of drugs and how dangerous they are.'

'Oh my God. It's not like everyone was shooting up under the stairs. Georgia was just showing off, trying to be cool. She probably had about two puffs of a joint before pulling a whitey.'

'What's a "whitey"?'

Phoebe grumbled under her breath. 'Nothing. Just something that happens sometimes when you smoke weed.'

I'd have to google it later on. Right now, I needed to find out whether Victor was involved. 'Did you see Victor smoking?'

Phoebe rolled her eyes. 'No, nothing anywhere near as exciting as that. I did hear him discussing how he was struggling with the coursework for his psychology A-level though. Perhaps you'd better run that past the censors.'

'So you don't think it was his weed then?' I half-closed an eye, waiting to see if I'd snuck in my main question and got away with it.

She turned towards me with a big sneer on her face and said, 'Um, let me think about that for, oooh, a nanosecond. No, I don't think it was Victor's. Why would it be his? Let me guess. Because he's black? You're worse than Nan. You're such a hypocrite. "It's not what you look like, it's who you are." "We're not a family who judges people on what we hear about them. We judge on what we *see* happening." Unless of course your friend Faye happens to think that Victor is a crackhead and then you go along with that.'

I hissed at her to keep her voice down, then opened the fridge and pretended to be looking for the butter while I summoned up the necessary conviction to cover up the tiny doubt Faye had managed to spark in me. 'Don't be stupid. It's nothing to do with the colour of his skin. It's just that he's a bit older than you and might be more likely to come across drugs if he starts going to nightclubs and pubs. We both just want to keep you all safe.'

Phoebe had articulated the tiny misgiving shimmering away in the back of my mind, which I was ashamed I'd even allowed to creep through the cracks. I mulled it over, sifting through what Faye and I had said to each other. Nope. Nothing to suggest that Faye had discussed Victor for any other reason than that he was older and had more big-city know-how than our daughters with their sheltered little lives. Which was just as well, because everything about having Victor here was turning out to be harder than I'd envisaged without him getting into drugs on my watch.

CHAPTER SEVEN

I spent the rest of the morning unable to dispel the odd feeling that Faye was annoyed with me, despite me staying up half the night with her vomiting offspring. I kept looking at my phone, hoping for a text saying 'Sorry about last night and thank you for looking after Georgia. By the way, I didn't mean to lecture you earlier, I was just worried and you're doing a great job. Am coming to the rugby match so will see you later.' I wondered how many people in the world knew exactly where their mobiles were because they were living in hope of a beep to smooth over an awkward moment without the need to have the conversation in person.

I tried to discuss Faye's attitude with Patrick after lunch.

He put the newspaper down, but I could tell he was itching to get back to it. 'She was probably just a bit embarrassed because Georgia had shown herself up and was trying to put the spotlight on someone else.'

I leaned forwards on the table and brought my face close to his. 'But she did kind of pluck the idea out of nowhere. That because Victor's lost his mum, we need to be on drug alert.'

Patrick took a slurp of his coffee. 'She does have a point. Some kids do go right off the rails when they've suffered a trauma. And Lee and Faye can be a bit preachy about parenting. They think they've got all the answers.'

'It really gets up my pipes that she can't ever look at her kids and accept they might actually be the ones at fault. Instead her answer is to start making insinuations about everyone else.'

Patrick sighed as though I was losing myself in a teacup. 'Why don't you tell her that her comments really annoyed you, then?'

There he had the ultimate trump card to which I could only huff and puff. I was a coward. I didn't know how to confront people without being afraid of them hating me for speaking up.

Now Ginny was gone, I wasn't awash with good friends. I didn't have Patrick's confidence, the assumption that any group would part slightly to make way for me. It took me ages to make a close friend. It had only really happened with Faye through the girls being in the same class at primary school. We'd spent a lot of time together, whispering through recorder concerts, catching each other's eyes at parents' evenings and volunteering at the same school events so we could have a bit of fun. I couldn't afford to lose her.

I took myself off for a walk, trying to concentrate on the autumn colours, the birdsong, the shapes of the leaves, the things that historically soothed my brain. Ginny had always mocked my default to nature in troubled times. 'What you need is to get yourself into town where there's a bit of life.' I did love visiting her in Cardiff, the sheer vibrancy of the place, but I was always glad to get back to the village, to my cottage backing onto the cemetery, full of names like Herbert, Gladys and Hector, where the horse chestnut trees outside my bedroom window walked me through the seasons.

I sat on a bench in the churchyard. My longing to speak to Ginny was overwhelming. I'd barely had time to examine the hole she'd left in the whirlwind of getting Victor settled and keeping Phoebe clinging to the straight and narrow. I closed my eyes and turned my face to the weak sunshine glinting off the church tower. For the first time since her funeral, I lifted the tiniest corner of the lid I'd jammed down on the great big messy emotions surrounding my grief.

The rawness of her absence, the desire to hear her say, 'You need to stop being so damn nice' engulfed me. And I surrendered to it, crying my heart out between Ernest (1899–1951) on my left and Nell (1897–1961) on my right. They'd both lived longer than she had and they were born in the nineteenth century when they were probably mainlining heroin for toothache.

Ginny would be furious if she saw me shuffling through life like someone who was afraid of disturbing the air around her rather than attacking every day with fierce determination.

With that thought in my head, I said goodbye out loud to Ernest and Nell, tracing their names in the worn stone with my finger. I wondered if people were happier then than they were now, now they supposedly had 'more', more choices, more possibilities. More freedom. And, it felt to me, so many more complexities in their lives.

I wandered back to cook a proper fry-up for Victor to give him some ballast to get through his rugby game that afternoon. I called him down, and Patrick followed, with a sheaf of newspapers under his arm.

'Wow, things are looking up since you came to live with us, Victor. Beats the cheese sandwich that I usually get.'

There was something lovely about having a boy who enjoyed his food, a stark contrast to Phoebe, swinging between the vast fads that I just about mastered before she moved onto the next no carbs/no dairy/'For God's sake, I told you I was a pescatarian' stage. It was so relaxing to serve up a plate of sausage, bacon and eggs without the microscopic inspection of 'Is this egg from a battery hen?'

Phoebe slid in, turned her nose up at the fry-up and fiddled about with a pot of cottage cheese for the whole time it took Patrick and Victor to polish off lunch and have a second bacon butty.

'Are you coming down to watch Victor play rugby?' I asked her.

'Dunno. Let me see what's happening.' And off she went into that world, the one of secret smiles, frantic typing and finally an aggressive silencing of the phone. Which all amounted to 'I'll come down for a bit.'

I still felt strangely nervous as I walked onto the rugby fields, a bit like I did when Phoebe was a tiny baby and I was around my friends who'd already had children. That curious pride, of wanting them to think she was the most gorgeous, best-behaved, ahead-of-the-curve baby ever. And, alongside, the fear of judgement from those more experienced in child-rearing that I was a bumbling idiot who made such a palaver out of breastfeeding. And now, just like I did then, I felt a novice at boy-rearing. And rugby watching.

Victor, on the other hand, was always at his most confident. I watched him walk over to the group and immediately get stuck in with the warm-up, snatching a ball, and hurling it at a boy who was standing with his hands in his pockets. There was something so primeval and animalistic about all those young men pitching their strength and speed against each other. I wondered if I'd ever relax into the game instead of wishing for it to be over before he hurt himself.

I whispered as much to Patrick, who tucked my arm under his and said, 'He'll get the odd knock, but that's all part of the game. I played for ten years and never got seriously injured. Well, apart from breaking my collarbone.'

The worst injury Phoebe had ever had was getting a piece of Lego stuck up her nose and that had turned me into a panicking idiot.

As the match kicked off, Faye arrived. I gave her a big hug and pretended to myself that she'd embraced me just as she always did, that the slight stiffness, the holding back, was all in my head.

Phoebe scanned the field. 'Is Georgia coming down?'

Faye shook her head. 'She's stayed at home to get on top of her homework. I think she's realised that partying and homework aren't a great combination. She's really decided to knuckle down this year – she doesn't want to miss any coursework deadlines.' I wondered if Faye knew that Phoebe was already two weeks behind with her English essays and the teacher had completely lost the plot in front of everyone. I tried not to take her comments as a criticism of my own attempts to get Phoebe to focus. I wanted to explain that I was doing my best, that the more I nagged and clamped down on

Phoebe, the more rebellious and difficult she became until I was frightened to push any more in case she dropped out of the sixth form completely.

Phoebe glared at me as though I'd been telling tales and said, 'See you later. I'm going to find Mia and Beth.'

As soon as she'd gone, I asked Faye if Georgia had had any ill effects from the party. 'No, she seems fine. Hopefully she's learnt her lesson.'

'Did she mention there being any drugs there?'

The image of that bag of weed burned brightly in my mind.

'No, but I doubt that she would recognise them if they bit her on the bottom. She's so naïve sometimes.' Faye said it as though she was criticising Georgia, but it felt as if there was an unspoken jab at Phoebe hanging in the air, that she'd be an absolute hotshot at the identity parade on all the Class As.

I let it go.

Faye's husband, Lee, joined us, slapping Patrick on the back. 'Come to watch the future contenders for the Six Nations again then?' he said, which led into an easy conversation about the form of the England players, followed by the chances of our school getting anywhere in the *Daily Mail* Trophy.

I searched for Victor, before I spotted him on the sidelines wearing a hoodie. I turned to Faye. 'I hope he'll get on at some point.'

'They'll probably swap him in at half-time, if not before. I suppose they want to get a few tries up before they bring on someone who's still really new to the team.'

As I watched the boys pile into each other, studded boots dangerously close to their young faces, I felt that familiar angst, torn between wanting Victor to get a chance to do what he loved and a wish for him to stay away from the action, safe from harm.

Patrick and Lee were shouting out incomprehensible things from the sidelines, with Lee getting increasingly agitated. 'Knock-on, ref!' 'Offside!'

I still couldn't get used to how seriously Faye followed the rugby. She was nothing like her normal chatty self, locked onto every move Jordan made, ignoring my attempts to talk about anything else in favour of commenting on the match.

About twenty minutes in, Jordan fumbled a pass, allowing the other side to commandeer the ball and score a try. Patrick said, 'He should have kicked that out. Didn't have enough support around him to make that work.'

He'd obviously overstepped the new 'father' on the touchline opinion quota because Lee pulled a face and said, 'It's not the Rugby World Cup, mate.'

Faye joined in. 'It's early in the season. He's just finding his feet.'

I'd have felt the need to apologise and spend the rest of the match cheering overloudly every time Jordan touched the ball, but Patrick just ignored them.

Then a player went off and Victor came on. For a boy that seemed so gentle in every other area of his life, he was a force to be reckoned with. There was something in his movements that reminded me of Ginny, that same fluidity and rhythm. Within minutes, he'd powered through the opposition with an aggression that surprised me, proper hand in face, shoulder-barge stuff. When he dived over the line to score, I thought I was going to burst with excitement.

'That was amazing!' I turned to Faye, all wide-eyed with delight.

'He's certainly getting a few lucky breaks today,' she said.

I frowned, that funny little prickle of anxiety flickering again. 'I think he's used to playing at county level where he lived before. I watched him a couple of times and there were some big old boys at the Cardiff club.'

'He's a great asset to the team. Black people are so quick on their feet. They've got that whole running thing in their DNA,' Lee said.

I felt a coldness settle on me. When Jordan got the captaincy, Lee saw it as the rightful outcome of years of schlepping to rugby matches, putting Jordan in rugby holiday camps, taking him to

Twickenham to see the greats. At no point did he shrug and say, 'Well, he was only made captain because being an English boy with blonde hair/Scottish grandparents/a few freckles across his nose means he has a superior ability to read the ball.' I scanned my memory. No, Jordan being captain was all about his amazing talent.

I caught Patrick's eye to see if he was reacting, but he just said, 'He's doing really well, isn't he?'

Maybe I was being too protective.

While we watched, several parents came over to speak to us, complimenting Patrick on Victor's rugby as though we had anything to do with it. I was amazed how everyone seemed to know so much about him.

Jasmine came bowling up, barely visible under a woolly scarf wound around her neck and face. 'Victor's playing brilliantly. It's so brave what you're doing. You're so generous to take in someone else's child. I'd be terrified. I've made enough mistakes with my own brood without inflicting my crap parenting on anyone else's.' She jerked her head towards her ex-husband who was busy booming out the statistics of how many rugby players ended up with broken necks and concussion to goggle-eyed mums. She leant into me and whispered, 'He'd never have let me take in someone else's child. Far too selfish.' She clapped her hands gleefully. 'That's why he's an ex. Arrogant pig.'

In a village where the only thing I ever heard about people's marriages was how many diamonds were on the bracelet their husbands had bought for Valentine's Day, I loved Jasmine for her honesty. At the same time, I was conscious of Faye separating herself, not joining in, as though Jasmine was too quirky, not mainstream enough for her to bother with. I kept trying to involve Faye in the conversation, but her face had a funny little expression that I recognised as her waiting for Jasmine to leave.

I turned away from her and filled Jasmine in, quietly, on how I didn't see myself as brave or generous and I didn't deserve for other people to see me like that either. Her kindness, her lack of judgement, had suddenly uncorked all the guilt I had swilling around in me. She didn't flinch when I said it was an action we'd been trapped into rather than embraced. That I'd been so small-spirited that I hadn't explicitly told Ginny, 'Victor is the last person you need to worry about, he'll be absolutely fine with us.'

Jasmine shrugged. 'You did step up though and, let's face it, if we're really honest, who does have the energy for other people's problems? Most of us are already hanging on by our fingertips.'

In the ten minutes I was chatting to her, she made me feel so much better, that I wasn't a poor excuse for a human being, that actually it was normal to worry about our imperfect family having to expand to include yet another complication. And now our lives were being played out with what felt like a whole crowd of critical assessors looking on, holding up their three out of ten scoreboards.

Jasmine went off to fetch one of her daughters from dance and Faye pulled a face. 'Got yourself a new best friend there. She'll be sending you over her mung bean recipes if you don't watch it.'

I smiled as though I was taking it in good humour, but really I wanted to say, 'At least she doesn't make out everything is perfect like you do.' Instead I said, 'I like her. I think she's got a really good heart.'

Faye looked at me as though I needed my bumps reading.

Before I could examine all of that more closely, the other side scored two more tries in quick succession and Jordan took a knock to the head straight afterwards. He was helped off the pitch and Faye and Lee went over to check on him.

'I thought all that stuff about Victor being good at rugby because he was black was a bit off,' I said.

Patrick said, 'He's just plucking any old excuse out of the air because Victor was outclassing Jordan. He's the best player on the pitch. By a long way.'

And as if to prove Patrick's point, Victor thundered down the field, did a neat dodge of several boys who were steaming over to halt his advance, and ducked over the line with several metres of clear space to spare.

Patrick went wild. 'Way to go, Victor! Woooooo!' His face shone with joy and pride as though he'd been responsible for throwing a rugby ball around with him as soon as he could walk. A wave of relief rushed through me that Patrick was showing some interest in Victor. Quickly followed by a sting of regret that I'd never seen Patrick embrace anything that Phoebe had done with such unbridled enthusiasm.

Honestly, as my mother would say, 'Jo, your ability to see a grey cloud on a sunny day is astonishing.' Or as Phoebe put it quite often when I was whittling about her being safe, 'Do you read books on how to infect people with your negativity?'

I needed to be more Patrick. Or better still, more Ginny.

Lee came back to grab his rucksack.

'Is Jordan okay?' I asked.

'Yeah, you know, a bit concussed. See him out of a few games though. Bad luck this early on in the season. Not sure who's up to skippering in his place.'

Patrick returned his attention to the field as Victor took out the other team's prop to a huge cheer from the home crowd. 'Victor's doing a good job. He could easily lead the boys.'

Lee waved dismissively at Patrick. 'I don't think they'll choose someone who's only been at the school five minutes.'

Patrick stood his ground. 'He's the best player though. Might be good to have some new blood in charge, take a fresh look at the team. If they've all been playing the same positions since the first year, might be time to have a shake-up.'

Lee cleared his throat. 'Come on, mate. I know the boy's had a tough time, but you can't just hand him everything on a plate.'

'Nothing to do with handing him anything on a plate. Look at him. He's head and shoulders above the others,' he said, turning away from Lee and focusing on the game.

I shuffled about, admiring Patrick for standing his ground but still fighting my own temptation to pat Lee's arm and whisper, 'Sorry, he's getting a bit carried away. He's never had a boy to cheer for before.'

Instead I stuttered, 'I hope Jordan's all right. Keep us posted.'

Lee didn't acknowledge I'd spoken and hurried off.

I shivered next to Patrick, a sick feeling in my stomach that even something that was supposedly joyful had become a battleground. In between cheering the line-outs, Patrick was muttering about how Victor 'read the ball' so much better than anyone else. I was relieved when the whistle blew.

Despite Lee, I couldn't help smiling at the boys lifting Victor up into the air. I'd never had that feeling of belonging, of everyone congratulating me because I had some outstanding talent or anything that made me the heroine of the moment. It was about time Victor had something to celebrate.

We walked over towards them, the chatter and camaraderie floating over to us. The head of games was saying, 'And I'm thrilled to present Victor Yaro with Man of the Match! Not bad for only his fourth outing with the team.'

A huge cheer went up and two of the sturdiest players hoisted Victor onto their shoulders.

Up by the car park, I saw Lee reach Faye and Jordan, then, after a moment, Faye craned her head round in our direction. I'd have to ring her and smooth things over. She was always going on about Lee flying off the handle over nothing. Hopefully we'd end up having a good laugh about our husbands squaring up to each other over a schoolboys' game of rugby.

When we got home, Victor went off to the shower and Patrick made us tea. 'Lee can be a right pompous idiot sometimes. We've spent years listening to what a brainbox Georgia is and what a sporting talent Jordan has. But he can't bring himself to acknowledge that Victor is far better than anyone else on that pitch. And he could actually cut him a bit of slack, give Victor something to be excited about rather than getting stuck on whether he's having it too easy. No other kids at that school are having to deal with their mum dying.'

Patrick's strength of feeling surprised and heartened me, appearing like it did as the first green shoots of spontaneous interest in Victor's welfare. I was the eternal malcontent though.

'You're right, but let's try not to fall out with anyone over it. I think people struggle with change. It's such a close-knit school. They've all been together since they were five. Maybe they're just threatened by someone new coming in. Lee's always been a bit pushy about Jordan's rugby.'

Patrick scowled. 'Well, tough shit. He'd better not trot out that "running in the DNA" line again or I really will take him to task.' So he had noticed Lee's comment. I was glad it wasn't just me being super sensitive.

For the umpteenth time, I wished I could apologise to Ginny for not understanding properly on the rare occasions she moaned about people thinking they knew what she was like because she was black. All that having to take it in good spirit when the lads at work used to sing 'Simply the Best' every time she walked into an editorial meeting. I'd actually been a bit envious that she got such a welcome, as though they were specifically waiting for her to turn up. Whereas people only tended to notice me if the coffee and sandwiches didn't arrive on time.

Now though, twenty-six years on, I really understood how offensive the constant references to something that was just the body she was born with must have been. A bit like those irritating people saying, 'You've got a spot on your nose,' in case there was any chance at all that you hadn't noticed. And that was before they made you the spokesperson for every acne sufferer in the world.

I sat at the kitchen table wondering whether I'd ever stop missing her.

CHAPTER EIGHT

The following Wednesday, Mum called me first thing in the morning when I'd just got back from the school run. 'I've caught you!' As though my life consisted of jollies to the theatre in London and trips to Brighton to check out new restaurants.

'How are you, Mum?' I asked.

'I wanted to talk to you about Christmas.'

'What about it?' I asked, glancing at the clock and sighing as I saw another half an hour of cracking on with my freelance report writing disappearing into a rabbit hole of what she should buy everyone before she came to the conclusion that a Body Shop voucher and some golf balls would take care of Phoebe and Patrick.

'I was wondering, as it's the first Christmas with Victor, if we should try and do something different.'

I immediately felt ashamed of being uncharitable but still flipped the laptop lid open and tried to type quietly while Mum rattled on.

'When I was on the way back from that charity committee I belong to with Edna, you know, over Higher Morsten way, we walked past that new place that's open, what's it called?'

'I don't know, Mum,' I said, reading down a column of figures.

'Anyway, it specialises in meat. Normal ones, beef and pork, but it had a few unusual ones, like goat and rabbit, and I thought Victor might like it. Or there was crocodile. That might be more up his street. Do they eat crocodile in Nigeria?'

I was pretty sure that Victor had eaten far more Nando's than goat or bloody crocodile. And Ginny was a right fusspot about meat – 'Nothing on the bone! I don't want to imagine it running around.' An email pinged into my inbox chasing me for a report. I didn't really have time to get into yet another explanation that Victor was as British as Phoebe so I limited myself to 'Victor eats what we eat, Mum. He doesn't need any exotic dishes.'

I heard the unmistakable sniff that preceded a huffy 'I was only trying to help.' I rushed in before I spent the day feeling guilty for snapping at her. 'It sounds like somewhere Patrick would like if they do a good steak. I'm not sure about Phoebe. Did you notice if they did any fish dishes?'

'They did chicken on skewers and spaghetti bolognese.'

Mum seemed to be overlooking the essential difference between plaice and pork.

'I'll talk to Patrick about it. Perhaps we'll go and have a recce at the weekend.' I was in that closing-down, getting-off-the-phone mode.

Mum plodded on, oblivious. 'Your friends were in there, so I expect it's quite good.'

'What friends?' Mum was wasted on tea making and doily watch at the old folks' home. She would be invaluable to the police as an unlikely surveillance expert.

'That Faye. She was sitting right in the window.'

'Oh, I'll ask her what she thought.'

'She was with a group of women.' Mum sniffed. 'I think they'd been drinking because I could hear them cackling through the window.'

I wondered who she was with. It could be anyone. Her book group? But she usually invited me along to that – 'Doesn't matter that you haven't read *the* book. You read loads. And anyway, we mainly drink wine.' They usually met at the curry house though. I wracked my brains for other groups of friends.

'Did you recognise anyone she was with?'

'That Andrea, you know, the pilot's wife. She was there.' Mum was so busy proving her sleuthing talent, it didn't occur to her to ask why I wanted to know.

Faye couldn't stand Andrea, so it couldn't be something Faye had organised.

Mum rattled on. 'And that physiotherapist who charged your dad ridiculous money to look at his back that time.'

'Rita Starling?'

'Rita Stealing more like.' Mum had never been in favour of any activity that she couldn't cut a coupon out of the paper for.

Although she would never admit it, Faye had never liked Rita, ever since her daughter 'took' Georgia's place in a public speaking competition and won. Rita had always been on the periphery of Faye's group of friends anyway so it was strange that she'd been included and I hadn't. I told myself not to be paranoid, that there would be a reason they were all out together. I didn't want Mum to twig I hadn't been invited and turn her detective skills on me. 'Right, Mum, I'll talk to you later. I've got lots of work to get in for this evening.'

'To my mind, you work far too hard. Patrick's a good man for not getting cross about the long hours you do.'

I put my head in my hands and bit back the 'Patrick's a lucky man that I work my arse off so he doesn't have to carry the entire financial responsibility for the household. And I do all the washing and cooking!'

I said goodbye, wrestling with a feeling of being excluded. I couldn't concentrate on my report. My mum had confirmed what I'd been trying to ignore. Over the last few days, Faye, who was always glued to her phone, had been slow to respond to my text messages asking how Jordan was. I couldn't help wondering whether her curt replies, with just one kiss rather than the usual stack of over-the-top emojis, were because she was in a hurry or distracted or because she was in fact grumpy because of what Patrick had said to Lee.

When I'd mentioned that I thought they'd fallen out with us to Patrick, he'd dismissed the idea. 'Faye maybe, but blokes don't fall out over stuff like that. We say what we have to say then move on.'

I logged into Facebook to see if I could work out what was going on. Nothing on Faye's page. I tried Rita's, but her privacy settings meant I couldn't see anything. Another click.

Like a blow to the stomach, on Andrea's page was a group shot of about ten mums from school, wine glasses in the air. When I read the caption underneath, I just kept staring. 'Happy fiftieth birthday, Rita. Well done everyone for not letting the surprise out of the bag – and great job organising, Faye!'

Underneath were comments from various people about what great fun it had been, including one from Faye, 'Fab food and company! Let's do it again soon, birthday or no birthday!'

I didn't even know it was Rita's birthday. Presumably they'd all had a whip round for a present but no one had asked me. I couldn't help imagining them slyly slipping tenners to the holder of the kitty, being careful not to do it when I was around. I got up and made a cup of tea. It seemed so childish at forty-eight to mind being left out. But Faye was supposed to be my ally, the person who had my back. I would have always made sure she was invited if I'd been in charge. I had a sudden rush of regret at the way I reacted when Phoebe came crying in about so-and-so not inviting her to a sleepover, brushing it away with a 'Well, you can't invite everyone every time.'

I wondered how I could confront Faye, depressed in the knowledge that I might drop in that I knew they'd been out without me and let her get away with a 'Oh yes, it was a last-minute thing and I knew you were really busy at work.' And somehow I'd feel I was in the wrong. It was easier to suck it up and say nothing.

I couldn't shake off the impression that there was a sizeable band of mums trying to distance themselves from me and my daughter, in case Phoebe contaminated their precious offspring with getting into trouble in class. Or maybe they didn't approve of me taking in Victor and inflicting my inadequate parenting on another poor child. I didn't want to believe that they had an issue with the fact that the school had engineered a place for him in an already over-subscribed sixth form.

I was just fiddling about trying to compose a text message that wouldn't sound clingy and needy, shaking my head at the thought I even needed to second-guess how to suggest meeting up for a coffee, when my phone went. I had a little stab of fright that it was Faye, calling to tell me exactly why I hadn't been invited. Then a much bigger stab of fright when the number of Phoebe's school popped up.

It was Mrs Grosvenor, Phoebe's head of year. 'Mrs Clark? I'm ringing about Phoebe – don't worry, she's not hurt – but she's been shoplifting in town with another student.'

My heart leapt with an equal burst of fear and fury. 'What? Where was she?'

'A security guard caught her pocketing some make-up in Teen Dream.'

Unlike me with my one eyeliner and one lipstick, Phoebe had a whole shelf full of make-up to keep herself tinted, lined and glossed for several years to come and certainly no glaring omission I could see that merited getting a criminal record. Stupid, stupid girl. I didn't know whether I was more disappointed by her stealing or by the fact that it didn't really surprise me. How did someone like me, apologising for the inconvenience if I returned the wrong size trousers to Marks and Spencer, unable to relax in my seat on a crowded train if there was someone even a couple of years older than me nearby, end up with a daughter who thought it was okay to steal?

'Was Victor with her?'

Mrs Grosvenor sounded puzzled. 'Victor? No. He's in his economics class. She was with Georgia Samuels.'

I didn't know whether it was my imagination, but there'd been a matter-of-factness about Phoebe's involvement but a hint of 'it's very out of character' about Georgia's.

'She's at Teen Dream now but was withholding her name, so of course they phoned us because they're in school uniform. We pieced it together because she was with Georgia, who was cooperating.'

Withholding. Cooperating. Despite my shame at Phoebe's behaviour, Mrs Grosvenor's sudden descent into police speak seemed a bit extreme, as though Phoebe was a key witness in a murder trial rather than a stupid sixteen-year-old who'd made off with a tube of Kisses Under the Stars.

'Are they calling the police?'

'I'm not sure, but I suggest you get down there *tout suite*.'

Mrs Grosvenor was veering into Hercule Poirot territory.

'Right. Yes. Sorry about this, Mrs Grosvenor. I'm really embarrassed.'

'We'll talk to them both when they get back here, but, clearly, we can't have pupils from the school playing truant and running amok in town, giving us all a bad name. There'll have to be some sort of sanction.'

'I completely understand. Of course. We fully support any sanctions.' I wanted to cry and say, 'I'm not a bad parent. I cook broccoli. I monitor screen time. I draw the line at (really bad) swearing.'

I ended the call and grabbed my coat. I stuck my mobile on speaker in the car, left a message for Patrick and drove the ten minutes to town. I tried to ring Faye, but her phone went to voicemail.

She was already there when I got there, in the manager's office. She had her arm round Georgia, who was sobbing her heart out. Phoebe's face was set, but there was no doubt a wave of relief passed over her when I walked in.

The manager wasted no time. 'We've taken their photos and will share them across our network of stores. They are banned from all our shops and if there is any repeat offending, the police will be called.'

My body sagged with gratitude that we would be spared the humiliation of sitting in a police station. It would be just my luck to bump into my mum's neighbour whose social life revolved around reporting the speed of the traffic through our village. This was one escapade that my mother didn't need to know about. 'Thank you. It won't happen again. I am really sorry.'

We walked out of the shop in silence.

As soon as we got out into the street, Faye turned to us. 'I'm grounding Georgia until Christmas and I'd appreciate it if you would keep your distance for a bit, Phoebe. I don't think you two are a good influence on each other currently and it's a very important year, so it's best if you don't see each other until you sort yourselves out.'

I nodded. 'I don't know what's got into you both. What on earth were you thinking?'

Georgia sniffed. 'Phoebe said she'd done it loads of times and got away with it.'

'Phoebe! Dad is not going to be impressed by this at all.'

I knew I'd just become a version of my mother's 'Wait till your father gets home', but Phoebe didn't acknowledge she'd heard any of it.

Faye wasn't cutting me any slack. There was no sense of 'We've both got a challenge on our hands.' Just an 'I will be keeping my daughter away from yours.' And I wasn't sure if it was my own shame at being the mother of a daughter who went on shoplifting jaunts, but I felt that the whole walk back to the car park was enveloped in a cloud of unspoken blame, laced with, 'Georgia is going to Oxford and I'm not letting your daughter derail my dreams.'

We reached our car first. I got in, waved to Faye and said, 'Speak soon. Give me some dates when you're free for dinner at ours in November.' There was a tiny beat. 'Or December.' My words trailed off and I made a point of not looking at the expression on her face.

'It's a busy time at the moment, what with Lee's mum and dad not making their mind up about when they want to come and stay and Lee's got a lot on with work.'

I opened the car door, nodding like I didn't know she was giving me the brush-off. It certainly wasn't the moment to investigate my exclusion from Rita's fiftieth.

In the end, Faye couldn't quite bring herself to draw a definitive line in the sand and muttered, 'I'll double-check.'

'Let me know when you know.' I got in the car, trying to ward off the feeling that I'd just confirmed a string of winter Saturday nights with *Strictly* rather than Faye and Lee.

The hurt that our friendship couldn't withstand a bit of trouble with our kids filled me with an anger that I directed towards Phoebe, becoming the raging woman snapping down the indicator at every corner, pushing through on amber lights, speeding onto the roundabout like I had a host of policemen on my tail.

'I mean, what were you actually thinking of? What did Georgia mean by you'd done it "loads of times"? What is going on with you? Do you want to end up in a young offenders' institution rather than university? Because the way you're going, that's what will happen!'

Phoebe stared out of the window, refusing to rise to my 'What? You must have an answer. Help me understand!' Though, in reality, I was beyond wanting to understand and far more intent on finding an outlet for my impotence that I'd done such a poor job at bringing up Phoebe.

She didn't say a word, just slammed out of the car and straight into the house.

I staggered out, light-headed with rage and weak with hopelessness. What I did know was that I hadn't improved anything. I chalked up a little tally in my mind.

Bellowing out my own upset and anger: tick.

Trying to find a way forward: a big fat zero.

Reflective listening skills: Room for significant improvement.

Victor arrived home soon afterwards. He always did a little tap on the door before he came in, even though I told him over and over again to walk straight in. There was something lively about him, just like Ginny when she'd nailed an interview with someone the bigger magazines had wanted or been asked to go on the radio about a feature she'd written.

I managed to say, 'How was your day?' even though I wanted to hang my head and say, 'I'm sorry you've had to come and live in this chaos. Would you like me to see if you could live with Cory?'

But Victor was grinning from ear-to-ear as though our little cottage and his box room were paradise. 'I've been made captain of the rugby team while Jordan is concussed. I might get to be co-captain when he comes back if I do well while he's off.'

I forced my face into a smile. 'That's fantastic. Well done.'

That wouldn't suit Faye and Lee at all.

CHAPTER NINE

Patrick was nowhere near as furious as I was about the shoplifting. 'Honestly, my sister got caught with a whole load of pick 'n' mix up her sleeve in Woolworths at Phoebe's age, but she didn't turn into a career criminal. I know it's not ideal, but I don't think it means she'll end up in prison.'

'But it's not a good time for her to get a reputation as trouble when the school are going to start predicting grades and writing university references.'

Patrick sighed. 'They're not going to be looking at any of that for another year. Sometimes I think you're too strict and that's what she's rebelling against.'

'Too strict? What, because I don't want to have to stand in front of some bloody security guard and store manager and say, "Yes sir, no sir, it won't happen again, sir?" Next time, you can go and feel like the shittest parent in the world. Perhaps you'd like to talk to her, see if you can get through to her. At the very least we should ground her.'

Patrick's face was blank and neutral, as though I was speaking in a reasonable, conciliatory manner rather than having a go at him. 'I think we need to be careful about giving her more reason to kick against us. And if she's grounded, it means Victor won't really be able to go anywhere either because he hasn't got his own social life yet.'

I knew what Patrick said about Victor was true but in that moment, I didn't want to have to consider what was right for him when I was so worried about Phoebe. I was working out how to articulate that without sounding totally heartless when Patrick said,

'Maybe we just need to take the pressure off and let her make her own decisions a bit more. Instead of encouraging her to go straight to university, perhaps she'd benefit from taking a gap year.'

My whole chest constricted with the horror of the idea of Phoebe lounging in bed until midday, watching Netflix all afternoon, bursting into my office willy-nilly and turning up her nose at any suggestion she might see if Morrisons needed any checkout staff. Meanwhile, Patrick would disappear off to his job as an HR consultant every day, imparting his wisdom about staff challenges at conferences and training courses, liberated from the tension at home.

'I'm really wondering if we've bitten off more than we can chew with Phoebe playing up and Victor needing our support,' I said, too stressed to care that I was dropping straight into the trap of Patrick's original objections.

Wisely, he decided not to remind me of that. But he still infuriated me by looking as though I'd found a tiny little issue and blown it up into a big fuss. Then again, he wasn't the one who had to go into the village and have Eileen who ran the newsagents peering over her glasses and tilting her head sympathetically, 'How's it going with that poor boy? It must be so hard for him. All of you. Not easy taking on another woman's child.' She'd pause, as though she was waiting for me to fill her in on exactly how difficult we were finding it.

I kept batting her off with platitudes – 'He's doing really well in the circumstances.'

'Your husband was very good to take him in.'

The fact that everyone, including my own mother, thought Patrick was some kind of saint irritated me to an abnormal degree.

'He's a lucky lad. You'll do a grand job of keeping him on the straight and narrow,' she'd conclude. She managed to make it sound as though we'd plucked Victor from the jaws of gang warfare.

For one brief moment, I'd nearly succumbed to the temptation of sweeping all the pear drops and sherbet dip-dabs off the shelves and shouting, 'He had a perfectly nice family. His mother loved him. He doesn't need keeping on the straight and narrow.' I'd love to see her face if I said, 'Actually the one who's going right off the rails is Georgia, you know, Faye's daughter. Drugs and shoplifting in one month.'

And over the next week or so, I noticed that it wasn't just people in the village who had opinions about our lives. At school drop-off, the women who always waved before, sometimes stopping to chat, were suddenly ducking into their cars as though they couldn't be a minute late for the Starbucks they'd ordered on their mobiles. When I said as much to Patrick, he thought I was being paranoid but he didn't have to face them all and ask himself if the whole school knew that Phoebe had been stealing. I'd pretty much got my answer the day before when Jasmine had knocked on the car window while I waited for Phoebe.

'How are you doing?'

I considered responding with a cheery 'I'm fine. How are things with you?' but there was something about Jasmine that just made me want to be honest. 'Not that great.'

Her face displayed no surprise, so I ploughed on.

'Is it common knowledge that my daughter's a thief?'

She laughed. 'I had heard that there'd been a make-up incident in town, but I don't think that makes her a Category A criminal. Isn't it just a teenage rite of passage? I used to nick the plastic mirrors off *Jackie* magazine when I was about thirteen.' She giggled. 'Can you even imagine a teenager now being bothered about a crappy old mirror or lipstick on the front of a magazine? Christian Dior eyeshadow or not worth the bother!'

Jasmine always made me feel so much better about things in a way Patrick did not. And for some reason, probably because it was beginning to sink in that there was no quick fix for Phoebe, that we'd have a lot more 'incidents' before we saw daylight, if we ever did, I felt so aggrieved that he was just getting on with life as normal. I wished I could do the same.

That evening, I tried to divert my energy into cooking rather than the row I wanted to pick with Patrick, opting instead to chop up peppers and onions with a satisfying smack on the wooden board. The next thing I heard was Patrick on his mobile in the sitting room saying, 'Cory! My man! How's it going?' Then, 'Yeah, all good. Victor's been made captain of the rugby team. Feels like he's been here forever. Come down one Saturday. In a few weeks? Sure. Be good to see you. Phoebe? Yeah, fine, just getting used to the bigger workload in the lower sixth…'

Then they went on to talk about a conference Patrick had coming up, the problems he had in getting good back-office support.

I stood marvelling at Patrick's apparent ability to brush over the whole shoplifting saga. I wasn't sure I'd ever be able to let her go into town again without saying, 'Make sure you don't walk out with anything you haven't paid for.' I tried to give Patrick the benefit of the doubt that he and Cory didn't really do emotional, seemingly much more comfortable in the arena of work and finances.

On the other hand, I wished Faye wasn't being all funny with me so I could ring and hear her say, 'Think how many calories worrying uses up. You'll be a size ten in no time.' And I'd come off the phone feeling a bit better, like this was a tricky time of life but it wouldn't last forever.

I peered round the corner and gave Patrick the ten-minute signals. He was waxing lyrical about Victor's sporting prowess. He'd never championed Phoebe in the same way. But then again maybe there hadn't been so much to champion.

I raked guiltily through my memory for times when we'd been really proud of her. I'd thought at one point she might go to drama school – the irony – because she loved acting and even at eight or nine had no problem remembering her lines and delivering them with aplomb. I'd basked in the reflected glory, congratulating myself on raising such a confident daughter. All that promise had dissipated by the time senior school rolled around, replaced by fussing over whether her shoes were 'in', the proclamation that acting in school productions was only for 'melts', with an accompanying sneer that left me in no doubt that I wouldn't be seeing her on stage anytime soon.

A change in Patrick's tone cut into my self-flagellation.

'Did Ginny ever give you any indication who he was? She was always so secret squirrel about it. Whenever I mentioned it, she always said Victor had the people he needed around him.' Then I heard him lower his voice. If ever there was a tactic to pique someone's interest for something they shouldn't overhear, whispering was the way forward. I stirred quietly, taking care not to scrape the spoon on the bottom of the pan, but all I could hear was, 'Interesting. I never heard her say that.'

Disappointingly, the topic moved on to the subject of pensions and I went back to pouring stock into the risotto.

When Patrick finally got off the phone, I said, 'Sounded like an interesting conversation?'

He glanced over his shoulder. 'Just the usual. Hoping to get together with him soon.'

'What were you saying about Victor's dad?'

'Oh nothing. Cory had some idea that Ginny really loved his dad, that it wasn't as casual as she made out.'

I shushed him as I heard a bedroom door bang upstairs.

'Well, even if that was the case, and she *never* gave me that impression, I don't know how we would find him anyway.'

Ginny had had that uncanny way of appearing to be really open, of encouraging everyone to tell her their secrets, while tightening a drawstring around her own business. She'd always shrugged when I'd asked her about Victor's father. 'He turned out to be married. I didn't even bother telling him I was pregnant.' I had meant to ask her for a bit more information so I could answer Victor's questions if he showed a desire to know more, but in my last few visits, I somehow never found the courage to deal with difficult subjects. It was so much easier to default into reminiscing about the backpacking holiday in Thailand in our early twenties when we'd shared a hut on Ko Samui with a resident rat. I loved seeing her face break into a smile as we remembered dancing at the Green Mango under the stars. I knew you were supposed to say all the things you needed to, ask all the questions that you'd never otherwise get an answer to, but sometimes I just wanted to tap into a shared experience that took us back to a time when we had sand between our toes and years ahead of us. And then she'd died before I found the nerve to pin her down.

Patrick said, 'I'm quite glad Ginny wasn't in touch with him really. It would be horrible for Victor to get really settled with us, then have some other bloke swoop in and cart him off to Toronto or wherever.'

I blinked at this total turn-up for the books and chose to shout up the stairs that dinner was ready rather than pick up on the fact that Patrick no longer felt we needed a six-month review of Victor's future here. I was disappointed that my reaction wasn't one of straightforward relief but before I could examine the thought further, Phoebe came bounding down the stairs, chatty for once about her friends learning to drive.

She said, 'I love those little Fiat 500s. So cool. I'd love one of those.'

Patrick said, 'You can forget that. You'll have to share Mum's Ka.'

I saw the hurt flit across Phoebe's face before she said, 'Don't worry, I never expect anything from you.' I wish I knew what the right approach was. Having more or less everything she wanted hadn't worked but Patrick was right that our clampdown in the weeks following the whole video debacle had led to more defiant and extreme behaviour.

After debating long and hard with Patrick about whether we should ban her from going out completely, we'd finally decided to try and win her over with kindness rather than punish her harshly and risk out and out warfare. Patrick seemed to have forgotten what we'd agreed, so I shot him a look and tried to keep some kind of tenuous connection going. 'I don't think Phoebe meant she expected a car, she was just filling us in on what people were driving.' I spoke gently. 'You're not even seventeen for another few months so we can look at it again then.' But it was too late. That tiny gossamer-thin thread from her world to ours had snapped.

Patrick mumbled something about how her behaviour would have to improve significantly before he felt minded to pay for lessons, let alone a car. 'An upturn in grades and a few less dramas and we might think about it.' He then invited Victor to go to a business conference with him in London in the Christmas holidays.

I did wonder why we bothered discussing what tactic to take with her when Patrick just seemed to ignore what we'd settled on. Of course, I didn't want to give Phoebe the impression she could get away with anything but in a different way from Victor, she'd also had to adjust to a lot of change. Maybe we were expecting too much of a sixteen-year-old. I smiled at her, trying to show her that I understood why she might feel left out, but before I could suggest going to the theatre or booking a spa day, she pushed her plate away and disappeared to her bedroom.

I should have been thrilled that Patrick was starting to come round to the idea of Victor living here, but instead I couldn't escape feeling that if someone was winning, there was a corresponding loss elsewhere.

CHAPTER TEN

Patrick suggested taking Victor to visit Ginny's grave on her birthday, 18 October. I hadn't forgotten, but I was hoping that by ignoring it, I'd somehow skip over the day without having to fall into the bear pit of emotion that I didn't yet dare indulge. And, shamefully, I was afraid of what going back to Cardiff might do to Victor and whether we were capable of dealing with the aftermath. I kidded myself that because he'd lived first-hand with the knowledge that Ginny was dying, he'd done most of his grieving. Whenever I tried to tell a story about Ginny, he listened but never chipped in with any memories of his own.

'Do you think that's wise? Reminding him about her when he's settling down here?'

Patrick put his head on one side. 'I don't think we'll be reminding him, Jo. I doubt he's forgotten that his mother's dead. I know he hardly ever mentions her, but this might be a way to help him talk about her.'

Patrick had obviously swotted up on the good guide to grief since my dad died nineteen years ago when his main response, after his patience during the first few months, was, 'He wouldn't want you to be sad,' as though that was the magic bullet for me to pull myself together and get over it.

'Her birthday's on a Friday, though. He'll be at school and you'll be at work.'

Patrick, the man who never took a day off for Phoebe's sports day, for her hospital appointments, who moaned if he had to drive twenty minutes at midnight to pick her up from a night out, was suddenly happy to drive three hours to stand by a grave. He said, 'I'm due a few days off. I'm sure the head will let Victor miss one day. I think it would be good to celebrate her life, make him feel that we won't forget her.'

'Why don't you ask him?' I said.

I knew Patrick was right, but I couldn't work out why I felt defensive and reluctant. I should have been overjoyed but Patrick's enthusiasm for 'Project Victor' had suddenly taken off in a direction I hadn't expected. I had the sensation of standing on the side of a track, watching Formula One cars scream past, instead of the horse-drawn carriage I'd expected to come labouring along.

On Friday, we dropped Phoebe at school. My heart softened as she said, 'I hope it goes OK today' to Victor. I was just allowing myself a moment of pride at her kindness when she demanded some money to buy dinner in town 'if you're not going to be home'. I was ashamed of being relieved that she wouldn't be spending the day with us.

As we fed onto the motorway, I tried to engage with Victor. 'How do you feel about visiting your mum's grave? Would you like us to leave you there on your own and we'll wait in the car? Obviously, it's quite a big cemetery, so we'll make sure you find the grave okay.'

'I don't mind, whatever you're happy with.'

Not for the first time, I felt a wave of irritation that Victor never seemed to give a straight answer, unlike Ginny who was sometimes breathtaking in her directness. When we worked on the magazine, I'd gone with her to a meeting she was putting together for a 'Best of British' feature to go with coverage of summer festivals with various people who wanted to push the Britishness of their products. At least two people in the room didn't quite manage to get their 'Oh, I didn't realise you were black' expressions under control. She'd laugh and say, 'You were expecting a white Virginia and here I am, a black Ginny! Still British though!' And then she'd watch them fluster and bluster while they inevitably said something like, 'I hadn't thought about what colour you'd be, it's not really relevant, is it?'

She'd let it go with good humour, but afterwards she'd moaned to me. 'Yeah, they hadn't thought about colour because they'd assumed I was white.'

Initially I thought she was overthinking it, but over the years working with her I saw it all: the automatic assumption that the best person to interview a black celebrity would be Ginny, the way she was wheeled out when the management were showcasing their diverse workforce. God knows how she put up with it all with such grace.

I realised that I really wanted to go to her grave. Wanted to stand near where she was buried and tell her that she had left such an enormous hole in my life. She wouldn't have let Faye get to me. I swallowed and stared out of the window, with tears sliding down my face.

Friday turned out to be a bad day to travel. Every time we thought that we'd finally cleared the traffic on the motorway, the speed restrictions flashed up again. And with every traffic jam, our mood seemed to sink further into melancholy.

When we arrived at the cemetery, stiff and aching after hours in the car, we took a few wrong turnings before we found Ginny's grave.

I stood back to let Victor put down his roses. I whispered to Patrick, 'Shall we leave him for a few minutes?'

Patrick went up to him and put his hand on Victor's shoulder with such tenderness, I felt an unexpected rush of love for him. 'Would you like some time on your own?'

'Could *you* stay with me?'

'Of course.'

I hovered, not sure whether to go or not, floundering in the unfamiliar territory of Patrick taking the lead in an emotionally charged situation. I wanted to step forward myself, to rub my hands over the newness of her name on the gravestone and feel her love through my fingers. I felt ashamed of missing her so much. Whenever I mentioned her to Mum or my other friends, there was this unspoken sense that unlike when my dad died, the death of a friend was something you could brush off in a week, as though lifelong friends like Ginny were two-a-penny, able to be replicated by a casual acquaintance you met at the tennis club or someone you had a coffee with who you'd never think about again if they moved thirty miles away. A proper friend knew about your pre-marriage astounding lack of judgement with Derek the disco dancer and still loved you. Or occasionally reminded you about *that night* on the Pernod and black, but in a way that made you feel an intimate part of their history rather than a stupid outsider. Someone to whom you could open the door in your pyjamas, hungover to hell and not be mortified about being braless. Most of all though, a friend like Ginny never left me feeling that I wasn't enough, that she'd ever decline a call from me because she wasn't in the mood to speak to me. Except for that weird period of life – after my dad died and she got pregnant – when I didn't feel she was there for me, or at least not in the way I wanted her to be. But we were young and none of us understood what losing a parent meant back then. If I hadn't experienced it personally, I'd probably have assumed that she just wanted to be left alone too.

Patrick glanced round at me as Victor started to cry. He put his hand up, as if to say, 'I've got this.' He rested his arm around his shoulder and said, 'Better out than in, mate. She'd be so proud of how you've coped. She loved you so much, your mum.'

For the first time since he'd been with us, Victor sobbed, proper from-the-heart howling, the sort that contained the desperation borne of realising that you're left behind and the only way to survive is to let go of someone you want to cling onto forever.

I watched, expecting Patrick to do that face he often did when Phoebe cried because she hated the way she looked in a new dress, or when my mum burst into tears when Frank Sinatra came on the radio and reminded her of my dad. The expression that signified

'Not really sure how to handle this, you'd better take over now.' But he didn't. He just stood firm, saying over and over again, 'You let it out. You're all right. We're here for you. Hang on in there.'

I wandered over to a nearby bench. I watched Patrick speaking to Victor, gently, until eventually he wiped the back of his sleeve across his face, placed both of his hands on the top of the gravestone and stood for a few seconds as though he was trying to absorb the essence of Ginny through the marble. They walked back towards me, Victor with his head bowed.

I got up. 'Are you all right, love?'

He nodded.

I tutted in sympathy. 'I hope we haven't made a mistake in bringing you.'

He shrugged. 'It's fine.'

'Let's sit here for a minute,' Patrick said. 'Jo, you go to the grave.' It felt less like something he thought I needed and more a dismissal. As I walked over, I didn't know why I had that sense of not being included so often these days. I forced myself to be a grown-up, to feel glad that someone was able to reach Victor, even if it wasn't me and even if Patrick never bothered to understand what was going on in Phoebe's head in the same way.

I crouched down by Ginny's grave, longing to feel her presence. I recalled her telling me how I had to do this one thing for her, had to make sure her boy was okay. 'He's got so much to offer, Jo. Don't let losing me be the thing that defines his life.' I screwed up my eyes, attempting to remember the feel of her bony hand in mine, the skin dry but her squeezing with all her remaining strength. 'Don't let me down. Live long and hard for my boy.'

I hoped she'd be pleased to know that he'd formed some kind of a bond with Patrick, even if I hadn't managed to get past that superficial politeness.

The bitter wind was whipping around my knees and instead of feeling close to Ginny, I felt foolish, distracted by Victor and

Patrick behind me, as though I was playing out a scene in a film, the cliché of the grieving friend seeking guidance at the graveside.

I stood up. 'Shall we go?'

The other two fell into step and we wandered back to the car, the light already fading. Victor asked if we could drive past his old school. I didn't want to be on the motorway in the dark, but Patrick showed a surprising level of flexibility of thought. 'Don't see why not. We won't hang about for too long, though.'

We drew up outside Victor's old comprehensive. The longing on his face for his former life caused a physical sensation of sorrow in my chest. That poor boy, forcing himself forwards while wishing he could turn the clock back to when life was simple, when he didn't have to think about anything, could just career along with no deeper thought than whose parents would allow a party.

Suddenly his head lifted. 'That's my mate, Dan!'

Patrick said, 'Go and say hello. We'll wait here for you.'

If ever there was a perfect combination of pleasure and pain, it was observing these two young men clasp each other in a way that didn't pretend to be cool, that held so much more than 'Good to see you, mate' in its embrace. Victor's face spread into a huge beam, his whole body seemed to loosen as though he was steady on the ground, back on familiar turf. A couple of other lads joined them, with much fist bumping and pretend sparring.

I turned to Patrick. 'I don't know whether we've done the right thing. Look how happy he is to be back with his friends.'

Patrick sighed. 'Jo, it is what it is. How could he have stayed in Cardiff? He couldn't have carried on living with Ginny's dad. The only real alternative would have been sending him off to her brother in Oz.'

'Do you think it's the colour thing that makes him feel at home?'

'What, being with other black boys?' Patrick considered my question for a moment. 'I don't know. I don't think so. Ginny always seemed perfectly happy to hang out with us. I don't remember her having loads of black friends or it even being that much of a subject for discussion.'

'It must be weird though, to have everyone know you in our village just because you're the only black person there.'

The conversation was cut short because Victor came over to the car with a couple of the boys.

Patrick got out. Victor did an awkward, 'This is Patrick, he sort of looks after me.' He suddenly sounded so much more Welsh, as though he'd remembered his tribe.

I didn't know whether to get out or not, so I ended up leaning across into the driver's seat, waving out of the door where they probably couldn't see me from that angle and saying hello in a voice that they would struggle to hear.

Victor suddenly seemed so different in the company of these young black men with their diamante earrings and semi-shaved heads. I had a horrible feeling that they'd take one look at me, a middle-aged white woman with my beige polo neck and sensible stud earrings, the opposite of Ginny with her big gold hoops and penchant for jewel-coloured scarves, and tilt their heads pityingly at Victor.

Patrick seemed to be doing okay, talking about the Millennium Stadium and what a brilliant day out he'd had there a few years ago. I didn't know what I'd say to them, but then I didn't have a lot of experience with teenage boys. Especially super-cool black kids who looked so urban streetwise. When Ginny was alive, I'm sure I would have said I didn't notice skin colour. I spent hours being outraged on her behalf when someone said, 'I don't think of you as black,' as though it was some kind of super-flattery. And now I'd become one of those people she used to laugh about, squirming because they were trying so hard not to be racist. 'I love it when I'm the only black person in the room and a white person tries to point me out – "That lady over there by the water cooler." "That lady with the red jumper." Woohoo guys! The woman with the *black* skin. It's not a disease! I've had over forty years to get used to it so I won't be surprised if you call me black and rush to look in a mirror. I promise!'

I wasn't going to be that person. I climbed out of the car, doing a half-wave in the direction of his friends. 'Hi there.'

Victor said, 'Dan's asked me to stay at his tonight. I could get a train back tomorrow, in time for rugby?'

I tried to sound self-deprecating and jokey, asking, 'What time's the match? Is your kit clean?' as though I knew it was silly to be fussing over trifling details.

'Two o'clock. The kit's in my bedroom. I also want to pop in on Granddad,' Victor said in a tone that pleaded to be allowed to do it.

His mates were fidgety, eager to be on their way, to dive into their weekend, to get the lowdown on Victor's new life. I had no idea if we'd come out of it well.

Patrick had his phone out, looking for train times. 'You should definitely try and see your granddad. Give him our regards. If you get the 8.55, I could pick you up from Crawley at 12.48.'

'How much is the ticket?' I asked, unwilling to let Victor just disappear off with these boys I didn't know. Whose parents I didn't know.

Victor pulled a face as though I was just delaying them unnecessarily, bouncing on the spot with impatience.

Patrick got out his wallet, huffing irritably as though I'd destroyed his street cred in front of Victor's friends.

'You've got a railcard, right?' I asked.

Victor shook his head. I felt a scorch of self-consciousness that made me want to dive back into the car, away from these lads who looked so much more clued-up than the boys at Phoebe's school. A Young Person's Railcard was the territory of parochial women like me, concerned with making savings, not spending unnecessarily, someone who'd buy from a solid high-street store, whose first thought was about durability and quality rather than style. So far removed from these lads, who were way too trendy to bother with anything as mundane as a debate about cheaper rail fares.

So I could have hugged the one with a wild mass of corkscrew curls who said, 'Get with it, Victor. You're wasting money. You get a third off, man.' He looked over at me and threw his hands in the air. 'More money than sense, huh?'

I did an over-enthusiastic nod and forced out a squeaky-sounding, 'You tell him.'

Patrick unfolded a bundle of twenty-pound notes, which made me cringe. I wished he'd discreetly slipped Victor the money rather than giving the impression that Victor was living in a household where our pockets were stuffed with wodges of cash. I tried not to have the thought, but I couldn't stop it – I hoped they weren't going to go to some seedy pub and blow the lot on dope.

With blinding clarity, I realised I was just as bigoted as those old duffers who complained about foreigners 'taking our jobs' in the village shop, and then said, 'We don't mean boys like Victor, of course,' as though he'd passed some invisible test that we hadn't known he was taking. I'd been living in my blinkered little village for too long. I had absolutely no evidence that Victor – or this group of mates – had taken a drug in their lives. Of all people, I should be above tabloid stereotypes.

With a cheerfulness I didn't feel, I clapped my hands together and said, 'Right. We'll get off then. Have a great time. Be careful. And I'll see you tomorrow. Text us when you're on the train.'

Victor was already turning to his friends.

I forced myself to speak up, to be better than I was. 'And if any of you fancy popping to visit Victor in Stedhurst, you'd be very welcome.'

They all mumbled a thank you, though I couldn't help feeling they were secretly going, 'No chance.'

By the time I got back into the car, the emotion of the day weighed me down. Patrick was in the mood to chat, upbeat, convinced the day had been a difficult one but ultimately a success.

'Great that he's letting his hair down tonight with a few old friends. He's done a fantastic job of slotting in at school with the rugby crowd, but it'll still be nice for him to spend time with people he's known for ages.'

I sat slumped against the door. 'I hope he'll be okay.'

'Why wouldn't he be?'

'I don't know. I just feel so responsible. And it's not like with Phoebe, where we know the kids and their siblings and parents. We've effectively left him in a big city with a bunch of lads who might or might not look out for him.'

Patrick gave a grunt of exasperation. 'For goodness' sake, Jo. He's eighteen. I'm sure he'll survive a night out in a big city and a train journey home. He's a sensible boy.'

Yet as Patrick sounded ever more confident that Victor would blossom with us, I was becoming more and more convinced that I was the wrong person for the job.

CHAPTER ELEVEN

In the event, Victor turned up on time not bearing any of the signs of a wild night out that I'd come to dread with Phoebe – love bites, a smashed phone, a lost jacket – though there was a distinct whiff of kebab and alcohol on him. I was so relieved nothing had happened on my watch, I practically flung myself at him when he appeared at the station. He didn't rush to elaborate on what he'd got up to or what time he got to bed, though he did make a point of saying that he needed to go and visit his granddad as often as he could, 'Because he wasn't looking too good.' I tried not to dismiss his worries with what he must have heard so many times when Ginny was ill: 'He'll be fine' and made a mental note to encourage him to go to Cardiff regularly and FaceTime in between.

Phoebe, for her part, seemed pleased to see him, insisting on coming to watch him play rugby. I suspected she was getting some kudos among the other girls for having the captain of the rugby team as a long-term guest.

As Patrick said, 'Anything that keeps her engaged with school is a good thing. It doesn't always have to be academic.' He squeezed my hand. 'You worry too much.'

In my view, he didn't worry anywhere near enough. While I lay there so many nights, my mind going down the alleyways of everything from unexpected pregnancy to liver damage, Patrick's chest would rise and fall with the even rhythm of a man for whom tomorrow was just a happy little picnic away.

During the rugby match, Victor's coach came over to speak to us. 'That boy of yours is really talented. I wondered how you'd feel about him trying out for Saracens or Harlequins next summer?'

It was such a rare occurrence for a teacher to be seeking our agreement, rather than us pleading for help/more chances/different sets away from the troublemakers, that my brain had a difficult time switching into that space. Patrick was far more on it, asking the right questions, what it would entail, how the training would impact on his final year at school.

After he'd left, Patrick was fired up. 'If he did well there, he might get a contract abroad, maybe even Australia or New Zealand.' He paused. 'Ginny always wanted him to travel, to open his mind to new experiences.' He looked down. 'She'd be so proud.'

I nodded and wondered whether the fuzzy outline of grief would forever surround happy moments with Victor, a reminder of everything Ginny had missed.

Phoebe and her friends were cheering on the other side of the field.

'She's turned out to be quite the rugby fan. At least it gets her off her phone,' I said.

Patrick shrugged as though Phoebe was of little interest to him. 'Is she going out tonight?'

'She said something about a group of them going out for a pizza. She's invited Victor, which is good of her. I think Helaina's picking them up.'

'Helaina?' Patrick sounded as though he'd never heard of her before. I didn't know whether it was a Patrick thing to only remember the names of two of her friends or a me thing to be constantly mapping Phoebe's network, making sure she was included, not sitting on the periphery as I had throughout all of my schooldays. I'd only really found my niche once I'd met Ginny and discovered that someone who was popular and didn't need my friendship seemed to enjoy my company.

'Yes, you know, the one who's going to Cambridge. Andrea's daughter. Helaina. She passed her test two weeks ago.'

Patrick didn't respond to that little bit of extra information. I worried all the time about Phoebe going in the car with her friends who'd just got their licence, but if I said anything, she replied, 'I'm not five, Mum. I'll be driving myself in a few months' time.'

Patrick didn't seem to have the same capacity for catastrophising as I did, imagining the radio on full blast, the front-seat passenger showing the driver some stupid photo on Instagram at the very moment careful negotiation of a sharp bend was required. He said, 'We all did stupid things and survived. It's part of growing up.'

I couldn't think like that any more. I'd lost all sense of the invincibility that I used to have. Ginny had lived a good and decent life but that hadn't stopped her dying young. In between worrying about Phoebe, I lay raging at four in the morning about all the people who never had a nice word to say about anyone, who automatically assumed anyone down on their luck had brought it upon themselves, who couldn't give without feeling something had been taken away from them. Those people seemed to live forever, their motivation to stay alive not to contribute to the joy of living but to kill us all off with their toxic views.

Ginny, on the other hand, was a great believer in paying it forward, the one who'd sit on the pavement and chat easily, lightly, with the homeless man who sat outside the Co-op near her home. Who'd step in when someone was a pound short in the supermarket. Whose frequent refrain was 'I have enough to share.' She taught me so much and the universe was worse without her. Now my naïve belief that being a good person gave me a free pass, that random bad luck could never be mine, was gone forever. Patrick was, by turns, compassionate – 'It's early days. You've lost your best friend' – and impatient – 'You being miserable isn't helping anyone.' But grief defied logic.

*

When Phoebe, Georgia and Victor had disappeared out for the evening in the back of Helaina's car, I couldn't settle. Patrick was trying to involve me in a discussion about the film we were watching, but my attention kept wandering to my phone. So when an unknown number flashed up, a little scream of fright escaped me.

A young voice said, 'I'm with your kids at the Windmill pub outside Higher Morsten. They've been in a car accident, but they're both okay.'

Patrick leapt up as soon as I asked, 'Is anyone hurt? Do they need an ambulance? Can I speak to my daughter?'

There was some kerfuffle, then Phoebe came on the phone, crying. 'Helaina was driving. She came off the road on a bend.'

'Are you okay? Is Victor all right? What about the others?'

'I'm fine, so's Victor, think everyone is. Helaina's walking, just got a bit of a cut to her head. Josh, the man who phoned you, gave us a lift here.'

'Why didn't you stay by the car and wait for the police?'

'We haven't called the police.'

'Why not?'

Patrick already had his car keys in his hand. 'It doesn't matter. Let's drive to the pub and we can take it from there.'

Phoebe put the bloke back on the phone.

'Thank you, thank you so much for helping them.'

'Just did what I had to do. They didn't want the police turning up when they were in that state. Never get insurance again,' he said.

I didn't really compute what he meant in my haste to get on our way. As we sped along, the picture began to fall into place. 'They've been drinking. That's why they couldn't stay with the car.' I started shaking, the fear of what could have been making everything in me loose and jittery.

My heart punched with relief when I saw Phoebe and Victor through the window of the pub.

I didn't wait for Patrick, running in as soon as he stopped.

They were huddled around a table in the corner with a couple of blokes in their early twenties. Both Phoebe and Helaina were blotchy with fright and tears, looking young and terrified, their veneer of adulthood discarded. Georgia was hysterical.

I put one arm around Phoebe, which for once she folded into. Victor was comforting Georgia, who was shuddering and hiccupping. 'Are you both all right? I mean, as in not hurt?' They nodded.

One of the older lads stepped towards me. 'Hi. Thought we'd better get them out of there. We was behind them in our van, just finished a job. I said to Pete here, they ain't going to make that corner.' He indicated Helaina. 'This one here nearly turned it into a plane, flying over that ditch. Been there myself. Don't want the police getting involved. Stuck them in the van and brought them here.'

The other lad pointed to Phoebe and said, 'She was lucky to get out alive. All caved in down her side. And him,' he said, pointing at Victor, 'if he'd been sitting any further over to the driver's side, he'd have been a goner.'

Patrick had joined us by now and was asking all the sensible questions about whether the other parents were on their way and whether the car presented a danger to anyone else on the road.

'Nah,' Josh said. 'Well and truly buried in the ditch. You can't even see it from the road.'

'Is anything hurting, Victor?' I asked, as Georgia peeled herself away from him and sank down into a chair.

He looked like he might cry but shook his head, silent. Even in my panic, I couldn't help thinking how much he must miss Ginny. My knees went all weak at the thought that it could have been so much worse, that I could have been attending more funerals, this time even closer to home.

I thanked the boys who'd rescued them, gave them twenty quid to buy themselves a pint – 'Next time, when you're not driving.' A look passed between them as though I'd said something old-fashioned and stupid. I wanted to get out of there, away from these lads who were slightly too enthusiastic about being part of yet another crisis involving Phoebe. I breathed a sigh of relief as they left and turned to Helaina. 'Are you sure you're not hurt?'

'No. Just banged my elbow. I'm sorry. Really sorry.'

She looked so upset that I said, 'You've all been very lucky. Everyone has a few near misses when they first learn to drive. Hopefully you'll learn from this and take it a bit more slowly. Are your parents coming?'

As those words left my mouth, Andrea and her husband, Rod, came steaming through the door, followed by Faye and Lee.

'Helly!' Andrea shouted before bursting into noisy sobs and causing the whole pub to swing round for a better look. Rod kept clearing his throat as though he would like to have tapped Andrea on the shoulder and asked her to tone it down, but knew from experience that wouldn't end well.

Faye rushed over to Georgia, who fell into her arms. I talked over Georgia's weeping, filling her in on what I'd gleaned so far. Faye kept shaking her head, saying, 'Honestly, this has got to stop. It's just one drama after another.'

I tried not to take her comments personally and said, 'I couldn't agree more,' but she didn't make eye contact or give me the complicit nod of recognition I was angling for, just pulled her lips into a tight, angry line.

Patrick was doing that whole matey, 'Teenagers, eh? Well, no harm done' before getting into a debate with Rod and Lee about whether or not leaving the scene of the accident was illegal when no one else was involved. There was a discussion about getting a farmer Rod knew to haul the car out of the ditch. 'Shan't be troubling the insurance with that one. Only an old banger anyway. Not worth screwing up her chance of getting insured.'

Patrick frowned as though a thought had suddenly occurred to him. 'Why did the lads that brought you here keep saying "the state you were in"? Had you all been drinking?' Given that it only mattered whether Helaina had been drinking, I left it to Andrea and Rod to get an answer to that one.

Rod suddenly seemed to raise himself up a few inches, as though Patrick had cast aspersions on their daughter. 'Helaina knows better than to drink and drive, don't you, darling?'

'I hadn't had anything to drink.' She was making all the right noises, but her eyes were trying to tell Phoebe something. She just lacked that certitude, that total conviction that the accident was purely down to inexperience at the wheel. And there was something slightly off about her speech, as though she was explaining a complex idea to an audience of limited intelligence, slowly and deliberately. I wasn't the only one to pick up on it.

Andrea paused in her histrionics. 'So why didn't you wait for us by the car?'

Helaina's eyes filled again. Out of the corner of my eye, I saw Phoebe do an almost imperceptible shake of her head and even Georgia stopped sobbing into Faye's chest to freeze for the answer. Eventually Helaina answered. 'We just panicked. We weren't really thinking straight. The lads that picked us up said we'd better get out of there before the police arrived and we were sort of in shock, so we went with them.'

Rod had gone into lawyer mode. 'But why? If you hadn't been drinking, it was just an accident.'

Helaina crumpled in a heap and said, 'We'd been hotboxing in the car.'

'Hotboxing?' I asked, my mind leaping to some horrendous sexual practice that I'd now have to erase from my memory bank of distressing images.

Victor spoke for the first time. 'Smoking weed with the windows up.'

There was a pause while all the adults absorbed that information. Then Andrea grabbed hold of Helaina, all the 'bless you, Helly, never mind, it's just a bit of metal at the end of the day' right out of the window. 'You were smoking drugs? Do you know what weed does to the teenage brain? You do that and you can forget about getting into Cambridge.'

Thankfully, Rod told her to quieten down and we all disappeared out of the pub to a pivoting of heads finding our literal and metaphorical car crash temporarily more fascinating than the two for one Saturday night special on onion rings.

My mind was reeling. Drugs. Jesus. I'd been so worried about the possibility of Phoebe encouraging Helaina to drive after a shedload of vodka, the whole drug-driving had slipped under my radar.

Andrea raged on, her face millimetres from Helaina's. 'What were you thinking of? You've no idea what's in those drugs. Did you even realise what you were taking?'

If I hadn't been so worried that it was about to come out that Phoebe was the instigator of this, I would have ridiculed Andrea and her desire to stop any blame drifting towards her family. Though, to be fair, Helaina had always looked as though a lemonade shandy was right out of her comfort zone. I couldn't imagine her slipping a grubby ten-pound note into a drug dealer's hand, but someone had got hold of the drugs and there were only four candidates. I didn't have time to puzzle out who was the likeliest culprit because Rod turned on Victor the second the pub door slammed behind us.

'You gave her drugs! You scum! You're lucky you didn't kill her. You'd have had that on your conscience, but people like you probably don't even have a conscience.'

Before I could even absorb the implication that he'd decided Victor was to blame, Patrick pushed his way between them. 'Calm down. You've no idea how Helaina got hold of the drugs. Why are you blaming Victor?'

'Well, who else is going to bring them into school? Never been a problem until he arrived at Edgewater.'

Phoebe crossed her arms. 'That's not true. Frankie got expelled last year for doing cocaine in the loo when she should have been in RE. And Victor wasn't even there then.'

Admiration that Phoebe would stand up to Rod in the face of his fury mingled with the shock that she recounted the story as though cocaine was no big deal, something that happened in every school. Did it? Even in a small town where the deli was crammed at pick-up time with parents bulk-buying garlic-stuffed olives and double-checking that the duck eggs were free-range? Clearly an organic pork pie was no insurance against the kids stuffing white powder up their noses.

Andrea put her hand up as though providing the voice of reason. 'Let's all calm down. It's not really Victor's fault, it's just the way he's been brought up, perhaps his mum wasn't as strict as we've been with our girls.'

Patrick stood shaking his head, while I had the sensation of my brain lagging behind the scene in front of me. Andrea even had the gall to look over to Victor and tell him that it was nothing to do with skin colour. She didn't even *notice* skin colour. She wasn't saying it because he was black.

'The midwife who delivered Helaina was from St Lucia and black as the ace of spades. She was wonderful!'

There was a look on Victor's face I hadn't seen before. Something between anger, disgust and pity. He glanced towards Patrick as though asking for permission to respond. But Patrick got there first. 'Bullshit. You ignorant, small-minded racist cow.'

I wanted to cheer as he carried on. '"The way he's been brought up"? Don't you dare even start to have an opinion about his mother. I don't know what weird notion you have in your head, but she was a fantastic mum, who knew how to teach her son right from wrong. But more than that she was one of the biggest-hearted, kindest women I've ever met.' Patrick was stumbling over his words with the ferocity of feeling. 'Not that I need to justify what she was like to you.'

Andrea kept trying to interrupt, while Rod was pulling at her arm and saying – though no one was taking any notice – 'We don't have to listen to this.' But Patrick was talking over them both in his determination to have his say.

'You have no idea who got hold of the drugs. You haven't even asked yourself if Helaina might have surprised you all and bought some weed herself. No, you've defaulted to "the boy's black. Must be him." Literally, fuck off and consider yourself lucky that your daughter doesn't have the deaths of three young people on *her* conscience. And when you're ready, we'll be very happy to hear your apology. It wasn't any of our kids who got behind a wheel stoned out of their heads.'

Leaving Andrea and Rod standing with their mouths open, Patrick started to steer us all towards the car.

Faye was trying to hurry Georgia to their Range Rover, but she'd ground to a halt, crying, 'It wasn't Victor. He didn't get the drugs. You can't blame him.'

Lee wasn't having any of it. He grabbed Patrick's sleeve. 'You're being a bit out of order. We haven't made a big deal of it because the lad's had a rough ride and obviously we're friends, but it's a mighty coincidence that your lad arrives and, voyla, suddenly the kids are turning into right potheads.'

I didn't think it was an appropriate moment to point out, 'It's not voyla, it's voilà.'

Faye directed Georgia to the car and then came to stand with Lee. She patted Patrick's arm and he all but batted her off.

He flicked his hands up in resignation. 'You two can believe what you want to. I think you're wrong about where the drugs came from, but I can't prove it, so we'll have to agree to disagree.'

And with that, he told Phoebe and Victor to get into the car before we had a whole bunch of curious onlookers crowding round us. I scuttled after them, mumbling a goodbye to Faye, who wiggled her fingers in my direction, though whether it was a dismissal or a wave, I wasn't sure.

Victor was the first to speak. 'I'm really sorry. I've let you down. I didn't realise how stoned Helaina was.'

Patrick, the man whose attitude to my endless whittling was always, 'Jo, don't sweat the small stuff,' could barely squeeze a word out. 'Let's talk about this tomorrow when we're all calm again.'

But I couldn't hold my anger in. 'Honestly, you're both a disgrace. People have loads of opinions on our family as it is without getting on the wrong side of Miss Philosophy at Cambridge! Where did the drugs come from?'

A silence stretched throughout the car as we headed home. Phoebe was no doubt working out what story to spin, what yarn to peddle to us. I felt my stupid heart clutch at the possibility that *this time* she might actually wake up to the fact that if she carried on like this she'd either blow her chances of getting any qualifications by getting expelled or end up shunned by everyone as too much of a liability.

I barely recognised my own voice. 'Where did the drugs come from, Phoebe?'

There was no answer.

Patrick sighed. 'Let's deal with it in the morning.'

My whole body felt on fire, as though I might break something if I didn't get an answer. 'No. I'm not having you sit there and brush things over as this being something that "teenagers do". Phoebe is going to answer us for once.'

Phoebe was uncharacteristically quiet. Eventually Victor said, 'We all agreed to do it. It wasn't Phoebe's fault.'

I tried to soften my tone. 'That still doesn't answer my question about where the drugs came from.'

Patrick turned into our drive in a silence that enveloped us all in a blanket of distrust.

I climbed out, suddenly weary right down to my bones. 'I will get an answer. Neither of you are going out again, ever, until I find out how you got drugs that made you so stoned you ended up in a ditch.' I stopped shouting when I saw Mrs Giles next door peer through her curtains. Her sister was Andrea's mother-in-law. The whole bloody street would know by next week.

Patrick stood in the hallway. For the first time, I noticed how drawn he looked. Those evenings when Ginny had whipped out her tarot cards and made us listen to our 'fate' or Patrick had made curry for the four of us in our flat in Hackney, regaling us with stories of how he'd had to haul his boss out of the fountain in reception seemed not decades, but centuries ago. I had a flash of insecurity that eighteen years of marriage hadn't extinguished completely. I'd never quite shaken off the feeling that Patrick had got sucked into comforting me when my dad died and then it was almost easier to marry me than hurt me by extricating himself. This couldn't be the life he'd imagined. Because it certainly wasn't mine.

CHAPTER TWELVE

I woke up the next morning feeling as though I was on the wrong end of two bottles of heavy red wine, even though I hadn't had a drink the night before. As soon as I opened my eyes, waves of anxiety rolled over me. I lay there, letting my mind wander around the sensation that a whole group of mothers would be on some WhatsApp chat picking over the latest disaster, with Helaina and Georgia somehow coming out of it smelling of roses. I kept sieving through my memory for the warning signs, for the bits I was missing. I itched to ransack Victor and Phoebe's rooms to see if they had a stash of drugs tucked in a drawer somewhere. Phoebe would be cleverer than that, probably. I had no idea how cunning Victor was.

I went through to the bathroom, resisting the urge to clatter about the bedroom and disturb Patrick for the sole purpose of not being the only one awake worrying. I didn't know how he managed to sleep. I found myself inspecting every inch of the cottage, trying to work out where they could hide drugs. I even lifted up the lid of the toilet cistern to see if there was a little stash of contraband in a waterproof bag.

I tutted at my own ridiculousness. I'd obviously transported myself to the set of a gangster movie rather than a bathroom with a shelf of shells collected on West Wittering beach in rural Sussex. I sat down on the loo seat. Maybe my grief over Ginny was making me paranoid. She would have made fun of me. She'd always subscribed to the philosophy that if people wanted to talk about her behind her back, she'd give them something worth talking about. 'Honestly, I couldn't give a shit. Let them have twenty minutes bitching about me and my shortcomings. I see it as a public entertainment service, brightening up their sad little lives.' And over the two decades we were friends, I didn't quite get to the dizzying heights of her nonchalance, but I thought I'd conquered my need to have everyone approve of me. Instead I felt like I did before Ginny blew into my life – anxious to fit in but hating myself for wanting to.

I went downstairs to make a cup of tea and was just sitting down when a message pinged up on Victor's iPad right in my eyeline. I didn't even know iPads could receive texts. I was more curious about that initially than the actual message and didn't really mean to read it, but the sender – Georgia – caught my eye and before I knew it, I was staring at *Does Jo know we're going with each other? I've told Phoebe not to say anything. I will tell my parents, obvs, but after last night, not gd idea yet* followed by a whole row of hearts and a couple of teeth clenched emojis.

Immediately afterwards my phone pinged with a text from Faye. It was as though she had a camera in my kitchen and somehow knew Georgia was trying to keep a lid on her relationship – if teens their age even had relationships any more – with Victor.

What an evening that was! Can you meet for a coffee this morning? Think we need to talk and make a plan for our girls going forwards. ☺

It was incredible how much that smiley emoji cheered me up. Maybe we could find a way to work together rather than setting ourselves against each other. I hurried to reply.

Yes! Shall we go to that little vegan café so we don't bump into Stedhurst's great and good?

She wrote back: *Yep, but don't try and convert me to chickpeas! Food of the devil!*

*

My heart felt a bit lighter as I slipped out of the house.

Faye was already waiting for me with a couple of soya lattes and vegan brownies. 'I ordered for us because I can't stay too long.'

And there it was, the little trill of alarm, that I was a tick on her to-do list rather than two good friends trying to find a solution together.

She leaned forwards. 'That was all a bit of a nightmare last night, wasn't it? How was Phoebe this morning? Did she shed any light on what happened?'

'I haven't seen her yet. They were both still asleep when I left.'

Faye looked surprised. 'I've been asking Georgia all morning where they bought the weed from, but she keeps saying that Helaina got it.'

I frowned. 'Well, that's possible, isn't it?'

She broke off a piece of brownie and sniffed it as though it might be laced with poison.

'Everything's possible,' she said, giving me the impression she knew the truth but had decided to hug it to herself for a bit longer.

I gabbled on. 'I just don't know how schoolkids round here would get hold of drugs though. I mean, is it as simple as someone hanging around outside school? Do you think it's something to do with these County Lines I keep seeing in the news?'

Faye did the sort of scoff she usually reserved for mothers who complained that their kids hadn't been made a prefect. 'I doubt that organised criminals have made it as far as Stedhurst. It's such a small school, hardly worth targeting.'

'So do you think they're going down to Brighton to score? Or do they get them in pubs? I wouldn't have the first clue where to look.'

Faye spoke slowly, as though she was talking to someone whose first language wasn't English. 'Jo, I know Lee was a bit over the top last night, but don't *you* think it's a bit of a coincidence that the drugs arrived after Victor moved here? Think about it. He lived in Cardiff, a big city, with all the opportunities to make dodgy connections. Fair enough, Phoebe wasn't an angel before, but since he's been here, she's started to be really off the rails…'

Faye's words made me feel sick. I'd obviously been clinging onto a thread of delusion that her behaviour was challenging but within the realms of normal teenage rebellion. To everyone else, she was 'really off the rails'.

My voice came out needy and feeble, almost begging her to take her words back. 'Is she any worse than when we were that age? Albeit with different things? I clearly remember two lads stealing their dads' cars and racing each other on the M23 and skidding across the central reservation after overdoing it on Woodpecker cider at a party. And everyone was smoking John Player Specials.'

Apart from me because my dad had said smoking made your breath stink and no boy would ever kiss me. I already thought I'd never get a boyfriend, so I couldn't afford to take any chances.

Faye clicked her tongue in irritation. 'Oh wake up, Jo! Helaina is not your average idiot teenage boy thinking he's Lewis Hamilton. She's a straight A student with everything to live for, not some loser raiding the cocktail cabinet for the dregs of the Christmas Galliano. If anyone can get into Cambridge to study philosophy it's her, yet she suddenly decides to get off her head on skunk? You're talking about the girl who spends her Saturday afternoons at the children's hospice, not a misfit looking for kicks.'

'Maybe it's because they're in the sixth form now and all the year above are doing it. I don't think we can assume that Victor has some hotline to a Cardiff drugs cartel. If he was such a crackhead, he wouldn't be the best rugby player in the school, would he?' As soon as the words were out of my mouth, I rushed to do a recall, kind of like stabbing at the 'close' button on an email in that split second when you realise you've sent it to the wrong person. 'I mean, one of the best players.'

Faye pursed her lips and did an exasperated sigh. 'It's really kind what you tried to do for Ginny, but you can't sacrifice your own family. Patrick was pretty aggressive last night. You must both be under so much strain. He wasn't in favour of having Victor in the first place, was he? I don't know many men who would be. No wonder it's taking a toll on your marriage.'

Just a few months ago, in the turbulence of Ginny fading away in front of me, I'd been very honest about Patrick's reservations: 'He's like a big grizzly bear, terrified that a young male in the family is somehow going to usurp his authority. Keeps saying he doesn't know anything about bringing up boys. He didn't know anything about bringing up a girl, but we've managed. He does have the advantage of being a bloke himself. And it's not forever. Victor will be at university in two years. And Ginny is also one of his oldest friends, it's not like we're just inviting the son of a random stranger to live with us.'

'Maybe he's terrified he'll have to do all the embarrassing man-to-man talks,' Faye had said.

'He's eighteen! If he hasn't worked out what to do with it by now, then God help us all. Anyway, they probably know far more about sex than us, judging by what I hear Phoebe and her friends talking about when they don't think I'm listening.'

It was incredible how relaxed I'd been about sharing the intimate details of my marriage with Faye. She'd been so supportive: taking Phoebe home for dinner, letting her stay the night so I could drive down to Cardiff to see Ginny and not have to fret about racing back. I'd really leaned on her.

Now, I felt that everything I'd said was being scrutinised, held against me, against Patrick. I felt a sting of injustice. 'Patrick's been great with Victor, actually. They've got a lot in common with the rugby. And, obviously, we've all had to adjust, but Patrick and I are pretty much singing from the same hymn sheet now.'

I wondered who I was trying to convince. If anything, I was lagging way behind Patrick, still failing to make much headway with Victor beyond the polite 'Have you got any washing?/Would you like an omelette?'

Faye's snort of disbelief that Patrick and I saw eye-to-eye on anything was not entirely unfounded, but this morning, I needed a soft landing, not a brutal reality check. She had obviously been storing up her little speech for some weeks. 'Jo, I know Victor's had an awful time, but you can't let him destroy Phoebe's future. The way it's going, she'll end up getting kicked out of school.' She sighed. 'I think you really need to start thinking about other options. He's got an uncle in Australia, hasn't he?'

'I can't send him there! He barely knows him.'

'But he's not your responsibility. He's not family.' Faye sounded impatient. 'If something happened to me and Lee, I wouldn't expect you to take in Georgia, yet you're my closest friend here.'

My heart did a pathetic little leap of joy at knowing I hadn't yet been usurped by the likes of Andrea and all the in-crowd whose mobiles would no doubt be buzzing away with judgement, somehow boomeranging the blame for the latest debacle away from Georgia and Helaina and towards Phoebe and Victor. I wished Ginny was here to stand in front of me squeezing the space between her thumb and forefinger to show how little they mattered. I could hear her rich Welsh lilt: 'Squeeeeeze them down and, pufffff, blow them away.' All those years I'd almost pulled it off, nearly become like Ginny in my thinking. Despite my own internal monologue about my daughter often turning into one big fault-finding fest, I wasn't about to open it up to a free-for-all.

Faye slurped back the rest of her coffee. I waited to see if she was going to tell me to keep Victor away from Georgia, but she simply gazed at her watch and got to her feet. 'I've got to shoot.' She hesitated. 'I know you're doing your best.'

We hugged goodbye and I remained at the table, wondering whether Faye was right and that we'd all go down with the ship if Victor stayed with us.

I scoffed down my brownie and the rest of Faye's too.

Jasmine was just coming up the road as I walked out and her face lit up. 'Jo! Didn't realise this was one of your haunts!'

'It's not usually. I just came here because I'm keeping a low profile at the moment.'

She raised an eyebrow. 'The car accident?'

I nodded. 'Stedhurst never sleeps, does it?'

No doubt our disgrace was making the rounds of Snapchat and all the other social media channels I had never heard of.

She laughed. 'I gather no one was hurt?'

'No, thank goodness.' I hesitated. 'Is Phoebe getting the blame for it?'

'Not as far as I know,' she answered, though she didn't quite look me full in the eye. And then, like a woman who couldn't bring herself to lie however bad the news was, she said, 'Unfortunately, I think there's a bit of a groundswell view that Victor is the source of the drugs.'

'And have you heard anything that makes you think he is?' I braced myself.

She shook her head. 'I don't know. My son reckons that it's that bloke on the market with the sunglasses stall who's supplying. You know, the kids go up, try on a few pairs of glasses and come away with a bit of folded cardboard or a little plastic bag.'

'Why is everyone so quick to point the finger at Victor?' I knew the answer, though I didn't want to believe that the community I lived in thought like that in the twenty-first century.

Jasmine looked uncomfortable. 'Well, it's not a very diverse neighbourhood around here, is it?'

I loved her for addressing the elephant in the room. 'You can say that again.'

'Kai thinks Victor's a great bloke. Says he gets a lot of banter at school but just shrugs it off. I think he's quite popular with the girls too.' She had a little smirk going on that told me that she was party to the Georgia/Victor romance.

'I think he probably is.'

She folded her arms. 'Don't let people get you down, Jo. You don't have to accept their ignorance.'

She made it sound so easy. I couldn't see how I could stand up to everyone without becoming totally ostracised in the place I'd lived in for most of my life. I wished I'd stayed in London now.

As though she'd read my mind, she said, 'It's quite liberating when you stop dancing to other people's tunes. I had a good old cull of all my so-called friends who disappeared over the horizon kicking up clouds of dust when my husband left. And do you know what? I don't miss any of them. I might have fewer friends now, but at least they're not looking at me to see if I've got the right handbag and whether I've painted my nails.'

'You're very brave. '

'I'm not brave. It was difficult to let go of those people I thought had my back. Honestly though, I'm glad I found out they weren't really my friends. It saved me wasting any more time on them.' With that, she said, 'Right, off to get one of their banana and walnut loaves. Have you tried it? You'll have to come round and have some one day.'

And I walked home, her words running around my head, making me ask myself questions to which the answers might turn out to be horribly inconvenient.

Back home, I went upstairs to see if Patrick was awake. He was still lying in bed, talking on the phone in a low voice. As I walked in, I heard him say, 'Yeah, it's not great. Jo's pretty rattled. I think she'd prefer Victor to go off to Ginny's brother. Not ideal but we might have to consider it. Don't think we're there just yet, but we had our hands pretty full with Phoebe already.' He sat up as I shut the door, 'Talk of the devil. Jo's back. I'll catch you later, Cory. Cheers, mate.' He put his mobile down, looking slightly sheepish. 'All right, love?'

'No. I'm really worried.' I told him about my conversations with Faye and Jasmine and launched into my concerns that all the other women might turn out to be right, that Victor was supplying the drugs. 'I mean, what if someone gets killed? Helaina was lucky last night. They all were. I don't want to be responsible for some other mother losing a child.'

Patrick's face clouded over. 'You're as bad as they are. How do you know it was Victor and not Phoebe or Helaina?'

I tried to take my blinkers off, to look deep into myself, to accept how things were rather than how I wanted them to be. To admit to myself what my own child might be capable of. However, try as I might, I found it easier to imagine Victor with his worldly-wise demeanour having the balls to negotiate with some weasel-faced bloke than Phoebe. I just couldn't see my daughter, who still slept in a furry onesie and loved a soak with a fizzy bath bomb, passing over cash to some grubby little scumbag in a woolly hat. When I said as much to Patrick, he snorted with amusement.

'You've been watching too much telly. You've only got Jasmine's word that it's the bloke at the market. She probably grows marijuana in her back garden and supplies him.'

I didn't laugh. 'You're just as bad as everyone else, judging by appearances.'

He threw up his hands by way of apology. 'Sorry. I was just having a joke. I'd still put my money on the kids ordering drugs online and getting it delivered in a neat little package to a supermarket dropbox.' Patrick stretched and swung his legs out of bed. 'Shall we divide forces? You try and have a calm conversation with Phoebe to get to the bottom of it and I'll talk to Victor.'

Again, I felt that stab of irritation that Patrick elected to tackle Victor rather than attempt to fathom out what was going on with his own daughter.

He didn't seem beaten the way I was. He looked every bit the man who saw this as a difficult stage of life, not ideal, but something well within his grasp to deal with. I, on the other hand, was trying to stop myself being swept away by a wave that no one saw coming but really should have predicted.

'What if this is just the thin end of the wedge though, Patrick? What if dope, weed, is just a diversion and they're actually taking stuff that's so much more dangerous?'

Patrick picked up his towel from the radiator. 'There's no point in getting carried away until we know what the score is.' He held out his arms to me. 'We'll get through it. I promise.'

I really wanted to believe that.

CHAPTER THIRTEEN

I hoovered the whole of the downstairs in an effort to control a tiny bit of my environment while I prepared myself to do battle with Phoebe. By the time she emerged, I was channeling all my good mothering skills. When she moaned about the little cut near her hairline, instead of snapping, 'You were lucky you haven't got a great big scar right across your face,' I said, 'Let me just pop a bit of antiseptic cream on that, it'll be gone in no time.' I made her American pancakes and the barely warm, notch-one toast she loved. I didn't comment, though it nearly killed me, about her scrolling through her phone while she was eating. I did worry that she would actually lose the capacity to focus on anything more than a foot away. I started well, with, 'You must have been really frightened last night when Helaina crashed the car.'

She spoke through a mouthful of food. 'Yeah.'

I gave myself a small pat on the back for at least getting her to agree with something I said. I plugged on. 'I feel' – large pat on the back for remembering not to leap in with 'You always…' – 'that you've lost your way a bit at the moment. Is there anything I could help with?' I left off the next bit of the sentence, 'Like hunt down the lowlife supplying you with drugs.'

She shook her head. 'No. Just got to survive school so I can get to university and get out of here.'

'Is it really that bad? Are we that bad?' I was nearly bursting with the effort of not listing everything we did for her: the running around carting her to parties in the middle of nowhere, paying for her phone, organising our family holidays around every must-attend, can't-possibly-miss music festival that then didn't even happen but left us with last-minute flights at exorbitant prices.

Phoebe closed her eyes as though the awfulness of our family was obvious to everyone apart from me. 'It's just so booooring here. You and dad banging on about working for my A levels and getting a Saturday job. Dad even suggested a paper round! Who does a paper round these days? It's like living with a couple of Tudors. And if I bring any friends round, you put on a stupid posh accent and start getting out napkins while making out you're a cool parent and anything goes. It's just really pathetic.'

Tears prickled at the back of my eyes. 'I'm sorry you feel like that. Dad and I are just worried that you don't understand the value of money yet and we know that living in debt is such a misery. We're just trying to help. I know you don't believe us, but we are. And the whole working hard for your A levels, well, no one is saying you have to be an A* student, but it's a springboard to the next step of your life.'

Phoebe folded over, like a rag doll collapsing in half. 'Like you've even done anything with your life. You didn't even go to university, but you talk about your copywriting business as though you're the founder of Instagram or Bill Bloody Gates. But nope, just a secretary for some crappo magazine no one's heard of, and now writing a few press releases for air freshener and moss killer. Whoop. Whoop.'

I resisted pointing out that I had been the personal assistant to one of the most influential editors in the women's magazine world. It was ironic that I'd left to set up my copywriting business so I could work from home and have more flexibility in terms of childcare after Phoebe was born. I forced my brain to remain on the task in hand: trying to find out the root cause of Phoebe's issues and whether the drugs were just a one-off experiment or the tip of the iceberg.

I scrubbed at the saucepan in the sink to give myself time to get my rage under control and to push back down all the home truths

I would really, dearly, have liked to point out to Phoebe, whose biggest disappointment so far in life was probably receiving the wrong charm for her Pandora bracelet last Christmas.

'Everything we say to you comes from a place of love, darling.' Though right now I was pretty sure I could also find a little residence of strong dislike. 'We'll do our best not to go on about things, because I know, I'm absolutely sure, that you'll find your way in life.' I aimed for a note of levity. 'There are plenty of ways from A to B and you're an intelligent girl, so I know you'll be fine.' I tried to sound confident rather than patronising, but I wasn't sure I'd pulled it off. 'Can I just say, though, that I am really worried about you taking drugs, because you never know what's in them?'

Phoebe flung her head back and lay spread-eagled on the chair like someone whose last drop of energy had drained out of them. 'Oooh drug-g-g-g-gs. Stop acting like we were injecting ourselves with heroin.'

'But because of drugs, you did end up having a car accident that could easily have killed you.' Keeping my voice conciliatory and calm was taking every ounce of my self-control.

'That's because Helaina is a shit driver and was showing off in front of Victor about how fast she could go, not because she'd been smoking.'

'So you don't think the fact that she was high on dope – weed – had anything to do with it?'

'No.'

I stopped fiddling about at the sink and sat down opposite her. Her angry little face took me back to when I'd tried to teach her to play table tennis on holiday. She'd become so frustrated by missing the ball that she'd burst into tears and stamped on it. I'd never known how to head her off, to rein her in before her emotions spiralled out of control. Yet there was still something vulnerable about her, though she hid it better these days. It seemed an age since she'd crept into our room with her duvet to sleep on the floor.

'Phoebe, I'm worried about you, love. You're embarking on a dangerous path and it's not going to end well. Don't throw your life away. You've got so much going for you.'

Her face softened slightly. My heart lifted as though something I'd said was making sense, that somehow I'd found the right slot in that complex teenage brain to post a wise word through. But she pushed back her chair. 'You're just so false, I can't believe anything you say. You even make out you're far too intellectual for *I'm A Celebrity* and you only watch it because I like it and pretending to Victor that normally you'd be reading the bloody *Economist* or something.' She stood up.

I tried, desperately, to bring her back to me, to create that tiny spark of connection, that fizz of understanding. 'I'm sorry you think that about me, but I'm being honest. You can be amazing when you put your mind to it.'

'Well, at least you've got two of us now, so if it all goes tits up for me, you've got another shot at getting it right. Dad is already practically falling over himself with pride that Victor's the rugby captain. Shame it's taken sixteen years for him to have a kid he can be proud of.'

Her words were like a slap. I'd thought a lot about what it might mean to try and integrate another child into our family, how that might put pressure on our time and maybe our privacy. I'd considered how Phoebe might be resentful – or possibly thankful – not to have our full attention. I'd worried about Victor feeling an outsider, playing catch-up to the sixteen years of family traditions, the whole unspoken modus operandi of a family where everyone knows where the cushioned soft spots are and the sharp angles, what triggers and what defuses an argument – although that was obviously still a work in progress. It had never really occurred to me that Phoebe would be the one who felt excluded.

'Of course Dad's proud of Victor for his rugby because that's his big passion, but he's proud of you for so much more. As am I. You're still our priority.' Well, my priority at least.

I vaguely registered the baritone rumble of male voices next door. I wondered if Patrick was managing to winkle more information out of Victor.

A wave of disgust passed over her face. 'Shut up. I've heard you talking to Dad about me. About how lazy I am, how difficult, how rude.'

It was incredible how Phoebe claimed never to hear me shouting that dinner was ready at the top of my lungs but had bionic hearing when it came to me hissing my frustration to Patrick behind closed doors.

'It's just a temporary feeling, a knee-jerk reaction just like you have when you get angry. Just me letting off steam when I've been worried about you or feel that you have been a bit ungrateful.'

Shame there wasn't a national prize for understatement. I could start polishing my podium now.

I blundered on. 'I'm sure you talk about us to your friends and sometimes not in a complimentary way, but it's all in the heat of the moment. Anyway, before you go, just so I don't have to worry myself to a frazzle, could you tell me where the drugs came from?'

Phoebe laughed, a nasty sound that reminded me of my boss when I got my first job in London. I'd asked her if The Ivy was a theatre. She'd made me feel parochial and stupid. And now, sitting there in front of Phoebe, I felt both of those things and old, too old, to have the energy to deal with someone who should love me but apparently hated me.

She marched out of the room, shouting over her shoulder, 'Why would I tell you that? So you can drive round and have a word? Give them a piece of your mind? Wooo… bet they're shaking in their shoes.'

I rested my forehead on the table. Why was this all so hard? I'd tried to do it all right. The sticker charts when she was in primary school. The pasta jar working towards – what was it? – some pack of cards they all used to collect, extortionate at a pound for five.

The praising the positive and ignoring the negative. I'd stayed at home when she was little in the belief that sitting with her pushing those circles and squares through the slots in a plastic cube, being on hand to make jam tarts with pastry that ended up so grey no one wanted to eat them, would somehow make all the difference. I suddenly wished I'd never left the job that took me out of the house for long, long hours and had delegated bringing up Phoebe to a nanny. They'd have done so much better than me.

CHAPTER FOURTEEN

Just when I thought my life couldn't possibly plummet any further down the scale of middle-aged satisfaction, the doorbell went.

'Oh hi, Mum.'

'Are you all right? You look exhausted.'

I was pretty sure I didn't look anywhere near as knackered and done in as I felt. 'I'm fine, just the time of year. Need a bit of sunshine, I think.'

I didn't want to let her in, but short of keeping my own mother shivering in the wind on the doorstep, there was nothing for it but to move back and wave her through to the kitchen.

She tutted her way in, taking in the pans on the draining board and dirty plates on the table. 'Just finished lunch?'

'No, breakfast. We had a bit of a late start.'

'Oh lucky you, being able to sleep in. I never could. Not even at your age. And now… well, I'm like Margaret Thatcher. Lucky if I get four hours these days.'

I couldn't listen to Mum's insomnia diatribe today. Whenever she stayed here, her snoring kept me awake from the other side of the landing.

I interrupted her. 'Cup of tea?'

'Only if I'm not holding you up,' she said, taking off her coat without waiting for an answer. 'Where's Phoebe?'

'Upstairs.'

'Not asleep at this time?'

'No, just getting ready. She works hard, she needs a bit of downtime.'

I spent my life defending her. I felt ashamed of wishing I had one of those shiny, glossy daughters, the sort everyone said, 'I bumped into your daughter. Isn't she lovely? So polite. So charming.'

Thankfully, that little spiral of thoughts was stopped in its tracks by Mum pulling two neon orange and lime green bobble hats out of her bag. She leaned towards me conspiratorially. 'I thought Victor would get chilly in the winter, so I've knitted him a hat. And, of course, I didn't want Phoebe to be left out. She must have her nose put out of joint a bit, what with him taking up Patrick's time, with all that rugger.'

I didn't know why when I had so many things to be annoyed about, Mum calling rugby 'rugger' made me grind my teeth together, but it did.

I forced myself to be grateful. 'That was really kind of you,' I said, knowing that Phoebe would immediately pull a face and say, 'I'm not wearing that.' And unlike my imaginary perfect daughter who would just wear it for five minutes to keep Mum happy and make some enthusiastic comment such as, 'That'll keep the wind off, Nan,' she'd make no attempt to disguise her disgust.

My thanks wasn't enough to satisfy Mum, who said, 'Will you call her down?'

'I think she might be in the bath.'

At that moment, Victor and Patrick emerged from the sitting room. Patrick managed a reasonably cheerful hello, as did Victor.

Mum leapt up, pressing her gift on Victor. 'I bet you find English winters cold, don't you? I knitted you this. Try it on. I did it a bit on the big side to fit over that hair.'

'English winters are a bit chillier than *Welsh* winters, aren't they, Victor?' I made a joke of it, attempting to catch Victor's eye to apologise. He had that weary look that I recognised from Ginny when people used to describe her as 'exotic'. She was brilliant at the quick putdown without labouring the point – 'Snow leopards are exotic, starfruit are exotic, but me, I'm born and bred in Cardiff.' I wished I'd paid more attention to how she'd handled other people's ignorance, how she made a stand without severing the relationship completely.

Mum carried on oblivious. 'Put it on! Let's see how you look.' She patted his hair, running her fingers backwards and forwards over his head.

I wanted to save him from having to put on the bloody hat. I didn't want him to have to appease my mother's need for validation. In a voice that had all the strength of a one teabag brew crawling out of the pot, I made some feeble protests about the poor lad being put on the spot and having to model for all of us and how I'd take a photo so she could see it later.

Mum waved me away, saying, 'You'll look just the part in it. Keep that bit at the back that you've shaved off nice and warm.'

I hated myself for not snatching it out of her hand and telling her to leave him alone. Gallantly, he put it on and made a show of going into the hall to look in the mirror. And yet again, I'd allowed my mother to get away with something that made him – made us all – uncomfortable because none of us had the guts to say, 'He's lived in the UK all of his life! He isn't any colder here than we are!' in case we actually had to face the truth: that even if she didn't intend to be, she was being racist.

Was he standing there in front of the mirror, swallowing back his anger? Was he pushing his grief that Ginny wasn't here to protect him down into some deep, dark place? But protect him from whom? From me? With my get-out-of-jail-free card that I'd sported all my adult life? 'My best friend is black.' When push came to shove though, I'd left it to Patrick to call out other people when they'd gone, 'Young black man, drugs, must be him.' And I'd allowed my mother to pat his hair. Actually pat his hair. Like some prize poodle with a bow in its fur.

I heard some muffled sniggering in the hallway, then Phoebe appeared in the kitchen in a pair of jeans that had more holes than fabric. Victor followed her in, still wearing his hat.

I tried to make eye contact to warn Phoebe about the knitted tea-cosy that was also heading her way, but she ignored me completely. I hoped Mum wouldn't notice the strained atmosphere between us and add fuel to the fire by deciding to investigate.

But she was a woman on a mission to distribute her bounty. 'Hello darling.' Her eyes dropped to Phoebe's jeans, but she omitted to comment in her rush to hand over another lurid creation.

Phoebe giggled but not unkindly. 'Thanks, Nan. See you've been busy.' She turned to Victor. 'Bet I look better in it than you.'

And with that she plonked it on her head, whipped out her phone, leant against Victor and took a selfie. Then she marched over to my mum. 'Right, Nan. Honest opinion. Who looks best? Go on, it's me, isn't it? You don't have to be tactful. Victor can take it. I am the one who bosses the orange woolly hat, yeah?'

I stood, waiting for her to say something horrible, something I'd have to repair afterwards, ashamed that I hadn't done a better job and simultaneously furious with my mother for having an opinion on everything. That rage was sitting there, primed, ready to spill, before Mum even uttered a word, a bubbling cauldron of pre-emptive anger.

But Phoebe didn't say anything mean. She made Mum's day, who was all, 'I knew you'd like it. As soon as I saw it in my magazine, I thought that's the hat for those two.' She grabbed Phoebe's hand. 'Your old nan knows you best.'

'I'm actually going to sleep in this. It's so cool.' Phoebe was twirling round the kitchen. I couldn't work out whether this was some kind of elaborate joke or whether I really did have no idea what Phoebe would like. The only thing I knew for sure was that Victor coming to live with us had magnified the cracks in everyone's veneer. And if I wasn't going to let him down, let Ginny down, I was going to have to stop being such a coward.

CHAPTER FIFTEEN

Over the next few days, Patrick and I danced around each other with our views about whether Victor was a 'contributing factor' to the problems with Phoebe or the main trigger. Or a red herring and, in fact, he was fine, it was our daughter who was out of control.

Patrick seemed a bit sparing with the details about what he'd uncovered from his chat with Victor, which led to me picking away at him. I didn't want to fall into Andrea's camp of blaming Victor for Phoebe's shortcomings but I couldn't deny that I was increasingly concerned that all the various stresses and strains of our domestic situation were only going to exacerbate Phoebe continuing to press the self-destruct button.

'He doesn't seem to do that much work, always seems so last minute, which probably leads to Phoebe doing a lot less,' I suggested.

Patrick frowned. 'He's still getting better results than her though. Don't you remember what Ginny was like with assignments? How many times did we get back from a night out to find her typing up a feature at 3 a.m.?'

I had to smile at the image that conjured up of Ginny in her pyjamas and fluffy bedsocks, swearing away in a shipwreck of coffee mugs and biscuit wrappers.

'It's not Victor's fault, but inevitably we're spreading ourselves more thinly and I think Phoebe's suffering as a result.'

'So what do you propose?' Patrick asked.

I wasn't sure I really wanted to suggest this, but I said it anyway. 'Should we see about him going to live with her brother instead?'

Patrick dropped his head down. 'Are you serious? You want to pack an eighteen-year-old off to Australia to someone he probably last saw when he was about ten? Her brother didn't even come to the funeral and I don't think we've been overrun with enquiries about how it's all going for his nephew so far.'

My shoulders sagged. 'I know.'

Patrick steepled his fingers. 'Phoebe started to get into trouble before Victor even got here. All that performance, if you'll pardon the pun, with that boy was just before she went on study leave for her GCSEs. April? May? Victor was still at home with Ginny.'

'I was up and down to Cardiff, though. I wasn't here for Phoebe in the way she perhaps needed me to be. I kept farming her out to Faye and Mum.'

Patrick pushed his chair back. 'That's life though, isn't it, Jo? Sometimes every last need doesn't get pandered to and you just have to accept that today's not your turn and get on with it. Most teenagers don't start shoplifting and taking drugs because their mum was helping out a dying friend for a few months.' He got to his feet. 'She's had your undivided attention for sixteen years. Maybe being a spoilt little madam is more of a problem than you being absent for a few days now and again. Honestly, I'm not quite sure what she's got to moan about. If she was in Victor's position, I could understand a bit of wayward behaviour. But she's not. She just needs to get a grip and take a leaf out of Victor's book: make the best of it.'

Although there were many days when Phoebe's selfishness left me open-mouthed, Patrick's unforgiving view of her winded me. Despite Victor being part of the whole hotboxing escapade, Patrick somehow thought he was less to blame. Back in June, I'd been desperate for Patrick to engage, to embrace Victor. But this about-turn was a direct lesson in being careful what you wish for.

I tried again. 'The drugs thing is a whole new escalation. And we've never got to the bottom of what really happened.'

'I have,' Patrick said, triumphantly.

'What do you mean?'

'Victor wasn't even in the car when they were hotboxing.'

I hated how we were suddenly using words we never even knew before. 'Why didn't you say something earlier? How do you know?'

'Because I've only just found out. He didn't want to be a snitch. He's finally admitted that he was playing FIFA in the house with Helaina's brother.'

'I don't believe that. He wasn't involved at all?' And there they were, my unfiltered – but as yet, unfounded – accusations for all to hear.

'Why don't you believe it? Is it easier for you to believe that someone has led Phoebe astray? It could be that she's the ringleader.'

Patrick had nailed my worst fears, but I couldn't yet admit them, not even to myself. 'I just don't think she was that bad before he got here.'

'You need to take your blinkers off.' He sounded like Faye. When had we become so harsh with each other? Where had he gone, that man who'd flown back early from Canada to stand beside me at my dad's funeral? Who'd left Cory to party on with Ginny in return for the chilly single bed at my mum's and a sitting room full of weeping relatives. The man who'd placed my hand in his and squeezed gently to remind me that he was there. His warmth in that cold church, the solid feel of him, holding me steady. The man who'd raised a glass of whisky to my dad, then to me, after the last well-wishers had disappeared and said, 'Do you know what your dad dying made me realise?'

And I'd lifted my head, peering at him through swollen eyelids and a fug of alcohol that I'd forced down to alleviate the ache in my heart but that had had the opposite effect, magnifying it, making me a mixture of weepy and belligerent. 'What?'

'That I can't stand to see you in pain.'

I had a flash of irritation then. 'That's what happens when someone dies. I'm pretty sure most people don't lose a parent and shrug it off like they forgot their gloves somewhere.'

In that moment, I wanted to claim the monopoly on grief. Cory, Ginny and Patrick still had both of their parents. And though we'd shared so much, knew each other so well, this thing, this huge adult thing, was a world away from a meeting with a scary boss, a bollocking at work, a break-up with girlfriends or boyfriends. And only I, so far, was familiar with this abyss.

Patrick had tutted at himself. 'I didn't express that properly. I meant to say, and this probably is not the day, but in some ways it is because I think your dad liked me....' He'd tipped the rest of the whisky down in one, grimacing at the burn. 'I love you, Jo.'

I'd rubbed my eyes. 'Love me, how?'

'When I was in Canada at New Year, I kept telling myself to make the most of being there, on that dream holiday we'd all promised ourselves. I hated you missing out. I couldn't stop thinking about you back here sitting with your dad, knowing they couldn't do any more for him. And I knew that, Vancouver or not, I'd rather be in Stedhurst to hold you and tell you that I'd be there for whatever you needed.'

I didn't say anything. I'd leaned forward and rested my face on my forearms. He'd kissed the back of my head, leaning into my hair. And somewhere in my bruised and bereft heart, there'd been a tiny flicker of hope.

He was the only one who'd really supported me during that time. Ginny had been rather distant and Cory had tried to redeem himself over the years but he just didn't do big emotion. Though tonight we'd see if the leopard had changed his spots. He'd issued a mysterious invitation, strict instructions to go over to his for dinner. I was in the mood for some of Cory's irreverent humour, to have a few hours where Patrick and I could relax, away from Victor and Phoebe and the bloody villagers peering up our drive with their Labradoodles peeing up the gatepost. I made Phoebe put Life360 on her phone. 'If I see that mobile leave the house for one single minute, I will be on the next train home. Otherwise we'll see you about midnight.'

CHAPTER SIXTEEN

Patrick and I took bets on what Cory had to tell us. We were giddy with relief at having something to talk about that didn't concern the kids. More often than not, we restricted our conversation to the banalities of life to avoid any conflict: who could pop to the post office and pick up a parcel. Otherwise when we were overtired, had had a few glasses of wine or I'd had an unsatisfactory text exchange with Faye, our discussion would turn into a bonfire of grievances, both current and historical. So Cory's call to arms felt like a legitimate reason to risk leaving Victor and Phoebe home alone.

As we got into the car, I felt nearly as shy with him as I had been when we first made the transition from friends to lovers nearly two decades ago. Despite sharing a flat for a good chunk of the previous ten years and witnessing everything about each other from bathroom habits to hangover traditions, shifting from a platonic to a romantic relationship was an entirely different dynamic. And so apparently was parenting one wayward child of our own and one bereaved child of our best friend.

'Does Cory know how hard we've been finding it with Victor and Phoebe?' I asked.

'I've told him a bit. He was pretty horrified when I said you'd brought up the possibility of sending Victor to Australia the other day.'

'Typical Cory. Falling on the floor with shock about what everyone else is doing while dancing through life with nothing more challenging than the Battersea bakery running out of almond croissants. I'd love to see him navigate all this shit.'

Patrick made a grunt of agreement.

I searched for a topic that wouldn't spoil these precious hours of freedom, pushing away the sense that Patrick had been disloyal to me, making me out to be the bad guy wanting to get rid of Victor. 'Do you think he's marrying Lulu?'

Patrick grinned. 'Maybe. That would be great. Ages since we went to a good wedding. Or even a bad one.'

I slipped my hand into his. 'She probably wants kids and intends to make sure his bachelor days are well and truly over.'

Patrick sighed. 'I'd like to see him settle down. We'd probably see more of him. If he had kids, he might not find it quite so dull to come out into the sticks for a weekend. Especially if we promised them a lie-in.'

We spent a few happy minutes reminiscing about what a shock to the system it had been when Phoebe was born. Patrick started humming 'Isn't She Lovely?' taking me right back to when he paced up and down the landing with her at three in the morning so I could snatch some sleep. My mum acted as though I'd won the husband lottery, 'Surely he doesn't do it when he has to go to work the next day?'

Most nights he did, though. He was so much better than me at soothing Phoebe – and soothing me when I was ragged with exhaustion. 'Just get some sleep. You'll feel so much better.'

And when I listened to my friends talking about how their husbands didn't even stir when their babies cried, I had the warm feeling of being firmly in a partnership, where it wasn't about duty or who should be doing what, it was about kindness, wanting the best for each other. Love.

As Patrick hummed on, I felt trickles of sadness, as though all that togetherness, that putting each other first, had faded away, life and its demands beating out of us that urge to consider the other. Now, we were surviving family life rather than creating a cosy cocoon for us all to flourish in.

'I'd like to spend more time with Cory anyway, even if he isn't getting married to Lulu,' I said. 'I want to go out more, have more fun.'

'I'm definitely up for that. I didn't think you were very keen on leaving Phoebe on her own in the house.'

'I'm not, but we've got to start somewhere. Let's see how she gets on tonight. I've got Mum nipping round about seven to cook them dinner.'

'I'm pretty sure even Phoebe could manage to stick a pizza in the oven.'

'I know. I just feel better about someone popping in to check up on them.'

Patrick made a face, but I didn't pick him up on it because I didn't want him to pull away from me, withdraw into silence.

I said, 'I probably am too protective and maybe if she felt we trusted her more, she might live up to our high expectations rather than endlessly meeting our low ones.'

Patrick was obviously in a flag of peace mood as well and said, 'You just want to keep her safe. I understand that.'

And the conversation turned towards the goodwill chunk of the marriage pie chart… where we might go on holiday when Phoebe left home, leading into a gentle tussle over whether my first choice, Venice, would be top of the list – 'I want to see it before it sinks' – or his choice, 'Caribbean. Don't care where. I just want to be on a beach with a cocktail in my hand. And snorkelling.'

We were still off in fantasy land when we drew up at Cory's. He buzzed us into the underground car park and we took the lift up to the third floor. As I pressed the button, I was tempted to throw myself on Patrick, be one of those couples that can't resist a quick fumble in the lift rather than the wife who says, 'Have you filled up with screenwash?' Disappointingly, after the endless conflict of the last few months, I didn't even have the confidence to reach up and peck him on the lips in case he stepped away from me.

Cory was already standing at his door. 'Come in, come in. What can I get you? Tea, beer, wine?'

I gestured to Patrick. 'You have a beer if you want. I'll drive back.' I turned to Cory. 'No Lulu?' I asked.

'Nah, she's at her sister's today.'

My hopes that this was the big announcement faded. Unless Cory wasn't sure how we'd react and was worried we might not be enthusiastic enough in front of Lulu. I thought I'd been really clear that I liked her.

I sipped my tea, while Patrick and Cory chatted about work and, irritatingly, about whether Cory's accountant would be able to take a look at Patrick's books to see if the business could be more tax-efficient. I was on tenterhooks, waiting to find out whether I needed to start planning a hat extravaganza. Something joyous to look forward to.

Eventually Patrick put down his beer and said, 'So, matey. What's the summoning us over to you all about? I'm assuming it isn't just because you've missed us? Could it be anything to do with "the next stage of your life"?' Patrick's face spread into a huge grin, eyebrows raised in expectation.

Cory shook his head and wriggled back into his chair. He looked uncomfortable and in that moment I realised that this wasn't going to be good news.

'Are you ill?' I asked, my stomach churning. I hadn't even begun to process what happened to Ginny, let alone find the resources for losing another friend.

'No, no, nothing like that.' He glanced from Patrick to me. I sensed his reluctance to speak and my heart started to beat faster, my excitement shifting into a brace position of dread. He looked down, took a deep breath and said, 'I need to tell you both something about Ginny.'

'Ginny?'

'Yep. She gave me a letter before she died to open only in very specific circumstances.'

I had no idea what he was going to say but became aware of hurt filling my chest, that despite me visiting, listening, helping her work through those final months when she was coming to terms with leaving Victor behind, she'd chosen Cory to be the holder of the knowledge. Simultaneously I told myself off for even allowing myself to consider a confiding hierarchy when poor Ginny had the right to do whatever worked for her.

When Ginny was dying, Cory was the one to make sure her will was in order, to look at setting up a trust fund for Victor that he could access at twenty-five – 'Hopefully he won't blow it on birds and booze by then,' she'd said.

But I still didn't think he would be anyone's choice for the full confessional. When my dad had died, he'd just about managed to look me in the eye when he said, 'Sorry about, you know, your dad and that.' And he never mentioned it again.

Patrick stuck his finger in the top of the beer bottle and twirled it around. 'Go on then. Don't keep us all guessing.'

Cory dipped his head down then looked directly at Patrick. 'It's about Victor. She told me to open it if it looked like either of you were having second thoughts about keeping him with you.'

Patrick pressed his thumb and forefinger into his eyes.

Cory paused as if he was reluctant to relinquish the last chance to change his mind about saying what he'd called us here for.

'He's your son, Patrick.'

CHAPTER SEVENTEEN

For a fraction of a second, I waited for Cory to burst out laughing. He didn't.

I looked at Patrick, who was sitting on the sofa, arms hanging limply at his sides. He kept screwing his eyes up, then blinking.

'Is that true?' I wished I didn't have to ask a question to which the answer might send a bulldozer careering through everything I'd taken for granted.

Patrick was biting his lip and frowning. Fear coursed through me, making my limbs feel weak and wobbly.

'How is that even possible?' I said, fright and fury combining to give me strength. 'Patrick? Presumably it wasn't artificial insemination?'

He jumped to his feet, banging his bottle down on the glass table. 'Cheers, mate, for not having a quiet word, you know, like giving me a moment to gather my thoughts about that.'

Cory flicked his hands in apology. 'Ginny's letter was very clear. She said it wasn't fair for Jo not to hear it at the same time as you. She said I couldn't refuse her dying wish.'

The man who had broken a million promises to women over the years. Who'd worn his unreliability as a badge of honour. Who'd actually promised to fly to New York to stay with a girlfriend and had texted her to say he wasn't coming when she was waiting in the arrivals hall. However, on this occasion, he'd been as good as his word. I didn't know whether I loved or hated him for that.

I tried to do the maths. Tried to work out when. When the man I married had slept with my best friend and got her pregnant. Before we were together? After? Confusion fuddled my brain, stopping me understanding whether Victor's September birthday, two months premature, meant a mountain-sized betrayal or just a great hill-sized one.

The shock was giving way to a feeling that scared me. Something that dragged in resentment, betrayal and anger all wrapped up in a poisonous parcel of being made a fool of by the people who were supposed to love me the most.

'When did you sleep with her, Patrick? Or were you having a relationship with her? An affair? Something you forgot to mention to me?'

'No! Nothing like that!' He was shaking his head, as though he couldn't absorb the news.

I got up and looked out of the huge window. The cars below. The women hurrying along the pavement, with nothing more exciting to worry about than whether they could get away with tomato pasta for a second time this week. Their mundane, magnificent lives.

Cory came and stood beside me. 'She wanted to tell you, but she wasn't sure any of you would ever need to know.'

'Why now, Cory? When I can't ask her anything? Why did she even tell you? And why did you tell us? What did you hope to gain?'

He stepped back. 'Gain? I didn't hope to gain anything. Do you think I wanted to do this? Christ, Jo. I know you don't think much of my morals, but I've always tried to be a good friend. To all of you.' He ran his fingers through his hair. 'I knew you were angling for Victor to go and live in Australia with Ginny's brother. In the letter, Ginny made me promise not to tell you unless it was absolutely necessary.'

The clues had been sitting there all these years – Ginny resolutely refusing to discuss Victor's father. Her subdued reaction when she'd discovered that I was going out with Patrick. Victor's blue eyes. My disappointment that she hadn't been more effusive when we'd announced our engagement. Her laughter, uncharacteristically unkind, when Patrick had got in a tangle with Phoebe's baby sling. An odd little moment when she'd shown no interest in the results of a family photo shoot I'd had done for my fortieth birthday.

It was as though, after many years, I'd finally knocked the winning ten pence off the shelf in the amusement arcade, nudging all the others to come cascading down. My mind wheeled back to the last days before she died, when the only time she rallied was to say, 'Victor belongs with you.' Even if the idea had terrified me, I'd been stupid enough to be flattered that she trusted me with her precious son. But now, I understood. It wasn't me. Nothing to do with me. She was sending him to be safe with his dad. The pain of her betrayal was physical, a sensation that made me dizzy and nauseous.

Cory pressed his palm against the window, leaving a greasy print. 'I wouldn't have even agreed to keep the letter if I'd known. I thought it was the details of Victor's Canadian dad. I was thinking, well, I'm not sure what I was thinking. I was hoping that we could involve him somehow. Take the pressure off you two.'

'Ginny was betting on what would happen if we learnt the truth, wasn't she?'

Cory nodded. 'I suppose so. I assume she thought it would mean that Patrick would never ask Victor to leave. And I guess she hoped you'd be big enough to accept it.'

I swung round to face Patrick. 'You knew. You must have known.'

He was pale with shock.

'I didn't, I promise. I'd asked her, before, ages ago, if the baby could be mine. She was adamant he wasn't.'

'Tell me when. How did you come to sleep with my best friend?'

Patrick looked to Cory for support. 'New Year's Eve. Remember Ginny's joke? That if she hadn't got married by thirty, she'd marry one of us? Cory had gone off with one of Ginny's publishing friends. And it was just us. We were drunk. We stayed up too late. She reminded me of the joke and we sort of dared each other. We were both single. We felt life was passing us by and I suppose we were just seeing if there was anything there. It was one of those things. We knew straight away it didn't mean anything. We just, you know...' Patrick shrugged.

'No. No. I don't know. I know that you slept with my best friend and never felt the need to tell me. I know my best friend slept with my husband and thought she'd send their son to live with us. I know that I feel like a total and utter fool.' I turned to Cory. 'I suppose you were privy to all this? Were you aware that my husband had had sex with Ginny? Was I the only one of the happy little band of four who was blundering along in blissful ignorance?'

I'd never really considered sympathy or pity as one of Cory's standout attributes. He was much more of the 'What's done is done, so get on with it' school of thought, but in that moment, he looked genuinely sad and sorry. 'Jo, Patrick wasn't your husband at the time, you weren't even going out with each other. Don't you remember what it was like back then? We were all a bit confused, trying to work out who we were and the boundary just got a bit blurred that evening. But, to answer your question, I wasn't even there. It won't surprise you that I'd "found a friend" and wasn't at Ginny's that night.' He walked to his kitchenette and filled the kettle. 'Look at it this way, if Ginny hadn't got pregnant and hadn't died, leaving you in charge of Victor, it wouldn't feel like a big deal at all that your husband slept with one of your friends before you got together with him.'

'All that proves to me, Cory, is how very skewed your moral compass is.'

'Come on. I've slept with half of my female friends just to get that whole sexual tension thing out of the way so we can go back to being good mates.'

I looked from Cory to Patrick. 'Honestly, when I read about blokes like you in the paper, I do a little shake of my head and think,

"No, most men aren't like that. They're decent human beings." But you're not. What bloke sleeps with his wife's best friend and doesn't tell her?' I paused, trying to get my head around the timeframe. 'Then declares undying love, what, barely a fortnight later when her father's just died and she's vulnerable and – obviously – gullible? Then pushes it so far that he ends up marrying her, without ever feeling the need to mention that he and her closest mate have got properly up close and personal?'

Cory opened his mouth, but I wasn't bloody finished yet.

'And you, with the morals of a sewer rat, are stupid enough to stand there and try and defend him!'

Patrick seemed to shake himself out of his stupor. 'Jo, I'm sorry. I should have told you, but I never found the right moment. There didn't seem much point in making a big deal about it initially because I didn't know whether our relationship would work out the way I hoped and I suppose I thought you wouldn't give me a chance if I told you. Ginny begged me not to say anything to you because she saw how happy you were. And then she said she was pregnant by a Canadian, which was pretty big news, so my sleeping with her seemed rather insignificant.' His voice broke. 'I didn't mean to lie to you. I didn't want to hurt you. And when we got together it all moved so quickly that everything else seemed irrelevant. And I swear, I didn't know he was my son.'

'How could you not have known? Didn't you do the bloody maths? Sex on New Year's Eve, born 25 September. Even a ten-year-old could add that up.'

Patrick cracked his knuckles. 'You know as well as I do that Ginny said Victor was nearly seven weeks premature. She was always joking that Victor was the result of too many Valentine's Day Sex on the Beach cocktails. Or "Sex on a Snowy Mountain" as she used to say.'

I didn't even want to hear Patrick make any mention of sex in relation to Ginny, cocktail-related or not. Though what he said was true, I could hear her now. 'No cocktails for me. You never know where it might lead.'

I'd always felt that she'd been too forthcoming with some details surrounding Victor's conception (the affair with the married man, the anywhere-and-everywhere sex and the drunken shagging resulting in her pregnancy) and far too sparing with others (who the hell the actual father was and why he wasn't paying maintenance). And now, like a child pulling the beard off Father Christmas, the difference between what Ginny had told me and reality was only too clear. Victor hadn't been premature. That little hospital bracelet had told the truth about his weight. That whole five pounds, eight ounces a total fabrication. She'd lied to me. Outright lied to put me off the scent. So had Patrick.

I had an overwhelming need to get away. The life I thought I'd planned so carefully, trying to do all the steps in order – job, property, marriage, baby – now resembled a pre-fab house thrown up in haste post-war, only to discover a decade later that the sewers and electricity supply were inadequate for the needs of the inhabitant.

'I'm going home. Patrick, you stay here with Cory. You can have a good old chortle about what a mug I am.'

Cory put his hand out to stop me. 'Jo, no one thinks that. Ginny kept it a secret because she didn't want to cause trouble between you and Patrick. She was worried that you'd react like this.'

'Don't you dare put this on me. Ginny lied to me. Patrick lied to me. And now you are trying to make out I don't have a right to be well and truly pissed off that I've been tricked into looking after my husband's son when it's all Patrick can do to remember that his own bloody daughter could benefit from a bit of his attention now and again before she ends up in prison!'

Patrick ran over to me. 'Jo, Jo! Don't leave. Come on. I know you're upset. I'm sorry.'

'Save it. I don't want to hear it. I'm too angry now. You keep the car and I'll get the train home. The walk will do me good.'

He tried to take me in his arms, but I pushed him away.

'Don't. Just bloody don't. If there's any hope of us surviving this, you will stay out of my way tonight.'

I snatched up my coat and stormed out, waiting until I got into the lift to fold over and cry.

CHAPTER EIGHTEEN

I walked up from the station, my head tucked inside my hood, praying that I wouldn't meet anyone I knew. The rainy November evening was my saviour. No other wives were wandering the street, marvelling at how life could change forever on one seemingly innocuous Saturday. No, they were tucked up watching the latest Netflix series with their husbands who hadn't fathered a child with their best friend.

I made my way along the pavement, past the church. There was something weirdly comforting about looking at all those graves, their stone crosses tilting to one side with the passage of the years. In the end, we all ended up dead, whatever our path through life. I considered walking among the headstones, searching for a woman who'd died at my age, forty-eight, with the sole purpose of consoling myself that, unlike her and unlike Ginny, I was still here. I wasn't quite ready for silver linings yet though. I was firmly at the stage where red-hot molten fury was burning through my brain, scorching off the neural pathways that led to forgiveness and fast-tracking to the depositories for grudges, resentments and bitterness.

As I panted up the hill to our cottage, I could hear a boom-boom of a bass. I marched on, aware of the thudding getting closer, almost vibrating through the ground.

It took me a little while longer and a couple of teenagers staggering around the corner with cans of cider in their hands to realise that the music was coming from our cottage. All the lights were blazing, the windows were open and Stormzy was telling the whole village about someone being too big for their boots.

Thankfully nosy old Mrs Giles's house was in darkness. I didn't hesitate at the gate, didn't ponder for a second what would be the best approach, what would allow Phoebe to save face in front of her friends. I simply walked up to the group of teenagers smoking and flicking their ash in my winter pansies by the front door and said, 'Party's over. Get out.'

One of them said, 'A-ll ri-ght,' as though I was being totally unreasonable and made a move to go in through the front door.

I grabbed him by the shoulder. 'No, now,' I said, pointing down the drive.

He wriggled free. 'Just getting my jacket.'

'Phoebe will bring it to school. Go on, get lost.'

After all the times I'd skulked about when Phoebe was FaceTiming her friends, trying not to be the uptight, frumpy mother inadvertently looming onto the screen, I suddenly found myself giddy with liberation. I was way beyond the boundary of hoot-giving about what they reported back to their parents. Mad woman forcing teenage boys out into the November evening in just a T-shirt? Bring it on.

I stomped around the side of the garage, tapping another lad on the shoulder, who took a couple of seconds to register that the girl whose bra he was jamming his face into was frantically trying to tell him that they had company. 'Go on, out. And you, love, a word of advice. Not a good look getting your tits out in the winter drizzle for any old bod that asks to see them.'

They stumbled off down the path, mumbling. I had no idea whether they were cursing me or muttering apologies and I couldn't care less either way.

I strode round to the front door, where news had started to spread that the 'rents' were home. A couple of girls staggered out on heels that my knackered feet could only dream about, no coats, screaming with laughter. They ignored me completely as though I was the garden gnome holding a wheelbarrow of marigolds.

I bellowed after them: 'You're welcome! Come again!'

They peered round, their faces screwed up in 'She talking to us?' puzzlement.

Before I tackled the house, I breathed in a huge gulp of the freezing cold air. For some reason it made me think of Ginny and I sitting in an outdoor hot tub when we'd gone skiing with Patrick and Cory, four or five years before that New Year's Eve. We'd kept ducking under the hot water, then sticking our heads up into the icy air, steam coming off our faces. I'd prided myself on living the life I was destined for, the one with adventures and experiences, making memories that would cheer me up when I was – as Ginny would say – sitting in the nursing home dribbling my soup.

A wave of missing her threatened to dull the heat of my anger. Her zest for life, her attitude of 'Come on! You might not ever get the chance to sit in a hot tub at midnight in the snow again!' had enriched my existence beyond measure. And now that same appetite for experimental sex had damaged my life beyond measure as well.

I rode another wave of outrage and burst through my front door. I flicked on all the lights, taking a grim satisfaction in seeing hands withdrawn from places they shouldn't be, the shape of 'What the actual...?' forming on teenage mouths that seconds before had been glued onto far more pleasurable pursuits.

I clapped loudly. 'Party is over. Everyone out.' I switched off the music that was reverberating right up into my stomach, making me feel sick.

That sudden death of noise brought a few teenagers scuttling to the top of the stairs like astronauts deprived of oxygen.

'Downstairs. Now. Off you go.'

Helaina slunk past, adjusting her bra strap. So much for Andrea thinking Helaina was a shining example of model behavior.

'Where's Phoebe?' I asked.

She shrugged. 'I don't know.'

That little peek behind her gave it away. I ran upstairs and threw open the door to her bedroom, slamming the lights on. The whole room stank of teenage hormones and trainers. Two bodies were in mid-grope on the bed but not Phoebe.

'Get downstairs. Leave now!' My woman-way-beyond-the-edge hiss made them spring up, gathering shoes and random items of clothing like something out of a *Carry On* comedy. Hilarious really if I could ever have imagined finding anything funny again.

I ran into my bedroom. There was Phoebe, topless, with a boy on top of her, shirtless but still with his trousers on. My bar for rejoicing was sinking ever lower.

'Mum!' She still managed to sound defiant as though I had no right to enter my own room.

I could barely get the words out. 'Get dressed. And you, my friend, get out.' I shoved his shirt at him. It was definitely an 'every man for himself' moment.

He didn't speak, just grabbed his clothes and scarpered.

Phoebe had leapt up, covering herself with whatever little scrap of material hadn't been covering anything in the first place. 'Don't start. I literally can't be bothered to listen to it. Yes, I know I shouldn't have had a party. Yes, I know I shouldn't be in your room. Yes, I know I should have more self-respect…'

For the first time ever, I was tempted to slap her. I interlinked my fingers in front of me. 'Shut up, you little madam! I am sick to death of you doing whatever you like and thinking that you can get away with it. Put your clothes on and go to your room. Stay away from me.'

'For fuck's sake, you're mental. Who the hell wants to be near you anyway?' She stumbled out, clutching her bra and slamming the door behind her with such force, I heard the glass shelf on the landing rattle.

Before I could take in the enormity of the gulf between me nuzzling Phoebe to my breast moments after she was born and promising to protect her from harm and the deranged woman I was now, yelling as though I wouldn't care if I never saw her again, I noticed a little fold of cardboard on my bedside table and the tiniest smattering of white powder next to it. Instinctively, I dabbed my finger in it and then stopped myself. What did I think it was? Lily-of-the-valley talcum powder?

I charged out of my bedroom feeling as though I might start smashing things and screaming, 'You want to ruin your life? You want to kill yourself? Here, let me help!' The minuscule fraction of sanity remaining acknowledged that a scene like that probably didn't need an audience of teenagers standing round agog.

Instead, I marched into Victor's room. He wasn't going to be immune from the mad mum rampage. For the first time ever I didn't knock, and he jumped as the door flung open. I don't know who was more relieved that he was just helping Georgia put her jacket on. Even in my anger, I recognised the chivalry of that gesture, though, of course, the rumpled bed suggested that it hadn't been an evening of unbridled politesse.

In a tight voice, I said, 'Everyone is going home now,' and slammed out again. Georgia and Victor. Faye wasn't going to like that. Then again, served her right for not carrying through with her big threat of grounding Georgia till Christmas.

I stormed downstairs. Teenagers were milling through the hallway towards the door. I went into the kitchen, taking in the floor tacky with drink, the chewing gum stuck on my worktops, the fags and joints stubbed out in my plant pots and little silver dishes that I'd brought back from Morocco, where Ginny had taken me for a long weekend for my fortieth birthday. The disrespect of that ignited another torrent of fury.

I grabbed a bin bag, chucking in half-empty bottles of beer and vodka, nearly full cans of cider, and lugged it, dripping, towards the garden, no longer caring that the sticky liquid was seeping down between the parquet tiles. I thrust it onto the lawn, hearing everything crash down with a satisfying smash, before slumping onto the wooden bench by my flower bed and letting the tears stream out into the freezing night.

I made no attempt to stifle my crying. I leant over and howled my hurt in a manner that Ginny would have dismissed as dramatic. At the most, even when she got the 'no more treatment options left' news, she allowed tears to roll silently down her face, muttering, 'My poor boy, I'm sorry I didn't live longer for you' to herself.

No doubt Phoebe would be teased about me when she got to school on Monday. But, right now, I was claiming centre stage of unhappiness. I couldn't begin to imagine how anything would ever be right again. Me and Patrick. Could I really sit by every day and observe the biological connection he'd had with my best friend? Could I witness the little quirks of nature that triumphed nurture without them underlining the big lie that had sat alongside our marriage for eighteen years? Would every shared gesture, every lightning-quick understanding that comes from a genetic bond act like the sun on a magnifying glass, angled directly at my wounds until I combusted under the strain of pretending it didn't matter?

And that was before I tackled the whole issue of how we would tell Victor without him bursting into flames himself. God knows how we'd explain it to Phoebe without creating more problems than the skyscraper of shit we were already failing to scale. On the upside for her, she'd have a great line to tell any future therapist. 'Yeah, well, when I was only sixteen, my half-brother, my dad's son, came to live with us, but no one told me… So, yeah, it's not to my credit but I did find cocaine helped me forget…'

I had a child who, by the looks of things, had taken coke. I couldn't figure it out. We were so ordinary. So unremarkable. Just two normal parents, not perfect, but until now I would have said good enough.

Footsteps coming closer stopped my train of thought. I didn't sit up. I didn't want to talk to anyone and I certainly couldn't trust myself to speak to Phoebe. Someone sat down next to me and, from my bent-over position, I recognised the trainers as Victor's. The bench creaked as he leant back.

'Can I do anything?'

That voice. The same intonation as Ginny. That Welsh inflection underpinned by equal amounts of steel and kindness.

'Nope. Thank you. I probably just need to be left alone.'

He did what Ginny would have done. Completely ignored me. 'You're shivering.' He got up and went inside. I had that strange sensation of asking to be left alone and then feeling abandoned when I got my wish.

He returned with a coat, which he handed to me without a word.

I pulled myself into a sitting position and wriggled into it. 'Thank you.'

He sat beside me. In a T-shirt. I tried not to study him, to search his face for similarities to Patrick, to think about the secret Ginny and Patrick had kept from me for all these years.

'I don't think Phoebe meant for so many people to come. It was sort of one of those things where she invited a few people and then they wanted to bring plus-ones and it got a bit out of hand.'

For a brief moment, I just basked in the rare sensation of someone defending Phoebe. It was tempting to dismiss it under the banner of the whole 'teenage inability to predict what a consequence might be', but I couldn't let myself. I had to accept that my daughter was on the verge of getting into big trouble that might be beyond my capability of fixing. What if she got pregnant and wanted to keep the baby? What if she didn't and had to go through an abortion? What if she got addicted to cocaine? What would that do to her brain? What would be next? Heroin? And these were tip-of-the-iceberg worries whirring round and round my brain, stoking up a sense of impending disaster as they went.

I turned to Victor. 'Tonight's not just a one-off, is it though? We've had the shoplifting, the car accident, never mind the video that went viral round the school last year.'

I watched him out of the corner of my eye. He displayed no curiosity on that front, so someone had obviously filled him in.

'I don't think I can pretend any more that we haven't got a huge problem on our hands.' I sighed.

I was finding it hard to speak to him without the image of Patrick and Ginny in bed together clouding my thinking. I tried to focus on the practical problem of what we did with the news that Patrick was Victor's dad. Gather the whole family together and announce it casually over the Crunchy Nut Cornflakes just before school? Let Patrick take Victor away on his own so I didn't have to be party to the father/son reunion? I conjured up a vision of myself at home, with Phoebe nagging to be allowed to go to a party, while Patrick clinked champagne glasses with Victor, promising to make up for lost time, stepping forward into a relationship I'd never share in the same way. A relationship that would always remind me that the two people who loved me most had slept together, lied – at least by omission – then produced a legacy that there was no escaping, no bundling back into the 'yeah we made a mistake but that was years ago and we never need to consider it again' cupboard.

A burst of pain shot through me. Could I be big enough to get past this? What if I couldn't? A picture of our cottage with a For Sale sign poking out beyond the old-fashioned tea roses by the gate flashed into my head. Throwing Patrick out wasn't going to improve anything with Phoebe. Nor was springing a half-brother on her, when she was already a rebel without a cause. God knows how bad it could get *with* a cause.

Victor had Ginny's gift for sitting waiting for the other person to say more than they'd intended. I wasn't falling for that one. And even though I wanted to rant and curse about how she'd stitched me up good and proper, I was relieved to discover I wasn't such a horrible person that I felt her son should have to hear it.

I thought of all the times Ginny had come to stay here with Victor, the holidays we'd had camping in France, the hundreds of times I'd happily crashed off to bed, leaving Patrick and Ginny drinking wine and chatting downstairs. Had she been biding her time waiting to tell him? Secretly hoping to lure him away? Sitting there jealous of everything I had? I couldn't make sense of it. Couldn't understand what Ginny's thought process might have been. The temptation to turn to Victor and say, 'Did your mother ever mention Patrick as an old boyfriend?' hovered so far over the edge of my lips that I barely dared breathe in case I blew the words out.

Victor cracked his knuckles. 'Loads of girls at my old school were a bit wild, but their parents didn't care, just gave up. Let the police or school deal with them. Phoebe knows you won't give up on her, though.'

'Why would she behave horribly in the first place?' I asked, hoping to get an insight into the mysterious and unhinged workings of the teenage brain.

Victor said, 'I don't know. Sometimes I think she just likes being centre of attention.' He carried on. 'Not in a bad way, but the sporty girls are the really popular ones at school and I think she does it to get in with the in-crowd. Just sort of pushes it a bit far to show off.'

Who knew that instead of wasting all that money over the years on guitar lessons, extra maths and a brief spell of horse riding, we should have been funnelling our cash into making sure she was in the A team for netball? I'd had my eye on good grades as the gold standard of parenting. No exam success was going to propel her to stardom if she ended up with a baby at seventeen or, even worse, behind bars.

'Does she have really close friends?' I realised I wasn't sure who she hung out with now, as I got the distinct impression from Faye bundling various giggling girls into her car at school pick-up that she was busy trying to engineer other friendships for Georgia.

Victor rubbed at his eyebrow in a gesture that reminded me so much of Patrick I couldn't believe I hadn't noticed before.

He screwed up his face. 'I don't want to snitch.'

'You're not. You're helping me to keep her safe.'

'She mainly hangs out with the boys in the year above.'

'Was the one she was with tonight in the year above?'

Victor hesitated.

'It's okay. You're not telling me anything I don't know. I found her in my bed with him.' A bitter little sound escaped me. The irony of pumping Victor for information that might help me protect Phoebe was not lost on me.

'He's the older brother of one of the boys in the upper sixth.'

Not even a schoolboy any more. What the hell was he doing with a sixteen-year-old who still screamed for Patrick to get a spider out of her bedroom? No point in pretending to myself that contraception was no longer an urgent issue.

I sensed Victor getting ready to make an excuse to leave.

'Is she still friendly with Helaina and the rest of that group?'

'Sort of. I think she's fallen out with some of the girls in our year.'

'Do you know why?'

'Not really. They can all be a bit bitchy and over the top.'

I had to agree. On the few occasions Phoebe cracked the door open slightly onto her Instagram/Snapchat world and all the pouting and posing and 'Gorgeous!/So sexy, hun', it felt like peering into an online version of *Lord of the Flies*. How a teenager viewed those pictures depended on whether you were smiling out of one or gazing enviously in. At least when I was her age, I didn't have photographic evidence that I'd been left out of all the cool parties.

'Georgia's nice though.' Victor smiled, that soft little smile I'd forgotten existed in the world. The smile of someone who was falling in love.

I looked at him. My heart shuttled back and forth between the ease of our lives if he went to live in Australia and the nightmare I had no idea how to resolve if we decided to tell him and Phoebe that Patrick was his father. I knew what Patrick would insist on, that sense of justice I'd always adored in him. He'd say that Victor was the innocent party and he shouldn't be the one to pay the price. I could hear him now: 'We're the grown-ups. We can choose to be kind.'

All of which was true. However, I wasn't sure I was magnanimous enough to risk sending Phoebe into even more of a downward spiral to protect the son my husband had had with my best friend.

Ginny should have told me. Or told no one. What she'd done was so cruel, burying a time bomb in our lives that she must have known would detonate at some point. What if I'd found out in three years, five, ten? Would it have made it better or worse? I hadn't even started to process grieving for her and now I had to review my entire friendship with her in a different light.

I jumped to my feet, wanting to stop looking at the evidence right in front of me. 'Time for bed.'

As we made our way down the hallway, our feet sticking at every step, Victor said, 'My mum would also have completely lost her shit at a mess like this.'

My eyes prickled at his sweet vulnerability, my heart aching for his blissful ignorance. Would telling him the truth help? Would pulling Patrick out of the hat as a consolation-prize parent dull his grief for Ginny? Or would it simply lift the lid off his pain and strike it through with brightly coloured additives like a macabre raspberry ripple?

I climbed the stairs behind him, bidding him an awkward goodnight at the top. The mother in me longed to reach out and comfort him, the wife in me wanted to recoil from the physical evidence of the two people I loved most in the world deceiving me. As he disappeared into his room, an extra level of hideousness occurred to me: perhaps Patrick had resisted Victor coming to live with us precisely because he *knew* Victor was his son and realised that the secret he'd been sitting on for decades would come out. Which would make him a coward and a pretty shabby father. I put that thought to one side to be picked over later in favour of dealing with the drama in hand.

I hovered by Phoebe's door. I turned the handle, bracing myself for a stream of abuse. The bed was unmade but no Phoebe. The window was ajar. I leaned out. Across the lawn, I could see footprints in the wet grass as far as the garden gate leading onto the lane beyond. I shut the window and closed her bedroom door.

I flopped onto my own bed, my mind flicking through possibilities. I debated texting her friends or ringing around. Even if I managed to find her, what then? Would she fight me? Would she swear at me? Refuse to come home? Was I really going to be that mother who knew her child was missing but did nothing? Was climbing out of her window and shinning down the wisteria to chase after a boy the same as missing? Probably not. Would the police even be interested? But what if something happened to her? I imagined answering a police officer's question: 'And what did you do when you understood your daughter had left the house?'

'Lay on my bed' didn't feel like the parent-of-the-year answer, but what was the alternative? Waking up everyone in the village and pushing Phoebe further to the top of the list of troublemakers? Running around the streets hoping to stumble upon her behind a hedge with the at least nineteen-year-old, whatever his name was. I pushed my head back into my pillow. I should phone Patrick, share the burden. I stared at the text he'd sent, before I'd even arrived home.

I'm sorry. I love you. So simple, yet so complex. But all of my love, all of my energy, veered towards my daughter. The triumph again of motherhood over marriage. It was incredible that any marriage survived the all-consuming needs of children.

And now Patrick had another child to prioritise. Would that mean he didn't care as much as I did about Phoebe?

I sent one WhatsApp to her. *Phoebe, I know I was angry and you probably are too. Please come home so we can talk. I love you xx.*

I looked at the word 'love' and wondered if I even understood it any more. Nothing in my life felt love-filled.

I huddled under the duvet, my ears straining to hear footsteps on the gravel, my mind circling round and round what particular alchemy of personalities had made my child the one who hated her parents. I kept looking at my messages waiting to see whether she'd read it. After about an hour, I could see she'd seen it but no response. It was a sad state of affairs that I was relying on two blue ticks to indicate that somewhere, God knows where, my daughter was still alive.

While I waited to see whether Phoebe would come home, I picked through the detail of the whole period around that New Year's Eve and when my dad died. I'd been hurt that Ginny had gone quiet between January and Easter. She'd phoned once or twice, but the time difference with Vancouver meant she was at work when it was our evening. We didn't yet have a computer at home and we weren't allowed to use email at work for personal things. Ginny flouted that rule spectacularly, but it made me nervous, especially as her missives were always peppered with expletives that I was terrified would flag up in the system.

I'd held off telling her that Patrick and I had become an item. That we'd even talked about marriage. From a friendship point of view, I'd been closest to Ginny, but now Patrick would know my deepest secrets. And Ginny was the one around whom we all orbited, the energy, the plans, the facilitator of our group. However, when she left a message on my answerphone at home in April, saying she had something important to tell me, I knew I needed to confess my own secret.

There was that little time delay where we overlapped each other, both bursting out with 'I've got some news.' I tried to get her to fill me in first, desperately hoping that it was something good and exciting that would leave her able to be generous and happy for us. But Ginny, who always loved a surprise, insisted on me going first.

'I'm not sure how you'll feel about this….' I was nervous, stuttering my way through how Patrick and I had been spending a lot of time together since Dad died because he was working in Chichester and it was convenient for him to stay at Mum's with me. I blathered on about how Mum was so happy to have a man around the house and Ginny had joked, 'Patrick's not really Mr DIY though, is he?' And then there'd been a pause when the penny dropped. 'Oh my God, when you say you're spending a lot of time together, you mean you're *together*, like a couple?'

I tried to play down my happiness. 'Yes. I know it's a bit weird after being friends for all these years, but he's been so kind. It's been a funny few months with Dad, well, you know…' There was a silence. 'Ginny?'

'Sorry, yes. Wow! Is it serious?'

'It's got serious so quickly I can't actually believe it.'

'Marriage serious?'

I hesitated. 'We haven't set a date or anything.'

'Jo! Are you sure? I know we joked about marrying the boys when we got to thirty, but I didn't realise you'd keep them to it…'

Her tone was a bit clipped, sounding like she did when she was expected to be the last word in so-called 'black people's issues' – 'I don't know anything about blood diamonds in Angola. I grew up in Cardiff.'

I'd felt wounded then, as though Ginny thought I was a desperate old spinster ready to settle for anyone. I was let down that she didn't sound more pleased for me. She probably just needed time to get used to it because inevitably it would impact on her friendship with Patrick as well. I jollied her along. 'Anyway, enough about me. So what's your big news then? Please tell me you're coming back to live in Britain?' I hoped to prove to her that she was still a huge part of my life, that I hadn't become all dull and boring now I'd fallen in love.

'No, I'm definitely not coming back to the UK.' She sounded almost belligerent about it. I struggled not to be offended, as though she was dismissing everything, including me, as unimportant and irrelevant. 'I've been offered a promotion to oversee two magazines rather than just being the editor of *FemmeQ*. I was wishing you could come and hit some bars in Gastown to celebrate.' But she didn't sound like she wanted to go out on the razz with me – or anyone else. Her voice was flat, fed up. I should have asked her what was wrong, but I didn't want to hear the answer, to have to face any reservations she had about Patrick and me. I felt my happiness draining away.

I forced some enthusiasm into my words. 'That's amazing. You should be thrilled. You've done so well. I wish I could visit. Maybe next year? I took so much leave when we lost Dad, I don't think I'm in a position to ask for any holiday from work at the moment. Are you planning to come home at all?'

'Have to see how it goes. Anyway, on that note, better go. Got loads of meetings to prepare for.'

I felt short-changed at the abrupt finish to our phone call. She'd left me with the impression that she felt my getting together with Patrick had happened just because we were two saddos stranded in Sussex making do with each other due to lack of other options. I wanted her to know that, at least on my part, I wasn't settling. That in a truly shitty year when I'd buried my dad, I'd woken up to the fact that life was short and sometimes the best things in life weren't the exotic unknown but there, right under your nose. I put the phone down feeling robbed of the chance to understand more about her life. Who she hung out with, whether she had real friends or just posh publishing acquaintances. Whether she was on a big fat salary and striding out in designer gear, if she'd met any fancy executives with cosy wooden lodges on a lake. I wanted to ask her if she missed me.

And now, nearly nineteen years later, I knew why that conversation had been so awkward.

*

I eventually dozed off in the early hours, woken up by a frantic ringing of the doorbell. My alarm clock said 6.30 a.m. I shot out of bed, running downstairs two at a time, the surge of adrenaline making me feel sick. I took a deep breath before I turned the key.

It was Phoebe. Dishevelled, wearing a baggy sweatshirt that didn't belong to her. Her skin was white and blotchy, dark circles under her eyes. She'd definitely been up all night.

Relief washed away most, but not all, of my anger. I concentrated on sounding conciliatory. 'Are you okay, love?'

She pushed past me in a waft of stale smoke and booze. 'Yep.'

'Do you need anything?' I didn't let the words, 'Like the morning-after pill' escape my lips, but the effort nearly suffocated me.

She turned to me. 'From you? I don't think so. I'm going to bed. Don't wake me up.'

I stood in the hallway, watching her stomp upstairs. My anger collided with my despair at her disrespect, her rudeness. Nothing good would come from insisting on a confrontation now. I put on my slippers and picked my way through the chaos of my kitchen. The fear that had engulfed me when the doorbell went drained away. For now, she was here. Safe. I frowned as my slipper stuck to the floor. My desire not to get into a slanging match wavered. I considered dragging her down to clear up straight away but I couldn't trust myself not to escalate the situation beyond repair. Far better to direct my energy to cleaning. I filled a bucket with hot water, located a scrubbing brush and got down on my hands and knees.

I was on my fourth bucket of water, finding a grim satisfaction in the white grouting reappearing from under the brown dregs of cider, when I heard the key in the lock. I carried on cleaning, my back tense.

I sensed Patrick standing in the doorway. I was torn between a martyrish 'look what happens when you take your eye off the parenting ball' and punishing him for – what? – not telling me earlier? Not using a condom? Having a son, a special bond with another child that excluded me? I couldn't ignore the fact that also in that combustible mix was a sense of the sturdy scaffolding of a long marriage, framing our fragile lives. My jaded brain swung between abandoning all faith in our relationship and trusting myself to its robustness.

Patrick sighed. 'Jo.' That concerned and gentle tone. It reminded me of when he'd come to Dad's funeral and not left for a whole week afterwards. My mum had twittered about, making sure he sat in the best armchair, delighted to find a home for the fruit cake left over from the wake. He'd taken one look at me in my dressing gown the morning we buried my dad and held his arms out. 'Oh Jo.' And that was enough. I didn't need him to tell me it would be okay, or come up with any platitudes about how time would heal and at least I had my memories and how Dad was now at peace. I only required him to hug me and to tolerate my pain without shying away.

Patrick stepped into the kitchen. 'Jo,' he said again.

I couldn't tough it out. I put the scrubbing brush into the bucket and faced him.

A second person in our family who looked like they'd slept in a hedge. 'You look knackered.'

'I am.' He paused. 'Let me guess. Phoebe had a party?'

'Got it in one.'

'Are they still asleep?'

I hated myself for the little stab of jealousy that came with him asking after both of his children.

'Yes. Phoebe was out all night. Came in at half past six this morning.' I was braced, defying him to ask why I hadn't got her home before then. Or why I hadn't called him. Or why I should have done some other bloody thing that would have stopped us being the people that everyone nodded at the mention of and said,

'I know who you mean.' Before putting on *that* face, so damn smug that they'd done it right.

Apparently Patrick hadn't been married to me for all this time without learning something. He might not know where to find the cheese grater, that a Hoover bag needed changing if it wasn't picking up or that no one other than me was allowed to use the turquoise towels, but he knew enough to recognise when not to poke the bear.

He sounded contrite. 'Let me get you a cup of tea, then tell me what I can do to help.'

I made the childish part of me – 'Look round the kitchen and pick a bloody job! Any of the thirty-seven that need doing!' – bow down to the last sliver of adult cordiality. 'Thank you. Perhaps you could go and pick all the dog-ends out of the plant pots outside. Or see if you can fix the leg on the dining room chair?'

I carried on scrubbing. I could hear my heart thudding in the silence.

Patrick passed me a mug of tea.

'I'm sorry. I'm sorry it came out like this.'

'You knew, didn't you? That's why you were so against having him here. In case your little secret came to light.'

Patrick stepped towards me, shaking his head. 'No, no. I genuinely didn't. Jo, you know me better than that. I would have taken responsibility if Ginny had told me.'

He tripped over her name and my heart dipped at the understanding that the very mention of her would always evoke complex and contradictory emotions. As much as I was in a place to assume the worst, I noted a little release of tension at Patrick's words. I instinctively recognised the truth.

I wasn't finished yet though.

'But the fact remains you did know you'd slept with her and chose not to tell me.' I sat back on my heels. 'I'll always wonder if it was really me you wanted or whether there was more to it, whether she turned you down and I was a convenient safety net. And I will never ever understand how you didn't know you'd got her pregnant. It must have occurred to you that you could be the father.'

Patrick sat on the floor next to me. I wanted to tell him to be careful not to get bleach on his jeans. 'Jo, I asked her as soon as she told you she was pregnant.'

'How did you ask her? Did you phone her? Send her an email? How *did* you both decide that you would just continue planning to marry me while she was carrying your baby?'

'I rang her.'

'When?' I imagined him leaving the office at lunchtime, sitting huddled on a bench, waiting to find out whether he'd got his girlfriend's best friend pregnant.

'I can't remember now. When did she tell you she was expecting? May? June? It was straight away after that. I'd proposed to you by then, hadn't I?'

'What did she say?'

Patrick looked up at me, his face, the one that I could pick out of a crowd – the face that said safe and home and family and roots and belonging – troubled and uncertain. 'It was nearly two decades ago, Jo. The rough gist was that I shouldn't flatter myself that I'd score a hit with a one-time only session and that the baby was nothing to do with me.'

'And then you agreed that neither of you would mention it to me?'

'We did talk about it, of course we did, but at the time, we just thought it would cause unnecessary bad feeling and awkwardness between us all for nothing.'

I grunted. 'You can say that again.'

Patrick stretched his legs out. 'I know you won't believe me because of what we know now, but it really didn't mean anything. And that's easy for me to say because I'm not the one dealing with the news that my wife has had a baby with another man. I promise it was no more important to me than say—'

I put my hand up to stop him. 'Please don't name any other one-night stands for me to be jealous of.'

'I wasn't going to. I was trying to think of an old boyfriend of yours that was just a fling. How about that weird intense bloke who used to cycle over to our flat with organic wine in his backpack and a tin of chickpeas? That didn't last longer than a couple of dates.'

'Shut up. Shut up. This is not about who I slept with or whether it meant anything to me. This is about you sleeping with my best friend and you both deciding never to tell me. The two people I trusted the most.' If I hadn't been so angry, I might have got my own back, teasing him about the girlfriend who used to handwash her underwear when she stayed overnight and drape it around our bathroom, culminating in her catching Ginny dancing around the kitchen with a leopard-print thong on her head. But with the lens of hindsight shining fiercely on the two relationships I thought I knew inside out, I no longer had faith in anything I once took at face value.

And round and round we went, with Patrick claiming that because it pre-dated us getting together, it fell under the get-out clause of past history that didn't need to be discussed.

'So you wouldn't mind if you found out I'd slept with Cory then?'

Patrick hesitated a moment before saying, 'No, I'd be fine with it.' However, I could tell from the way his jaw tightened that he wouldn't like it either. He marched over to the sink and started rummaging in the cupboard for a cloth. 'Did you sleep with him?'

I stared at him. 'See, feels a bit different when the boot's on the other foot.'

'Are you going to answer the question?'

'Why should I since none of it means anything? What does it matter to you? What was it you said? "It's nearly twenty years ago."'

And so it carried on, although the closest I'd got to sleeping with Cory was collapsing into each other on the sofa after too much red wine.

Patrick and I wrestled the house back into some kind of order against a soundtrack of Patrick pleading his case and me hissing accusations, as jealousy and hurt clouded my judgement. In the end, I snapped. Having to keep my voice to little more than a whisper so Victor didn't overhear was adding to my fury. 'Look, I don't think we're in a position to play families reunited right now. Let's concentrate on sorting Phoebe out – if you're still interested in your daughter now you've got a much easier son – and we'll work out how to break the happy news to Victor that you're actually his dad at a later date.'

We both fell silent when we heard Victor coming downstairs for breakfast.

As he walked in, Patrick made a pathetic attempt at disguising the misery vacuum-packing his adoptive family by being all hearty. 'Bit of a party last night then?'

Victor grimaced. 'Yep. Sorry. I probably should have rung one of you.'

Patrick spoke gently. 'It's not your fault, Victor. You were in quite a difficult position. Given how things have been lately, we were probably a bit optimistic in going out.'

I couldn't bear to watch the interaction between them. Couldn't stand to see how Patrick was looking at Victor, his eyes sweeping over him, as if he was seeing him in a completely new light. I almost sensed Patrick shifting perspective, the irresistible, primeval pull towards protecting your own.

I knew that what would be right for us as a family – me, Patrick and Phoebe – would alter direction now. His loyalties would be stretched and corralled down a different path from mine. I could look at our situation rationally, intellectually, with empathy, but I'd have to get past the fact that my feelings for Victor would always have a slight shadow over them, bound up forever in an odd sense of betrayal. If Patrick eventually experienced the same ferocious love for Victor as we did for Phoebe, I didn't know whether I'd be able to join him or would endlessly lag behind on the journey.

I reminded myself that Victor was the innocent one in all of this. That whatever complex feelings his presence stirred up, none of this was his fault. In a bunker of dread lay the knowledge that he had a right to know who his father was. And Phoebe, to know that she had a brother. That left just me, with my nose pressed against the window, wondering where I fitted into the puzzle.

CHAPTER NINETEEN

Over the next couple of weeks, Patrick really made an effort with Phoebe, laying down the law, what he expected of her, how he hoped to see her behaviour change, but also taking her out on her own, praising every little thing she did: 'Your hair looks nice today/I like the music you were playing/would you like me to drop you off at the cinema?'

I, on the other hand, was staggering along, narrowly meeting my work deadlines, numb to all the barbed comments and insults Phoebe tossed my way. I no longer had the energy to remonstrate or to investigate where she might be compared with where she said she'd be. It was as much as I could do to manage not to run out of milk, toss some carrots and broccoli onto our plates and not rampage through the rooms sweeping every bit of wedding Waterford to the floor.

Throughout the last half of November when it was already getting dark and I knew I had only an hour to get my work done before the kids came home, my heart was so heavy that it wouldn't have taken much for me to jump into the car and drive. I imagined headlines in the newspapers: Middle-aged Mum Disappears Without Trace. Sometimes I'd even take it as far as fantasising about what eccentric trail I could leave behind to make me more interesting than the stupid woman whose best friend had tricked her into becoming a mother to her husband's son. Perhaps I could leave a note: *Don't bother looking for me. I've taken the pinking shears, the onion storage jar and *something* from the garage.* I imagined turning up as a mysterious stranger in the Outer Hebrides, living in an isolated house on the edge of the cliffs, before remembering that when Patrick was away for work, the clematis flapping against the bedroom window had me leaping out of bed with my finger poised over 999.

For now, Patrick and I were existing like guests in a B&B, raising our eyebrows at each other in acknowledgement but avoiding any meaningful conversation. At night, we'd lay in bed, tension humming in the space between us. Occasionally I'd blurt out a 'Had any thoughts about when or what you're going to tell Victor and Phoebe?' No matter how I tried to get the tone neutral, enquiring rather than accusatory, I couldn't.

Patrick would sigh and mutter something like, 'I don't know yet. I can't talk about this now, I've got a busy day tomorrow.'

And mostly, I'd limit myself to a sarcastic 'Haven't we all?' but once or twice I'd pushed. 'When will you be ready to face it? Or are we just going to be living in limbo waiting to see when the big man decides to own up to his mistakes?'

Patrick would either go really quiet and respond with a deflated, 'I don't know what you want me to say' or his anger would escalate with mine, both of us hauling each other further up the ladder of spiteful blame. We hissed about cowardice, hypocrisy and any number of things that seemed a million miles from slipping my hand into his on our wedding day and feeling the ground steady under my feet. For several days after each brutal run-in, the bruise of raw emotion ached around us, another withdrawal from our stability bank, the creeping recognition that this wasn't a spat about who'd loaded the dishwasher wrongly, who'd left the milk out, who'd put a red sock in with the whites. This was an issue that could sink us, and like Venice in November, we were running out of options to resist the rising water.

Some afternoons I'd ignore the emails chasing me for my upbeat prose on the latest eye cream and get out my old photos, as though those blurry pics of the four flatmates serving up great vats of chilli con carne would somehow shed a light on how we'd got from there to here. I'd always banged on about how the photos we had before digital cameras were so much more honest than everything we saw now: photoshopped, filtered, fiddled about with, inspected for double chins, half-closed eyes, the best angle. But now, I saw lies everywhere. Was Ginny doing the conga around our kitchen table with her hands on Patrick's waist an excuse to hold onto him? Was he staring into her eyes in that photo of him cracking the champagne when she got promoted?

The album that nearly finished me off though was the one of our wedding. Patrick married me on 30 December – the day after the first anniversary of my dad's death – and nearly a year to the day he slept with Ginny. I studied her, a bit chubbier than usual, but she'd given birth just three months earlier. I tried to read her face when she'd been snapped watching me marry her son's father. Did she want Patrick for herself or as a father for Victor? Did she envy my stable life, a solid home to bring up any children we might have?

On the day I remembered that she'd been a bit distracted, but I'd assumed that was because she was nervous about leaving Victor in Cardiff with her mum. She seemed happy enough for us. Or maybe I was so caught up in the circus of my big day, I didn't pay attention.

I studied the picture of Patrick and me, Ginny and Cory flanking us. I'd had a rush of love for them all, even pointing out in my speech that they knew more about me than anyone else in the world. Those words made me feel so idiotic now, so duped.

I raked through the memories, straining to recall the precise reactions of that one phone call, when I knew I was definitely getting married. I'd written to Ginny in May to tell her Patrick had proposed. I told myself it was the most sensible thing to do, rather than the rigmarole of trying to pin her down to a phone call in between what sounded like an exhausting merry-go-round of film premieres, grand lunches and product launches (though I did love it when she sent me samples of gorgeous make-up I'd never be able to afford myself). In fact, I was opting for the easy way out. I was wary of a curt response taking the shine off my joy like a watermark on a mahogany table. I couldn't shake off the sense that she didn't think Patrick and I were a great match for each other. Though when Patrick asked me to give a concrete example, I couldn't.

'Why don't you ask her outright? "Am I making a mistake?"'

I'd reached up to kiss him. 'What if she says, "yes"?'

'You'll just have to tell yourself that her judgement is totally questionable. Shall I remind you of that bloke, the one who always banged a saucepan every morning to wake her up, who she thought was her Prince Charming for about three months?'

I'd laughed at the memory of Billy the pan banger and we'd slid into bed, my worries soothed but not eliminated.

So when she rang at the crack of dawn one Saturday morning, I was on the back foot, nervous of what she was going to say. Thankfully she made all the right noises and I even dared bring up the question of her being my bridesmaid. 'I picked Christmas to get married because I thought you might be able to get a bit of time off.'

Ginny had hesitated. 'I'm not sure you're going to want me as a bridesmaid…'

Everything in me had sagged. It would be a real statement if she refused. I was her closest friend. Well, I used to be anyway. 'Why ever not?' I steeled myself for a rejection, working out how I was going to make it sound like it didn't matter.

'The thing is – it's a bit of a biggy really – I'm pregnant.'

'Pregnant?' My stomach had lurched. That was a game changer. Something that meant she might stay in Canada and never come back to the UK, that our friendship would forever be confined to snatched phone calls and holidays.

'Yes!' There was a snappy edge to her tone. I remember wishing we could wipe this conversation clean and start it again face-to-face over cocktails and crisps.

I didn't know which question to ask first, so I managed to make it all about me. 'You didn't tell me you were seeing anyone.'

'I wasn't keeping it a secret. It's quite new, the last three or four months. I didn't say anything before because I didn't think you'd approve.'

'Why wouldn't I approve?'

'Well, he's sort of married.'

'How sort of?'

'Very.'

We'd both stayed silent for a second while I absorbed the news.

I gave it my best shot at not appearing critical, but I was too closely aligned with my mother in that department to pull it off with any aplomb. 'So what are you planning? Does he know?'

'He does know but doesn't want to know.'

'Oh Ginny. What a cliché. Are you…' I stumbled on the words, 'keeping it?'

'Yes I am. It's not what I planned, but I'm thirty this year so it could be last-chance saloon.'

I had to applaud her courage in deciding to have a baby on her own. Since my dad died, I felt panicky about getting the train up to London by myself. In fact, I realised with a jolt, I only really felt safe when Patrick was with me.

'Will you stay in Canada? Would you be able to manage on your own if you've got to work?' I'd asked.

'God, Jo. You're such a harbinger of doom. I haven't made any decisions yet.'

The whole conversation was weird, the opposite of how Ginny normally was with news, good or bad. She was a blurter, not an eker. I never had to work this hard to glean the basics.

'When is the due date?'

'About the third week of November.'

'November? That soon? How long have you known?'

'Not long. A doctor here told me it was fine to take the pill for three months without a break, so I didn't realise I was pregnant for ages.'

'Will you come back home to have the baby at least?'

'I'll have to see what work looks like. Might have the baby here then see how it goes. I need to look into the finances of maternity leave and childcare. I suppose I could go home to Mum and Dad until I work out what to do, but I'm not sure I could stand her fussing over me.'

'You could come and live with us for a bit. We'll have moved out of Mum's into our own place by then.'

'No. No.' The forcefulness of her refusal offended me. I couldn't see how we'd be worse than her parents. Her mum had never made any secret of the fact that she had high expectations of her clever firstborn. I was pretty sure a baby out of wedlock wouldn't chime with her ambitions for Ginny. She paused. 'Thank you though. You won't want me there with a screaming baby in the lead-up to getting married.'

'We'd manage. I'm sure we'd muddle through. I'd prefer that than you on your own in Canada with no one to help you.' I felt selfish asking the next question. 'But you will be able to come to the wedding, won't you? Will you still be able to be bridesmaid? The baby will only be a month old.'

'At the rate I'm putting weight on, I'm going to be a right heifer by the time the baby's born. As long as you don't mind me looking fat in the photos, I'll be there.' The words sounded forced and monotonous, nothing like the excited bridesmaid begging to be allowed to make a speech that I'd envisaged.

And as often happened when I managed to speak to her, she'd rung off suddenly, leaving me vacillating between concern, puzzlement and resentment.

The front door opening dragged me away from the ghosts of grievances past. I snapped the album shut.

Victor was home first. He tapped on the door of my office. 'Have you got a moment?'

Those eyes. Patrick's eyes.

I ignored the tight feeling in my chest. 'Of course. Are you all right?'

'Yes. I just wanted to talk to you about something. I don't want you to take this the wrong way or think that I'm really unhappy here or anything…'

My heart did a complicated dance of bracing myself against him leaving and hoping that he might, if only to release me from the conflicting feelings that bustled into the room every time he appeared. I longed for temporary relief from the emotions that swelled and scraped and suffocated when there was an instant connection between Patrick and him, an offbeat joke they both found funny.

He looked down. 'I'm not sure I should even ask because Mum wasn't, well, she didn't ever really speak about it.'

I felt something soften inside me, this poor lad with no other choice but to trust us to put whatever he needed in front of the mess that the three adults he depended on had made.

'You can say anything to me, Victor. I'm not that easily shocked, as I think you might have gathered. Can't be worse than anything Phoebe's come up with.'

'I'd like to try and find out who my dad is.'

Dismay enveloped me. 'Is there a particular reason?'

Victor fiddled with the leather bracelet round his wrist. 'I'd never really thought about the white bit of me before. Mum was black, my grandparents were black, lots of my friends were black and everyone looks at me and, guess what, they think I'm black. I mean, I'm not thinking I'm suddenly going to meet my white dad and start seeing myself as white, but I suppose I'd just like to know where I came from.' He frowned. 'Maybe I'd just like to know who my dad is full stop.'

'I understand that.' I breathed in and out as evenly as I could. My mind was racing as I tried not to lie. 'Your mum didn't speak much about your dad to me.'

'Cory said that when I was ready, he might be able to point me in the right direction.'

'When did he say that to you?' I swallowed, wondering if Cory had known long before he told us and dropped a big fat hint in Victor's direction.

'He mentioned it when we all went out for a curry for my birthday. That he…' Victor frowned, trying to remember. 'That he wasn't sure, but he thought he might have some papers from Mum that might give me a clue where to start.'

I remembered the whispering between them at the table. I'd dismissed my unease, thinking that Cory might have grown up sufficiently to be giving Victor some sound advice on his university choices. But no, he could never resist being the one in the know. Cory and his big bloody mouth. Totally adept at keeping his own secrets, a girlfriend in just about every country he did business in, and rarely getting caught out. Typical that the one flaming secret we needed to manage, if not keep forever, turned him into a five-year-old levering the lid up a crack without any concept of the trouble that would force its way out.

'Let me talk to Patrick and we'll take it from there.'

Victor turned to go.

'Are you okay with us, though? I know it's not easy for you. You must miss your mum.' I ignored the surge of bitterness, pushing back the unfairness of it all.

Victor said, 'I'm fine, thank you,' as though he'd exhausted his opening-up quota for the day and was ready to scuttle off and lose himself in mindless scrolling on Instagram. I, on the other hand, couldn't afford to be mindless. I needed to think with scientific clarity.

I debated calling Faye and pouring it all out, making her laugh about the utter absurdity of it all. I could hear her now – 'You could be on *Oprah*!' But since the car accident, she took longer to reply to my texts and, unless it was paranoia, the mobile she always had glued to her hand seemed to go to voicemail far more often than it used to. In any event, I couldn't say anything before Patrick and I had reached an agreement on what approach to take.

Every time I considered the options, I wanted to shut myself into a big box to escape the test of whether I was generous-spirited enough not to project my hurt onto Victor.

These huge existential questions should have obliterated the petty considerations that had held me back in life, made me put up with other people's crap, stopped me standing up for myself. Incredible that I still cared what people thought about me given that my life was sitting on the side of the toilet just waiting for a flush, but I did. And though I fought against it, tried to chase it away, hated myself for giving it headspace, the concern that crept in at 4 a.m. alongside how we were going to survive as a family was always 'What will people say when they know Victor is Patrick's son?'

CHAPTER TWENTY

As soon as Patrick got home from his trip, I told him what Victor had said, whispering to him in the sitting room as he flopped into an armchair with a beer, looking worn out and grey.

'I'll tell Cory not to say anything until we've come up with a plan,' he said.

I couldn't sit. I was fidgeting around the room, picking up the little felt donkey we'd brought back from Spain, the blue glass vase from Sicily, the trinkets that I'd mistaken for evidence of a family life. Now I was flabbergasted that I'd found the early years with Phoebe so draining. Note to younger self: teaching a toddler to swim can be a little boring, helping a reluctant seven-year-old learn to read is a bit repetitive, playing table tennis with a nine-year-old inevitably ends in a tantrum if you don't let them win, but don't complain, you're in the golden age of parenting.

I turned back to Patrick. 'Will Cory keep his mouth shut? He's the one who's piqued Victor's curiosity by making out he knows something.'

Patrick shrugged. 'He's a decent man, Jo. He was devastated that you were so upset. I think – because he doesn't have any experience of marriage and kids – that he thought once you'd got over the shock, you might even be pleased that Victor was related to us in some way?'

I stood with my mouth open. 'Did Cory actually say that or is that you putting words into his mouth? What you would *like* to happen?'

Patrick put his glass down. 'Jo. I don't know what you want me to do. I wish I'd dealt with it earlier and it hadn't blown up in our faces. I'm sorry I've hurt you. I love you and that hasn't changed. I didn't love Ginny except as a friend. It's a long time ago and I really hope you'll forgive me and let us be a family. I need you on my side to sort out what we do next. We can't tell Victor without telling Phoebe, so we can't just improvise.'

Patrick apologising and acknowledging that he could have done it differently made my heart thaw slightly.

He stood up and held his arms out. I wasn't sure whether I was that defrosted yet. 'Jo. Come on. Stick with me. We'll find a way through this.'

I put my head into his shoulder, hingeing forward at the neck rather than relaxing into him. But the smell and warmth of him fired all the synapses in my brain that recognised safety and comfort. Within moments, I'd leant into him and the tears I'd refused to let him see, entrenched as I was in my sense of injustice, poured out of me.

He nuzzled into the top of my head. 'Jo. I'm sorry I've dragged us into this mess. I wish I could fix it. Victor has a right to know, but I'm really worried about how to broach it with Phoebe.'

'Can we not think about it for one evening? Just watch crap TV and deal with it again tomorrow?'

He kissed my cheek. 'Good plan.'

And for the first time in a month, since that horrible evening at Cory's, the chill that had been pervading our house dissipated, though every time I heard the creak of the floorboard in Victor's bedroom above, something snagged in my chest. This wasn't going to go away with us sticking our heads in the sand. And it wasn't as if we only had that one issue to resolve. Despite my best efforts to talk to Phoebe about whether she was experimenting with drugs and sex, nearly keeling over with the effort of not sounding judgemental but approachable and caring, any conversation inevitably ended with her slamming out. I veered between draconian sanctions – 'Right, no more going out in the evenings until I know you can behave' – which on current performance would probably be 2030 – and trying to allow little freedoms so that she could build up trust and I could praise her for it.

I'd been encouraged by her desire to take part in a musical production at school, and, at 9 p.m. I was just about to fetch her from a rehearsal, when my phone beeped.

Going for fish and chips with Georgia. Jordan will drop me home about 11.

I relayed the message to Patrick, who said, 'She shouldn't be out that late on a school night.'

'So should I go and get her?' My irritation that I'd have to be the bad guy because he'd been drinking threatened the fragile truce.

'I'll ring her,' Patrick said.

The phone rang and rang. One of the miracles of modern technology and teenagers that despite them being glued to their screens 24/7, they never actually picked up when you needed to talk to them.

I texted: *Phone me.*

Nothing. I shifted from text to WhatsApp, our TV programme long forgotten.

'I'll text Faye and double-check what's happening.'

The response came back immediately. *Georgia went to bed half an hour ago and Jordan is staying in Southampton on a university open day. Do you want me to see if I can find out where she is?*

I relayed her message to Patrick, my heart plummeting at yet another scene which would keep the Stedhurst mums in gossip for at least another week. I'd deliberately kept a low profile after the party but I was sure that more than one mother had made full use of her unlimited text allowance to discuss my unseemly meltdown on the night of the party. No doubt they were polishing their bargepole to push us, the troubled family, far from their doors.

'Where can she be at this time of night on a schoolday?'

Patrick sighed. 'For God's sake. Why can't she just do what she says she will do when she says she'll do it?'

I texted Faye. *Could you see if Georgia knows? Sorry to involve you in our dramas. Thank you.*

I imagined Faye reluctantly putting down her iPad, padding across her seagrass hallway, clucking about Phoebe, opening Georgia's bedroom door quietly in case she was already asleep. Georgia would probably sing like a canary rather than pull the duvet over her head and shout at her to 'Piss offffff'. And helpfully run through Instagram or Snapchat rather than look at her as though she was a complete idiot for asking. Faye wouldn't have to hang her head and wonder where in the labyrinth of reminding her to say please and thank you, floss her teeth, be grateful to the teachers for looking after her, her daughter had taken such a wrong turning that she wasn't sure they'd ever get back on the right road again.

Faye's number flashed up on my mobile. 'Georgia's not here!' She sounded panicky, but also accusatory.

'What do you mean? I thought you brought her home?'

'I did. She must have sneaked out through the garage.'

'To go where though?'

'I don't know. I bet she's with Phoebe somewhere.'

The way she spat out 'Phoebe' left me in no doubt that she blamed Phoebe for leading Georgia astray.

'At least they're together.' I paused. 'Let me think.'

Faye spoke first. 'Is Victor at home? I don't think he's particularly friendly with Georgia, but he might know something.' If I hadn't been so stressed, I'd have taken some petty satisfaction from the fact that Faye was always 'Georgia and I are so close, she tells me everything' – except that Victor was her boyfriend.

I rushed on. 'Victor's been at home since about five. I'll ask him and ring you back.'

I knocked on his door. I always gave him plenty of time to answer, unlike the way I barged in with Phoebe.

'Come in.'

I pushed the door open, feeling a bit embarrassed to find him sitting in bed bare-chested. We were a pyjama sort of household and it was just odd to be somewhere intimate like a bedroom with a child that wasn't mine in a state of undress. I wondered whether Patrick would feel the same.

'Sorry to disturb you. Phoebe hasn't come back from the rehearsal and Georgia went home but snuck out again. Faye's really worried and so am I. Do you have any idea where they might be?'

His face dropped. Ginny had never been able to hide her feelings either. Indecision clouded his face as he dithered between what was worse for the girls: dobbing them in or attempting a cover-up. 'I'm not sure where they are.'

I sat on the bed. Boundaries be damned. 'Victor, I know you won't want to get them into trouble, but they're so young and silly. Phoebe looks so much older and doesn't understand that men of twenty-five will expect her to have the life experience of someone their age. I'm not going to go off the deep end like I did the night of the party, but it's not safe for her to be out late at night doing God knows what.'

Resignation washed over him. 'Georgia invited me to go to a party on the industrial estate. I've got to get up early for rugby tomorrow so I said no.'

'The Flatland Estate? By the railway bridge?'

I hadn't been down there in years, but I couldn't see any good coming out of a party in some rank old warehouse surrounded by bathroom fitting units and drainage companies, none of which would be open at this time of night.

'I think so. I didn't bother with the details. I didn't think they'd actually go.'

'Was it a party of someone from school?' I asked, the uncoolest mother in the world, phrasing it as though I thought they'd all be playing musical bumps with cake in a napkin to take home. God, how I yearned for the security of those tedious afternoons in the village hall.

'Maybe an older sibling of someone at school. Sort of friends of friends.' Victor reminded me so much of Ginny when she didn't want to offer any information. He had inherited her talent for vagueness.

I waved my hands about in frustration. 'She definitely said the industrial estate? And she meant round here? They weren't getting any transport, like a train or a bus?'

Victor screwed up his eyes as though he was replaying the conversation in his head. 'No, it's near here.'

My brain was racing down the avenue of rusty old machinery falling on them and killing them outright, a gas explosion, police raids, drugs, how many drugs and what sort and who knew what they'd be cut with, never mind what the bloody people supplying them might do.

I pointed ineffectually at his phone. 'Can you look at Instagram and see if there's anything to give us a clue? Was it in an old factory? Or some kind of empty unit?'

I was probably forcing him to break all sorts of teenage codes of honour, but if I had to bully it out of him, I would. Victor was hesitating. But I wasn't in the mood for being messed about.

'Sorry, but you have to do it. I'll take full responsibility and I'll try and keep you out of it.'

Eventually he looked up. 'The Rising Sun? Is that possible?'

'Oh my God. That's a disgusting hovel. It's always in the local paper for raids and fights.' I held onto a ray of hope. 'She wouldn't have been able to get in without ID, though.'

Victor raised his eyebrows as though I still believed in fairies. 'Um, most of the sixth formers have fake ID.'

'How do they get that?' I flapped my hand at him. 'Doesn't matter. I need to get down there.'

I ran downstairs, texting Faye as I went, wishing I had the nimbleness of teenagers rather than my fat old fingers writing a load of gobbledygook.

The response was instant: *I'm on my way.*

Patrick leapt up and grabbed his coat, just as Victor came flying down the stairs, fully dressed. 'Shall I come with you? They might let me in a bit more easily.'

I didn't stop to think how screwed up all of this was, relying on my husband's secret son to be the knight in shining armour for our daughter. I shuffled them out to the car and screeched off, with Patrick shouting at me to slow down and not kill us all.

I sped as fast as I dared along the little high street, all but deserted bar the occasional dog walker, and down the narrow lane leading to the industrial estate. I would've preferred anger to have the upper hand, but I just felt fear, cold and all-consuming, the headlines of those teenagers who'd tried drugs just the once and died running through my head like a slideshow. And yet, there was still room in my brain to want to get there before Faye, before Georgia had spun her spin, placing the blame firmly on Phoebe.

The industrial estate was pitch black apart from the occasional yellow street light that served to make the whole area look as spooky as hell with its discarded old tyres on patches of wasteland and huge steel doors fronting the warehouses. Thankfully, it wasn't difficult to find the pub. We followed the noise to a dingy dump sandwiched between a used-car garage and a fancy-dress shop, gaudy clown faces with plastic ginger hair hanging pathetically in the window. A girl was throwing up in-between a Mini and a Kia on the forecourt, the ultimate romantic date for the gangly lad holding her hair back. I bet the garage owners were fed up with jet-washing the effects of too much vodka and coke every morning.

Outside the main door stood a gang of boys and girls, most of them smoking and all looking intimidating in their biker boots and leather jackets. A few were sucking on balloons, which, judging by the little silver cannisters discarded on the floor and glinting in the light, was NOS. I'd found tiny cannisters littered in the flower beds for days after Phoebe's impromptu party and, as usual, she'd made out I was the ultimate party-pooper, having a fit about nothing. 'It's just a bit of fun. You can buy NOS on Amazon! God, it's just laughing gas. It's not even illegal.' When I'd read up on it though, there was a suggestion that large amounts of nitrous oxide could cause damage to the brain, which didn't seem like a bit of fun. That new and unwelcome knowledge hopped into the queue, number seven hundred and sixty-three, behind the other worries already on my radar.

I geared myself up for yet another showdown, another humiliating tussle, another test of my will against hers.

I drove past and parked a little way up the road.

Patrick said, 'You stay here. I'll see if I can find her.'

I don't know whether Victor was terrified of being stuck where I could interrogate him with no escape but he leapt out. 'I'll come with you.'

In the rear-view mirror, I watched them walk across the road. Victor strode along, his gait confident and relaxed, whereas Patrick was padding along, tense and hurried. Maybe Patrick and I had been living in the sticks for too long, getting sucked into thinking any loud music or gatherings of young people was evidence of something illegal or dangerous going on. When we lived in London, we probably walked by, even frequented pubs like these without batting an eyelid. Maybe I was so middle-aged, I'd forgotten what it was like to be young, to party, to mix with edgy people who I wouldn't necessarily want to give me a lift but who didn't represent a threat to safety or sanity. Perhaps I was more like my mother than I thought, wanting to control Phoebe, mould her into the person I had in mind, rather than giving her the space to be who she was.

That little moment of liberal thinking was shattered by a fight breaking out right in front of Victor and Patrick, who ducked away from the shouting, swearing and glasses smashing. In the mirror, I saw headlights sweep round the corner.

Faye's Range Rover came into view. I waited until she pulled up behind me, then hopped out. None of the usual hugs. 'Are they in there?'

'Patrick and Victor have just gone in to have a look. They'll fetch Georgia too if she's there.'

Faye stabbed at her phone. 'Don't really want to try and get past that lot. I can't understand her doing something like this, especially when Lee's away. She knows how worried I'd be.'

We shrank back behind the car as the fight between the two boys started to gather more bodies, more arms and legs flailing about.

Faye ran her fingers through her hair. 'What the hell made them choose here? Surely there are plenty of other places for a bit of underage drinking?'

I made a non-committal noise that she interpreted as agreement. I daren't tell her my biggest worry. That they weren't here for tequila slammers. That they were here for the drugs.

The minutes ticked on with no sign of the girls or the men. We got into Faye's car.

'Does Georgia often sneak out like this?' I asked.

'No, I don't know what she's thinking of. She's never gone out without telling me before. I don't know how they even got here, do you?'

'Uber?'

Faye shook her head. 'God knows. I haven't had to deal with all the stuff you have. Georgia's never lied to me like this before.'

I sat, listening to Faye reframing this as an aberration on Georgia's part. I, on the other hand, was the mother of a troublemaker, party to zero daughterly confidences and producer of a wayward child who wouldn't know the truth if she ate it for breakfast.

'Maybe it's just how teenagers are these days?' I tried to lighten the atmosphere. 'I'd have had to run the gauntlet of ringing my friends from the landline in the hallway hoping that Mum and Dad had *Beadle's About* on full blast.'

Faye snorted. 'I don't think there's any universe where it's normal for two schoolgirls to be in a pub where— Jesus Christ!' she shouted as one man chased another up the road with a broken bottle in his hand. She pulled on the door handle. 'I'm going in. I can't sit here with all this kicking off. Surely someone should have called the police by now?'

'What if the girls are taking drugs in there? They might get arrested.'

Faye's mouth dropped open and she let the door swing closed. 'Drugs? Well, that would be the end of her getting into bloody Oxford. I did talk to Georgia about that whole hotboxing thing the other week and she said they'd just been curious to see what happened, that it was a one-off and they'd learnt their lesson.' Then as though an unguarded thought had escaped her, she said, 'At the moment she seems more interested in hanging around the rugby pitch fan-girling with Phoebe than studying anyway.'

The suspicion swept through me again, that somehow Faye held us responsible for everything that Georgia did wrong. I wanted us to be united in this, not start apportioning blame. All the way through school, we'd prided ourselves on not being those mums who complained if their children sat on the sporting sidelines or were overlooked for presenting an assembly. We'd derided the mothers who seemed oblivious to their time slot at parents' evening, running over their allotted five minutes and delaying everyone else. We'd made a pact to be brave enough to turn up to school without going anywhere near a lipstick or mascara and agreed never to join a gym. But now, when it really counted, it was every mother for herself, shooing the shit away from her own daughter and not caring how much it stuck on mine.

Before I could articulate any of that in a way that wouldn't make it sound as though I was trying to do exactly the same, Patrick appeared at the door of the pub, frogmarching Phoebe out. My shoulders dropped with relief.

Victor was a few paces behind, leaning down towards Georgia's tiny frame. He touched her upper arm, gently, in a gesture of reassurance. She looked up at him, woozily, her face all soft, the light of the pub sign reflecting down onto her. I recognised that expression on her face, the one that meant everyone else around you was just white noise. Alongside any cocktail of chemicals she might have taken, there was the biggest drug of all: love. I hoped her mother hadn't noticed.

Faye went flying out of the car and stormed over the road. I trotted behind her.

'What the hell do you think you are doing? Get in the car now. You can explain to Dad what you were thinking.'

Georgia was braver than I'd expected in the face of Faye's wrath. 'We were just having a bit of fun.' Then she doubled over giggling as though she was competing for a role as the Laughing Policeman in the music-hall variety performances my mother loved.

Faye was shouting, 'Fun, that's what you call this, is it?' Her arm swept round the broken glass on the forecourt and a gang of girls with more underwear than clothing on display. She grabbed Georgia's arm and we marched back towards the car before we picked up any more trouble. A slanging match with that lot would be like building barricades with blancmange.

Next to me, Patrick relaxed his grip on Phoebe, who I couldn't even bring myself to speak to.

I was ashamed that I was enjoying the temporary reprieve from being the most embarrassing mother in the world as Faye peered into Georgia's face, bellowing, 'What have you been doing? Have you taken drugs?'

Georgia kept opening her mouth as though she was going to answer, then clamping it shut again and snorting helplessly.

Faye pushed Georgia into the car, who, between giggles, was screeching, 'Bye, Pheebs! See you at rugby, Victor!'

Victor put his hand up but didn't say anything. I let Patrick settle Phoebe into the car. Victor followed.

I walked over to Faye as she slid into the driver's seat.

'Talk to you tomorrow, yeah?' I knew my face was searching hers, all needy and pathetic, looking for a glimmer of complicity, that we were working together, not ripping apart.

She leaned towards me and hissed, 'She's only been like this since Victor came to live with you.'

I tried to stay calm, but the injustice of her words made me tremble. 'Victor wasn't even out tonight. You can't blame him for this. Blame Phoebe if you must, but it's nothing to do with Victor.'

'That's where you're wrong. Everyone knows he's encouraging the girls to try drugs.'

'Everyone? Like who?'

'Everyone,' she repeated. 'All the mums are worried about what he's supplying the kids with at school. Andrea's worried sick about Helaina since she had that accident.'

I couldn't get my brain to find the right words. The thought that all that little posse were stoking each other up with their stupid prejudices and converting them into facts trapped me into a rage that felt both white hot and paralysing, a fire just before the door opened and made everything explode.

I worked hard to keep my voice even, reasonable, unable to give up on the hope that one day we'd be laughing about 'that time there was all that hoo-ha over a few spliffs'. 'I know they're your friends, Faye, but I think it's a racist thing with Andrea and Rod. You heard what they said the night of the accident. They've gone, ooh, black kid from a single-parent family whose mother died equals out-of-control youth peddling drugs to innocent little white girls.'

Faye took a step back. 'I'm not sure that's true. I don't think it is a racist thing with them. And it's certainly not with me, I'm pretty sure you know that. I take as I find. I've got nothing against Victor, I've got friends from all walks of life, all different backgrounds.'

I wanted to believe her, wanted her to convince me that it was circumstance, not prejudice, that made them point the finger at him. But Faye's friends from 'all walks of life' were white, relatively affluent families with kids who would probably go to university. Plus, of course, her Slovakian cleaner.

I was flailing about, struggling to stop the rush of resentment pulsing through my brain and find calm, grown-up arguments to show Faye she'd made a mistake.

But before I could get there, she said, 'I know it's hard when you've invited him into your home. I feel really sorry for you. But you've got to look at the facts.'

My throat was tight as I forced the words out past the indignation lodging there. 'Whose facts? The facts according to Andrea? She doesn't know what she's talking about. Victor wasn't even in the car when they were smoking.'

'He didn't need to be. He just had to get the drugs for them.'

And there it was, the funnel of oxygen right onto the flames.

'Faye, the only person who I know for definite has been in possession of drugs, is your daughter. That night she threw up at mine, when you went away with Lee, a packet of weed fell out of her skirt. I didn't tell you because I wasn't sure you'd want to hear it. The reason she got so sick was because she'd been smoking weed and when I tried to have the conversation with you, you shut me down.'

'What? Georgia was taking drugs as far back as that weekend?'

'Yes. You seemed adamant that Georgia would never be involved in any drug taking and I didn't think you'd believe me, so I decided to drop a few hints and let you find out on your own.'

She paused for a minute, then did what she always did if anyone criticised her daughter. She moved the spotlight onto someone else. 'I'd be worried if Victor was living in the house with my daughter.'

I made one last attempt to move my anger from rampaging to rational. 'You've got him wrong. I don't know why you've all decided to single him out. He's a fantastic young man.' I didn't dare examine the feelings I had about Patrick's son being a teenager to be proud of, but his daughter currently not.

A sneer crossed her face. 'I hope you've got a lock on Phoebe's bedroom door.'

And that was the grenade that transformed the fire into an inferno. That whole judgmental crap when she knew absolutely nothing about what was going on in my life.

I leant right into her face and whisper-shouted into her ear, 'I don't think that's very likely. He's her bloody brother!' There was no way I was going to admit that the wrongness and hideousness of that possibility had occasionally disturbed my nights.

Her eyes flung open as I turned on my heel and stormed off to the car, the brief release of, as my mother would say, 'giving her something to think about' immediately ceding to a panic so intense, I had a physical sensation of falling.

On the drive home, Phoebe kept trying to get my attention by making provocative statements such as, 'Victor, they've got a band playing tomorrow. Me, you and Georgia could go down there.'

Patrick kept doing imperceptible shakes of the head, as if to say, don't rise to it. But I couldn't speak anyway. I'd crossed a loyalty boundary that I wasn't sure I could ever repair. I gripped the steering wheel, focusing on the road in the dark, wondering if tomorrow morning I'd wake up as a soon-to-be-divorced woman.

CHAPTER TWENTY-ONE

As soon as I got in, I ran into the loo to text Faye. *Sorry about earlier.* Although it was best to be vague about what I was apologising for. I was overjoyed that I'd wiped the smugness off her face for a moment, but sorry that I'd told her something that could damage my whole family if it came out before we had worked out how to manage it. And even then, we might all end up in smithereens. I went for the humble-pie approach, in the hope it would give me time to come up with a plan. *It's been a very stressful time. Victor is Phoebe's half-brother.* I couldn't bring myself to write Patrick's son. *Phoebe and Victor don't know yet, so please please don't say anything to Georgia or anyone else until we've had a chance to tell them.*

Just a few months ago, I would have trusted her with my life. Now it felt as though the power to wreck it lay in her hands. I swung between reassuring myself that we hadn't actually fallen out, that she wouldn't deliberately do something to hurt us all and fearing that it might already be too late. I stared at my phone, willing dots to appear, desperate for the beep of confirmation that my secret was safe with her. Nothing.

I thanked Victor for helping out, which he dismissed as though his part in finding Phoebe had been betrayal, not protection. I left him talking to Patrick. Then I knocked on Phoebe's door.

'What?'

I paused before I pushed the door open. I didn't know what I'd do if she was sitting there with a bong or snorting something. As I'd just proved, any mothering skills I possessed had morphed from reliable old caterpillar to reckless butterfly. Miraculously though, she wasn't doing drugs. She was lying on her bed, on her phone.

She jerked her head round with such ferocious anger. How? How did we even get here? What stopped us being the family that had a few spats over the length of school skirts or pick-up times from parties but still maintained enough common ground that we could watch a film together or talk banalities about our day in the time it took to shovel down a chicken stir-fry?

'What do you want, cos I'm going to sleep?'

If my mere presence in her room engendered such hostility, I didn't even dare to imagine what she'd be like steaming in from school next week, next month, demanding to know whether it was true, whether Victor was actually her brother. Before I could arrive at that cataclysmic event, I needed to understand whether it was just Georgia who'd taken drugs. I had no idea how long they took to work, whether there could be a delayed reaction. Phoebe hadn't looked particularly stoned. But did that mean she hadn't taken anything or that it wasn't something that was easily detected? I'd tried to put the idea out of my head, but I had to know whether the night still held the possibility of a reaction to a dodgy tablet.

'Phoebe. Can you tell me if you've taken drugs tonight? I'm not going to blow my stack, I just need to know in case you get ill.'

She looked as though she was waiting for the punchline, caught between raised eyebrows and a burst of laughter. Eventually she said in a voice that was weary, as though we'd been through this a million times. 'Just go to bed, Mum.'

'Can you answer my question please?'

She tilted her head on one side. 'Why? Why should I tell you anything?'

Defeat dominated every one of my words. 'Because I love you and I want to keep you safe.'

She rolled away from me, with an exaggerated yawn.

I walked out. Somewhere, long buried, was my little girl, but really, who knew where? Where was that girl who even three years ago would still come for a hug when skies were grey? How did it all slip by? How did I not recognise that last time she'd willingly folded herself into me, that smell of fusty corridors and school lunches on her hair? That in just a few short years I'd be hovering outside her door afraid she might be flailing about on a trip from some substance I wouldn't recognise if it was sprinkled on my muesli.

I could hear Patrick speaking to Victor downstairs, but I didn't have the energy to go and find out whether it was something I needed to be involved in. I bloody hoped he wasn't doing the long-lost father schtick right now. Just thinking about that made my stomach churn.

I wondered whether it was too late to ring Faye. I sat on the edge of the bath in our en-suite, feeling as though I'd never know what the right thing to do was again.

I undressed and slid into bed. I lay there, listening to the hum of them talking below, that blokey baritone. I should tell Patrick that Faye knew the truth. There was still no reply from her. Maybe she'd gone straight to bed. Or maybe, as Phoebe would say, she was 'airing' me.

Eventually Patrick climbed into bed beside me. 'What a night.'

I grunted in agreement, vacillating between continuing my Berlin Wall protest by remaining resolutely on my side of the bed and snuggling in for a crumb of comfort that might quash the anxiety swamping my body.

'Do you think Phoebe needs counselling?' This from a man who wouldn't go to the doctor unless his leg was hanging off.

'Probably. But how the hell are we going to get her there? I can't get her to have a bowl of Cheerios for breakfast.' I pushed my head back into the pillow. 'Maybe we could do, I don't know, family therapy?'

I was relieved to hear Patrick make a groan of horror. I wasn't bursting to sit in front of a stranger and lay out our stall of mistakes. However, if that's what it took to get our daughter back, then I wasn't going to discount anything.

Patrick sighed. 'I don't know. I wish I had some answers. Let's look into it if things don't improve.'

His hand reached for mine. I held onto him, savouring the reassurance in his grip. I hoped it wouldn't be the last time.

CHAPTER TWENTY-TWO

The next morning, I had approximately one second before the realisation dawned again that my ship was sinking, followed by flying out of bed to find a lifebelt, in this case, a text from Faye.

Wow! You kept that one quiet! Let's try and grab a coffee at rugby and you can tell me about it. Secret is safe with me ☺
Hope you're okay though xx

I stared at my phone. Sent at 7 a.m. this morning. Lee had been away the night before and Georgia was all over the place, so hopefully she hadn't said anything to anyone yet.

I texted her back. *Thank you. I knew you wouldn't let me down. See you later xx* I hadn't known she wouldn't let me down. She'd gone from being the person I relied on to the one who at a stroke could destroy us.

I showered, trying to come up with a plan. Patrick would be furious that I'd told Faye before the kids. I was furious with myself. And then, in a complexity of matrimonial anger ping-pong, I was utterly pissed off that he'd put me in this position in the first place. And that Ginny had.

As I spread that thought out on my truth table, I knew I'd never have believed I wasn't second best, convinced that he was just trying it on with me because Ginny had rejected him. I was pretty sure that had I known, I would never have accepted that he truly loved and wanted me, stupid me who at forty-eight still blushed when

I bumped into people I knew in the street. Patrick thought it was cute. Phoebe thought it was pathetic.

I'd never have married him and never had Phoebe.

What was in Ginny's head? Why didn't she phone him as soon as she knew she was pregnant? Was the 'married Canadian' complete bullshit? I tried not to wonder if Patrick had known Victor was his from the beginning whether he might have swerved the marriage to me in favour of a far more adventurous life with Ginny, with her great talent for getting the party started.

By the time I'd got dressed, I was no further forward, just more filled with dread.

Patrick was already downstairs in the kitchen with Victor, flicking through the papers in a companionable silence. Right behind me, Phoebe appeared in a nightie that was so short, Patrick and I competed in a tie break for 'Go and put your dressing gown on,' which she did with so much fuss I wasn't sure what would have made Victor feel more uncomfortable, Phoebe's arse cheeks hanging out near his toast or the unmissable implication that his presence was inconveniencing her liberal vibe.

Finally we were all ready to leave for rugby. Just as we were walking out to the car, Mum came up the drive. 'There! Just caught you. Haven't seen you for ages.'

Ages being a week or so, but it still drilled into my parent guilt.

Patrick gestured to Victor. 'We're just off to rugby.'

'Mind if I join you?'

I was itching to speak to Faye so I did mind. Hugely.

But Patrick welcomed her, trained as he was by me to include my mother without making a fuss. 'No problem. Are you going to be warm enough? It gets very cold on the field.'

I nodded vigorously. 'It really does. It's nearly December, Mum, not a great time to be standing out in the wind. I could pop round to see you afterwards.'

Mum pulled a purple woolly hat out of her bag and jammed it on her head. 'I'll be fine.'

I had no choice but to let her come. On another day, I'd have been delighted to dilute her with the other grandparents who came to spectate. But today my mind fizzed about wondering how I could give her the slip so I could talk to Faye on my own. It had been difficult enough planning how I could ditch Patrick.

Mum turned to Phoebe. 'I like your stripy jumper. Horizontal stripes can make you look so fat, but lucky you being so thin. I couldn't wear those. You never could either, Jo, could you? You were always a bit solid, took after your dad.'

Mum was like a blueprint for inducing anorexia. Phoebe really didn't need Mum commenting on her body shape. No wonder I always walked out to my sunlounger on holiday assuming every bloke around the pool was whispering to his mate, 'Don't fancy yours much.' After Phoebe was born, I'd made a point of rarely commenting on what people looked like, good or bad. Though I'd still produced a daughter who was determined to have breast implants when she was eighteen.

Luckily, the sunshine had come out in Phoebe's world and we moved on from my body failings to which boys to look out for on the rugby pitch – 'You need to watch the boy with blonde curly hair, he's got quite a big arse, I mean, bottom. That's my friend Leah's brother. He's quite good, isn't he, Victor?'

'Yeah, he's up there. Bit slow sometimes. Freddie's a better winger. Fast.'

Mum turned to Victor. 'And are you quite good?'

'I'm all right. Settling into the team now.'

'Nan, Victor isn't *quite* good, Victor is a *legend*. Harlequins are interested in him for next year.' And just for a moment, Phoebe's championing of Victor, the proof that she could be kind, almost outweighed what I tried to reject but often succumbed to: jealousy that they shared a father. I hoped – desperately hoped – that I could be bigger than that.

As we pulled up to the rugby field, I scoured it for Faye. She came over immediately, greeting Mum with a big hug. So few friends of mine had that familiarity with my parents, that extra notch up in belonging. None with my dad now Ginny was gone. To be fair to Mum, she had an extraordinary memory for the minutiae of my friends' lives, their kids, their ages. As she machine-gunned her questions to Faye, I had the sense that I should intervene to stop Mum banging on. Just like Phoebe did with me when I was around her friends.

Thankfully, the match kicked off and I spotted my opportunity to go with Faye to get coffee for everyone from a van that was selling burgers in the car park. Normally I'd have been all Arabica-blend beans or die, but right now, I was trying to save my marriage.

I stuck Mum on Patrick, hissing at him to keep her occupied for a minute. These days, he didn't put up much of a fight about anything, as though he thought by keeping the peace, I'd somehow forget that we needed to address the fact that his son was living with us.

As soon as we got out of earshot, Faye said, 'Just run past me how Victor came to be Phoebe's half-brother?'

I glanced around nervously in case we were overheard. I kept the details to a minimum, but even saying those out loud had the effect of making the thing that had grown and grown, taking over just about every waking thought, shrink back slightly.

Faye put her hand on my arm. 'That was a bit of a shocker for you. When are you going to tell them?'

'We haven't decided yet. It's early days.'

And we reflected about never knowing what was round the corner and I felt the friend I'd trusted all these years come back to me, my ally rather than my adversary.

We bought our coffees and, on the way back, Faye said, 'I did ask Georgia about the drugs you found. She said she was keeping them for someone from a different school. Last night was the first time she'd taken anything since the accident and even that was by mistake. Apparently someone had given them some birthday cake and she didn't realise it had cannabis in it.'

I stared at her, waiting for her to burst out laughing at the preposterousness of her story. Instead she turned to me, her eyes defying me to disagree with her version of events.

'Good job I didn't come steaming round to tell you she needed to go to rehab then.' I became aware of our feet squelching on the ground. As we neared Patrick, Lee and Mum, I stopped. 'You won't say anything about what I've told you. Obviously Victor – although he's doing brilliantly – has had a lot of change in the last six months, so we need to be a bit sensitive in how we manage this. And Phoebe, God knows how she'll react.'

Faye wrinkled her nose. 'Yeah. You're going to have to be careful with that.'

I was going to have to accept that Faye would always have a slight 'tone' when she talked about Phoebe. On the other hand, who was to say that if she hadn't been my daughter I wouldn't have had the sighing-eyebrow-raising-head-tilting malarkey going on?

I took a tiny shred of comfort that all the spectators erupted into excitement, clapping and shouting Victor's name as he swallow-dived over the touchline.

Even Lee was clapping. 'He's good.'

I didn't look at Patrick. I didn't want to see that puff of pride of 'It's all in the genes.'

I scrutinised Faye in case she was giving the game away by making some kind of 'Wonder where he gets that from?' wink, wink, type comment, but she played her part perfectly. My heart softened towards her. Yes, she was fiercely protective of her kids, but in the end, so were we all.

On the other side of the field, Phoebe was cheering with her friends. They were surprisingly focused on the game, given that even when she watched a film, she had one eye on her phone. She looked so natural and happy. It was hard to believe that she was taking drugs. What was so lacking in her life? What had I missed, failed at, reacted wrongly to? I watched as Victor ran over to her to get some water. She hugged him. Hugged him! She never let either of us within two yards of her these days. But it was so natural, a genuine, joyful, congratulatory hug. Despite all the conflicting emotions that Victor engendered in me, knowing that there was some genuine affection somewhere in Phoebe's life cheered me. And, by the looks of her friends gathering round, some street cred from existing in the rugby players' inner circle as well.

The game drew to a close, with another win for our school and Faye's son, Jordan, pronounced Man of the Match. Secretly, I thought Victor had played better and it seemed I wasn't alone, judging by the noise that ensued when the coach announced that he'd been voted Players' Player.

Within a few minutes, Phoebe and her friends were mingling with all the lads and I wondered if Faye noticed the long moment when Georgia hugged Victor and the chemistry between them nearly singed the grass to a cinder. I asked what plans she had for the rest of the weekend to distract her.

Phoebe, who usually pretended she was an orphan at any school event, came bouncing over to us, not at all abashed about seeing Faye, who in fairness managed a reasonably pleasant greeting. 'Guess what?'

'What?' I asked.

'Victor's setting up a girls' rugby team.'

I bit back the 'Really?' and swerved into a 'And are you going to play?' despite failing to imagine Phoebe risking nail breakage, let alone getting covered from head to toe in mud.

'I definitely am. So's Georgia. Rhiannon. And Kat, you know, Jasmine's daughter.'

I didn't comment but was surprised to hear Phoebe mention Kat as one of the crowd. I loved Jasmine's daughter. She turned up in purple flares to non-uniform days with her hair held up with a pencil. Nothing about her suggested that every social occasion triggered a refusal to eat carbs for a week beforehand, an emergency fake-tanning session that led to the demise of every white towel in the house or several hours parading every outfit she owned before declaring that her mother was far too stupid to know what teenagers looked good in. Kat, mud and having to stop worrying what you looked like would be a stride in the right direction.

'When do you begin training?' I asked.

'Next week.' And she danced off, back to her friends.

I wanted to have faith that she'd really get involved, that she'd become part of a team and realise that the best bodies weren't the 5' 11", size six ones but the ones that were fit and strong and capable. That she'd direct her fierce energy into something worthwhile, get her highs from exercise rather than drinking and drugs. A shamefully larger part of me was doubtful, burnt by the brand new guitar discarded after a few weeks, by the self-defence classes which turned out to be for 'losers', by the latest, newest, must-haves that were urgent, that she could no longer survive without, that if she could 'just have', she'd never want anything else again. Until the next time.

I hoped that I'd be proved wrong.

CHAPTER TWENTY-THREE

As the days led into December, a month I always hated, carrying as it did the anniversary of my dad's death, I felt a wash of grief as strong as when he'd first died. The last few years I'd registered the date, but the rawness had faded. I'd been able to take a few moments to think about him, invent an imaginary commentary from him about my life – 'You've got a lovely little family there, pet' – and almost be glad that I had him, rather than devastated that I'd lost him. But this year, my sadness was back with a vengeance. He'd have understood all my complex feelings. Unusually for a man of his era, he was so good at talking things through, telling his stories of how he reacted to losing his brother, to being made redundant, to discovering that my mum was pregnant with me after six years of dashed hopes. This year, try as I might, I couldn't feel grateful. My heartbreak at losing Ginny seemed to compound the death of Dad, as though my losses were accumulating and crushing the life out of me. And that was before I allowed myself to enter into the lion's den of associating Patrick and Ginny together with when Dad died.

Every time Patrick said, 'Shall I get the tree out of the attic?' I snapped that I couldn't think about Christmas yet. What I really meant was that I didn't want to contemplate a Christmas where Patrick would be sitting in the middle of his family, with his shiny new son, but I would be on the fringe of it without my dad, who would have urged me to be generous. I tried to tune out his voice in my head saying, 'Be the one to give someone a hand up when they're down.' If he'd been here, I could have explained, had him listen and *hear* me, unlike Patrick who'd now reached a point of greeting every comment with, 'What do you want me to say?'

The rows about how/if/when to tell Victor recurred with depressing frequency. Usually I'd have talked this over ad nauseam with Ginny, though goodness knows how this particular issue would have resolved itself if she'd still been alive. I sidestepped Faye's curious questions and kept saying we were working things through. Which, as truths went, was rather flimsy: I was stuck in a never-ending loop of jealousy and betrayal sitting on one side of the scales with protectiveness on the other. Not just for Phoebe but also for Victor, who shouldered none of the blame and all of the consequences.

I couldn't walk through the village without being asked, 'How's it working out with the lad?' Never 'Is Victor doing okay?' No one ever seemed to spare a thought for the fact that he'd lost his mum in his teenage years, so much to process so young. All the attention centred around how we had coped with the trauma of having a teenager come to live with us.

Patrick alternated between 'I understand this isn't easy for you, Jo, but we can't keep it a secret forever' and 'I can't regret it. I'm glad to have Victor in my life,' which made me want to lash out, book Victor a ticket to Australia, pass the misery baton over to Patrick for a bit and see how much he didn't regret it then.

In the second week of December, Patrick was called to Cardiff on a training course. I heard him say to Victor, 'Shame you've got school and can't come with me. Never mind. I'll take you up there in the holidays.' The thought of them driving along the motorway, debating which music to listen to, creating memories, should have filled me with happiness, but I had a petty urge to come up with a million reasons why that wouldn't be possible.

Before Patrick left, he gave strict instructions to Phoebe to 'be good for your mother. No parties, no climbing out the window, no drugs, no shoplifting.'

She managed a ghost of a smile, and said, 'I'll be good. Got to keep fit for my rugby.' Which had, to be fair, outlasted my expectations. In fact, it seemed to lift her mood no end, despite her coming in freezing and filthy. She'd been a bit more settled, less combative than usual, which fed right into my dilemma about the great unveiling of a half-brother.

I invited Mum round for the evening and tried to reel Phoebe in by asking her to make a cheesecake for her grandmother. 'You know how she loves a bit of black cherry cheesecake. She'd be so impressed if you made one.'

Phoebe agreed, then marched in from school on the Friday and said there was a party that night and if she made the cheesecake, could she go?

I shook my head. 'I'm sorry, love, but I can't risk any trouble tonight. Not while Nan is here and Dad's away.'

It didn't take much for the storm clouds to roll in. 'I suppose you're going to let Victor go?'

'It's a bit different for him. One, I don't mind him getting an Uber back on his own. You're still a bit young to be in a cab by yourself. And two, I've never had any evidence of him taking drugs or getting totally off his face.'

'Oh bloody saint Victor.'

I wished it would be enough to say, 'I'd really like it if you stayed in just this once, with Nan and me and we had a quiet evening without any drama.' Experience had taught me that Phoebe was gearing up for a fight and unless I nipped it in the bud, it would unfold in front of my mum, who wouldn't hesitate to offer her wisdom.

'Phoebe. No. The answer is no.'

And with that, she said, 'Fair enough' and started crushing the ginger biscuits and melting the butter in a pan. Which immediately had me on red alert, wanting to block every potential escape route. 'Stop watching me like a hawk. I'm not going. You never trust me.'

'The trouble is, love, you've broken my trust on quite a lot of occasions, so it takes a bit of time to grow back.'

'You never look at the good I do.'

'That's not true, darling. I know you do lots of good things.' I wanted to cut the oxygen off to this conversation. I was just too tired. I knew that I should grab the moment to reason, to talk things through, but right then, I just couldn't be bothered to say the things I'd said a thousand times before.

Fortunately, Mum came bustling in with another random item that she was terrified I'd give to charity when she died so she was parking it in my house as a preemptive strike. 'I found this little snow globe for Phoebe.'

I expected her to mouth 'I'm not bloody nine' behind Mum's back, but she said, 'I *love* snow globes' and started dancing about shaking it.

Victor came into the kitchen and gave my mum a hug.

She put her hand up to his face. 'Such a handsome young man. Have you got a girlfriend?'

He did that cheeky grin that reminded me so much of Ginny.

'Mum, privacy!' I said.

'Oh, he doesn't mind me asking. Expect he's got all the girls after him.'

Victor did one of those funny little dances that teenagers did, even when you were asking whether they had any washing that needed doing. He didn't answer, just got some milk out of the fridge and did a swaggering walk to sit down. I did love seeing these little signs of happiness in him.

Phoebe started sing-songing. 'I know who it is…'

I raised my eyebrows at him. 'Is it a certain someone with long blonde hair, beginning with G?'

And we all laughed and for a moment, I just enjoyed the hope, the energy, the boisterousness that came with young people.

Mum clucked about. 'You eating enough, young man? And you, Phoebe, all this rugger Mum tells me you're playing. Better build you up! You look far too skinny. You'll snap in two.'

I gritted my teeth against the commenting on appearance. Sometimes I broke my own rule, but even saying, 'Your hair looks nice' to Phoebe meant she'd immediately respond with a negative about herself, 'Look at this spot, though' or moan about how her jeans were giving her a camel toe.

Victor pushed his chair back. 'I'll be off then,' he said, making an apologetic face to Phoebe.

She shrugged. 'Say hello to everyone for me.'

I wobbled, nearly weakened, then managed to stay, if not stuck to my guns, within grabbing distance in case of an ambush. I followed him out, double-checking that he had money for an Uber and a key to get in.

Mum proved a good distraction with her anecdotes about her over-65s fitness class, giving us just slightly too much information about how she had All Bran for breakfast, 'Just to make sure I go, you know, before.' She carried on. 'My friend Dolores gets dreadful wind when she does a squat.' Phoebe and I were both impressed when Mum showed us how she could do the plank, then the tree pose. 'My instructor says it's good for your pelvic floor, definitely improves things.'

Phoebe looked suitably horrified that Mum might segue into a discussion about either the importance of the pelvic floor in sex or for not wetting yourself and leapt up to show her how she could do one hundred sit-ups without stopping. I clapped her through the last twenty, properly impressed.

'Amazing! You are so fit!'

She told Mum all about Victor's training sessions and how she was drinking banana smoothies and eating peanut butter on toast every day to give her energy. 'I never even used to eat breakfast.'

Mum tutted at that. 'Most important meal of the day.'

Phoebe nodded. 'Yeah, I can't believe I didn't know that before.'

In my mind's eye, I pictured a sewing machine doing zigzag stitch across my mouth in order to stop myself shouting, 'I don't know why you didn't as I've probably been saying it every day for about five years'.

After dinner, we even managed to find a film without swearing or sex so I didn't have to cringe and sit in frozen silence until it got so bad, I had to fast-forward. We'd had such a peaceful evening, I couldn't help wondering if what Phoebe really needed was a bit of time with me, without competing for attention with Victor, or indeed, Patrick. I was just about to walk Mum home about 11 p.m. when the doorbell went.

'Have you got friends coming round, Phoebe?' I asked.

'Er, no. They're all at a party…'

I opened the door to find Faye, dishevelled and wild-eyed.

'Hello. Are you all right?' I asked.

'Is he here?' she shouted.

'Who? Patrick?'

'No, Victor!'

'No, he's at a party. Has something happened?'

Faye thrust a little plastic bag of coloured pills at me. 'I've just found these in Georgia's room. We've got a new desk arriving for her tomorrow and I was shifting her bedside table and they were under her lamp. With this!'

She shoved a mini Polaroid print of Victor and Georgia kissing at me. It was a proper tongue down the throat job, but despite that, my immediate thought was 'Thank God they're not naked.'

'Why don't you come in?' I said, deciding that inviting her in was a lesser evil than the neighbours overhearing what she was yelling.

She stepped into our hallway, trembling with anger and flapping the tablets at me. 'God knows what he's getting her hooked on.'

I sensed a movement behind me. 'Phoebe, can you just keep Nan in the sitting room and shut the door?'

I turned back to Faye, put my finger to my lips and whispered, 'My mum's here,' as though that had any chance of making it through the fog of her fury. I bustled her through to the kitchen, where she slammed the little pill packet on the table.

'This can't go on, Jo. What will it take for you to sort this out? Will one of our girls have to die before you do something?'

I tried to get my brain to hurry up with a response, but the force of her accusations was paralysing me.

'Hang on, do you even know what the pills are?' I picked them up and peered at them but knew immediately that I wasn't going to add value.

'It's ecstasy.'

'Are you sure?'

'Yes, I looked it up on Google.'

'OK. So what does Georgia say about it?'

Faye put her hands on her hips. 'I haven't spoken to her. She's at a party right now and not answering.'

'So why did you come round here?' I felt my fear dissipating and the stirrings of my own anger sparking about at the bottom of my stomach.

'Oh my God, literally, are we going to have this conversation again? No one – absolutely no one – had a problem with drugs before Victor got here. Now, not only has he got into some sort of relationship with my daughter – I dread to think what's going on there – but he's supplying her with drugs.'

I was still trying to dampen my rage, to stop it spiralling out of control and engulfing us both. 'Just keep your voice down. I don't want to involve Phoebe and my mum.'

Faye looked at me with such disgust. 'Do you actually think that Victor has specifically chosen my daughter? That he isn't peddling this shit to Phoebe as well? You need to open your eyes.'

'So what concrete evidence have you got that it's Victor?'

'Jesus, Jo. How can it not be? Our girls aren't going to have the nerve to go to some grubby little flat on the Talford estate and meet a bloody drug dealer, are they? Victor's eighteen already. Georgia's only sixteen, whatever she says, she's still impressionable. God, I don't know, she probably thinks Victor's really cool. Honestly, if I find out she's sleeping with him…'

I steadied myself on the edge of the table, trying to steer us back from the brink. 'Look, none of us wants our daughters to be having sex – and I've no idea whether they are or not. I know we'd all love them to wait for Mr Right and do it all perfectly and tastefully – and preferably without us having to be party to any of the finer details. And I'm not just saying this because, well, you know the whole history with Victor, but as far as I can see, he really loves her.'

If I thought I was offering something vaguely appeasing to Faye, I couldn't have been more wrong. She slammed her palm on the table. 'Oh well, that makes it all right then! Every mother's dream to have a big black man shagging her daughter and slipping her the odd ecstasy tablet.'

I heard myself gasp. 'Don't make this about race. Just don't. What Georgia and Victor are doing or not doing has nothing to do with him being black.' I threw my hands up. 'You must know that.'

Faye wasn't having it. 'Well, Jordan's the same age and he's not having sex with sixteen-year-olds and giving them drugs.'

'How would you know if he was? Actually, don't even answer that. You've got it in your head that Victor is some kind of drug baron grooming your daughter and I don't think you're going to listen to anything I say.'

I'd barely finished that sentence when Phoebe flew out of the sitting room. 'For fuck's sake, Faye!'

For once, I was beyond caring what Faye thought about Phoebe's language. 'Georgia buys her drugs from the bloke on the sunglasses stall at the market. Goes along, tries on a few Guccis and Raybans and Bob's your uncle. Just so you know, Victor never takes drugs. He's always telling her off about it, thinks it's for losers, and going on about how clever she is and how she'll kill all her brain cells off.'

Faye was flushed with anger. 'That's rubbish,' she shouted.

But Phoebe was going to have her say. 'You're wrong. Georgia and Helaina make a big thing of gathering up the money from everyone who wants drugs in our year. The bloke will only deal with them because they're pretty and he says they're a good advert for his "business".'

Faye glared over to me. 'Blood, even half-blood, is thicker than water, after all.'

My heart somersaulted. She wouldn't. Phoebe glanced over at me, puzzled. I put my hand up. Before I could react, Mum appeared.

'I'm not yet so deaf that I can't hear what you're saying about Victor.' She marched straight up to Faye and poked her finger at her chest. 'I've seen your daughter making a spectacle of herself all around the village. What's that boy called with the ginger hair? You wouldn't want to know what she was getting up to behind that grave with the angel with the broken wing. Talk about forward. Right by my Ted's plot too. Soon scuttled off when she saw me, that she did.'

Mum had never mentioned that to me. I couldn't help wondering if it was some elaborate revenge on Faye, though I wasn't sure my mum had that much imagination. But she hadn't finished yet.

'So here's my thinking. You might not want your daughter going out with Victor, but to my mind, she's got gold dust there and you ought to be bowing down in gratitude that she isn't with one of them scummy rascals who are always up to no good on the rec. Right proper gentleman Victor is, lovely boy and nicely brought up too.'

I didn't know whether it was the revelation that Georgia wasn't quite the vestal virgin Faye had imagined or the fact that my mother had caught her in flagrante, but Faye was silent for a moment.

Unfortunately, my mother had never liked a silence. 'So my suggestion, love, is that you get off home and have a strong word with your daughter before you go flying round the neighbourhood accusing people of all sorts.'

Faye tossed her head. 'You're all deluded. I mean, let's call a spade a spade here – literally – and look at who the real problem is.' And she allowed herself a little smirk at her own joke.

In that moment, I realised that I'd been holding onto something, a fragile edifice of a friendship in which I'd suffocated my instinct, dismissed all the times that she put me or my family down as tactlessness, over-protectiveness of her own family, no malice intended, just a bit clumsy but no harm done. Now I couldn't pretend to myself any more. And with a soaring feeling, a mixture of flinging my arms open on the first sunny day of spring and standing in the loudest most intense storm, I grabbed her arm and propelled her towards the door.

I didn't yell. Didn't swear, even though it was tempting. I said quietly, 'I'd credited you with the ability to judge a person for who they are, not what skin colour they happen to have. Please leave now.' I was shaking, adrenaline coursing through me.

She laughed, a horrid raucous sound. 'Oh don't come the martyr with me. Making out you give a shit about Victor now. You were all ready to pack him off to Australia, when you… Oh yes, sorry, I forgot that no one else knows about that.'

I saw her look round, judge her audience, rattle the power she had over me and put it down again. A surge of terror.

'Don't. Just go. Please.'

She leaned towards my mother. 'You can slag off Georgia as much as you like, but at least we're not all lying to each other. My daughter does actually know who her parents are.'

And with that, she flung the door open and clattered down the path.

Phoebe turned to me. 'What was she on about? Did you really want to send Victor to Australia?'

'I did consider it, yes.' Something in me capitulated, as I resigned myself to whatever was heading our way. I couldn't quite believe that I was going to say the words out loud. 'There's something you need to know.'

'Well, whatever it is, let's have a cup of tea. I'll put the kettle on,' Mum said.

I loved the way she assumed she was part of the great unveiling, but I didn't argue. I was grateful to have someone with me, though that could change at any time depending on Mum's reaction. I contemplated calling Patrick but decided that he couldn't do anything from Wales. This was something I'd have to deal with on my own, which was my punishment for opening my big mouth in the first place.

I took the Marks & Spencer chocolate selection I'd been saving for Christmas from its hiding place on the top shelf.

Phoebe clapped her hands. 'Oh my God, this is going to be huge!'

I wished I could have seen the funny side, but I couldn't stop trembling.

Phoebe put her hand on my arm. 'Mum, you're frightening me. Are you and Dad getting divorced? What did she mean about Georgia knowing who her parents are? You're not going to tell me I'm adopted, are you?' She was trying to make light of it, but panic was tapping a drumbeat in her words.

My mother put three large mugs of tea on the table and I attempted to speak, but clouds of tears kept sweeping across my throat.

'Phoebe, it's not you.' Like someone finally plucking up courage to jump into a choppy sea, not knowing whether they'd clear the rocks below, I said, 'It's Victor. He's your half-brother, your dad's son.'

Mum was slowest – or quickest – off the mark depending on which end of the telescope you chose to look down. 'Patrick's son? But he's black?'

'He's mixed race, Mum. Black and white.'

Phoebe didn't say anything. Just sat there frowning as though her brain was shuddering between the different hideous scenarios that could have led to this outcome.

'Dad and Ginny were…' I hesitated, the times I'd repeated to Phoebe about having respect for herself, about not having sex with just anyone, about being responsible with contraception, were echoing in my head. 'Dad and Ginny were in a relationship, before I got together with him.' I allowed myself that little diversion from the truth. I didn't think any child would benefit from knowing that their origins were in too many New Year's Eve cocktails, rather than love, however fleeting.

'You both went out with Dad?' She was frowning, hovering between disbelief and disgust.

Mum's eyebrows were somewhere only her rollers usually reached. I was so thankful that Phoebe had chosen the Mum-friendly euphemism of 'went out with' and I didn't have to have my mother and the word 'sex' in the same small space.

I made a noise that could probably pass for a 'yes'. 'Not at the same time though, of course.' I felt myself blush, as though I'd been denying a threesome.

Phoebe seemed stunned rather than the furious I'd expected. She went quiet.

'Is there anything you'd like to ask me?' I couldn't look at Mum.

Phoebe's voice when it came was small, reticent. 'Have you always known Victor was Dad's son?'

'No! Dad didn't know either. Ginny was in Canada when Victor was born. She didn't tell either of us, for whatever reason. We thought his dad was Canadian. We only found out when we went to Cory's a few weeks ago. We would have told you straight away, but there's been such a lot of trouble since then. We were just waiting for a calm moment.' I paused. 'Unfortunately we haven't really had one. I didn't mean for you to find out like this.'

Mum reached for a chocolate biscuit. Her uncharacteristic silence was most unnerving. Then suddenly, as though she'd been sieving for a splinter of good news in the catastrophic mess before her, she clapped her hands. 'How exciting to have found a brother you didn't know you had. I used to love Cilla Black on *Surprise, Surprise* when she used to get families back together. There was one woman who hadn't seen her son since he was six weeks old…'

Phoebe clearly had no idea who Cilla Black was. And even if she did, Cilla, God rest her soul, had no place in our personal *Surprise, Surprise.*

'Mum!' I was absolutely not in the mood for a long-winded story about someone else's dysfunctional family dynamics.

'Sorry, love. I was just saying that Phoebe wouldn't have to be an only child any more, that she's got a lovely brother. Might not mean much now, but when you and Patrick – and me – are six foot under, she'll be thankful. Lucky girl.'

And in that moment, I loved my mum so much. I'd expected her to rant about Ginny, even Patrick, but she'd surprised me. She'd seen the one good thing. And unlike me, she'd spotted it straight away with generosity in her heart.

'Phoebe?' I said gently, terrified that she'd storm out before she'd made any kind of attempt to sift through her feelings with me.

She sat picking at her nails, great whorls of dark emotion scudding across her face. Then she burst into tears and clambered onto my lap, sobbing into my shoulder. I held her, just held her, while my mum was all big eyes and 'It's a lot to take in…' For me though, it was like excavating memories, so long buried that I could never have brought them to mind without this sensory prompt. The time when Phoebe looked to me to fix things, instead of assuming I was the enemy. When her body ran to mine, the shelter, the safe haven, instead of being the one who ruined things, who spoilt her fun, who had no idea about anything. And all that love that I'd kept locked up in a vault, protected from her scorn, her sarcasm, and yes, her lies and let-downs, flowed out of me, enveloping her.

She gulped. 'I'm too big to sit on your knee. Am I hurting you?'
'Not at all. Quite the opposite.'

She sniffed. 'Does Dad love Victor more than me?' A fresh storm of tears ensued.

I pulled her tight. 'Not at all. Love doesn't come with a limit, darling. Dad loves Victor, but that doesn't take anything away from you. He adores you and he's had all that experience of seeing you grow up. He's only just getting to know Victor, so maybe it seems as though he's more interested in him, but that's just because he's trying to catch up on lost time.'

Her crying subsided. Mum reached for Phoebe's hand and I covered them both with mine. There was something about the little pyramid of hands on the table, Phoebe's smooth fresh skin, my short square nails and chapped knuckles and Mum's, wrinkled but soft, Nivea'd to within an inch of their lives. All that love held and passed down the generations, imperfect, sometimes antagonistic, often frustrating and annoying, but in a predicament, nothing said, 'I've got you' like a mum who's endured the worst of you and still carries a seemingly refillable, recyclable, indestructible well of love.

Just before I got carried away, one step removed from thinking up my own quotations about adversity, triumph and tragedy and turning them into fridge magnets, Phoebe yanked on the tether that brought me back to earth.

'Did you mind that Dad had shagged Ginny before you went out with him?' She made an 'ewww' noise as though the thought was too horrible to contemplate.

This was not a conversation I wanted to have in front of my mother, and one that I was only mildly more comfortable having with my daughter. I decided not to get in a tangle about dates and let them work that out for themselves when we'd got over the initial hurdles.

'To be honest, I don't think there's a woman alive who loves knowing that the man she married has also been involved with a close friend, even if it was a long time before they got together. I think that's just human nature.' I decided to adopt the 'long time' relative to a teenager's life when a week seemed like forever. Thankfully, she seemed to assume that I'd always known about their dalliance.

Mum piped up. 'Why didn't Ginny tell you about Victor though? I mean, it's not like Patrick had an affair with her when he was with you, did he? He wouldn't have done that.' Mum could never see any wrong in Patrick, not even now, with a random son dumped in her lap. I was pretty sure that if Patrick killed someone, she'd pat him on the shoulder and say, 'Oh never mind, you didn't mean to do it, your finger slipped on the trigger.'

I still managed to recognise that nothing good would come of her badmouthing Patrick to me or Phoebe. I followed her party line. 'No! No, his relationship with her was over before we got together.' I did my own internal eye-roll at 'relationship', but there was no backing out of that now.

Phoebe sat up but kept her arm round me. 'You're not going to make Victor leave, are you?'

'We have to talk to Victor and understand what he wants. Not a word to him yet, though, Phoebe. We really need Dad here when we tell him.'

'Do you think he'll want me as a sister? Is that just weird?'

I hugged her, struck by how most of her thoughts were about how she wouldn't live up to what people expected of her, that they'd be disappointed in her. All that bravado stripped away and the kernel of a vulnerable young woman struggling to find her place in life exposed.

And oddly, in this most complex and unwanted of moments, hope flickered that my daughter, who'd felt lost to me for so long, might be taking the first steps back to us.

I might come up with some witty wisdom for a fridge magnet after all.

CHAPTER TWENTY-FOUR

About midnight, I walked Mum home. I wanted to get her out of the way before Victor came back. I didn't yet have the stomach for her studying him and doing stage whispers of, 'You can see Patrick in him. How I didn't notice the similarity between them before, I don't know. Those eyes!'

As soon as we got out of Phoebe's earshot, she grabbed my arm and said, 'Are you all right, darling? It must have been a shock for you to find this out.'

'It was. I still don't know how I feel about it. I don't want to punish Victor – it's not his fault – but I just wish I'd known before I married Patrick. I feel so betrayed, especially by Ginny. She out and out lied to us.'

'How do you mean?'

'She always said Victor was premature.'

Mum slowed her pace. For someone who never stopped talking, her mastering of the art of walking and speaking at the same time left a lot to be desired.

'Well, wasn't he?' She paused. 'I do remember at your wedding thinking he was very bonny for a premmie baby.'

'No. I saw his hospital bracelet. He weighed over 7lbs. Phoebe was only 6lbs 3oz.'

'I always said you should have stopped work earlier. No wonder Phoebe was small, the way you ran yourself ragged.'

This was why I could never have a discussion with Mum. Her ability to allow irrelevant details to become her focus was legendary.

I'd had enough drama for one night. I didn't feel up to justifying any other areas of my life to date, so I let it go. We walked the rest of the way with Mum musing about her astonishment that Ginny had kept Victor's parentage a secret. 'Imagine not breathing a word for all those years.' I was pretty sure Mum would never find herself in the position of keeping something to herself for so long.

I unlocked her front door. We didn't do a lot of hugging, but she flung her arms open.

'They're all lucky to have you. And if that Faye causes any trouble, I shall put everyone right about that daughter of hers.' Mum leaned forward. 'She had her head in his, you know...' she said, waggling her finger downwards. Thank goodness she'd never overheard Phoebe giving the rundown of who'd done what with whom at their parties. Enough to make Mum's evaporated milk curdle.

I bundled her inside and disappeared, with a warning not to mention anything about tonight until I told her it was okay.

I was just walking home when I saw an Uber turn into the drive. I hung back, giving myself time to consider my options. Tell Victor now, without Patrick, before anyone else did? Phone Patrick and tell him what had happened? Hope that there wouldn't be a domino effect of Faye telling Georgia, who would then tell Victor. I'd never make a living as a government strategist.

I leant on the church wall, staring up at the stars. My mind was pick, pick, picking at why Ginny had acted the way she had. I didn't want to believe that my lifelong friend had intended to hurt us. Even so, there was no escaping the fact that she'd deliberately sat on a secret that had gathered more and more power to inflict damage as the years went by.

What if she'd phoned me on New Year's Day and told me she'd had sex with Patrick, before I'd got involved with him? What if he'd just come clean, as soon as it became apparent we had feelings beyond simple friendship? I wouldn't have loved it. But I might have been able to live with it. Anything would have been better than decades of believing Ginny was my safety net, my go-to listening ear, only to discover she was my betrayer.

In the meantime, I had to stop wallowing in what it meant for me and protect Victor, to make sure the next cataclysmic shock in his life was delivered as gently as possible.

I hurried up the hill. I'd have to ring Patrick, tell him that I'd let him down, that word was out before we were ready for it. I mourned the decades of my childhood when however angry you made someone, no one else heard about it in the time it took to vent in a WhatsApp group, a Facebook post or any of the myriad ways Victor might find out who his dad was.

I crept into the house. I heard talking in the kitchen and hoped Phoebe wasn't filling Victor in just yet. Instead, at my table sat Georgia, crying her eyes out, with Victor kneeling on the floor, trying to calm her down, and Phoebe making hot chocolate.

'What's happened?' I asked, despite being tempted to run away shouting that my trouble trove was already full and closed to further crisis.

Victor stood up. 'Georgia's had a bit of a falling out with her mum.' He brushed his hand over his face. 'Faye drove off in a temper when she came to pick up Georgia because, well, she kind of accused me of something and Georgia stood up for me, but it got a bit nasty. I didn't want to leave Georgia on her own so I hoped it might be okay if she stayed here for the night.'

My heart went out to this boy. Whatever Ginny had done wrong elsewhere, she'd instilled in him such a sense of responsibility and kindness. God knows, the world needed more people like that. 'Yes, of course.'

I bent down to Georgia. 'Does your mum know where you are?' She did a big sob and shook her head.

'Right, let me text her so she doesn't have to worry about you and I suggest you all go to bed. Phoebe, can you make up a mattress on the floor of your room?' Although I was tempted to throw caution to the wind and let Georgia share a bed with Victor. What that girl needed was comfort from someone who loved her. I wasn't sure anything in the world brought peace like someone who thought you were wonderful cuddling you to sleep. But already full bucket of shit and all that. I dismissed the thought immediately when my slug-slow brain came round to the question of consent. It was a jolt to realise that Victor needed my protection as much as Georgia, especially at the moment. It frightened me to think someone I'd considered such a close friend could turn so vicious.

Tempting as it was to leave Faye stewing in her own toxic juice, beside herself with worry about where her daughter was, I didn't want to stoop to her level. I tapped out a text.

Georgia's here. Gone to bed in Phoebe's room. She's okay. Best to let her stay till morning to give everyone a chance to calm down.

I pressed send. 'That's for you, Dad. Not her,' I said to myself. The reply came through immediately. *Thank you for letting me know.*

Stupid to feel an involuntary stab of sadness at the lack of kissing emojis. I'd lost my two best friends in one year. I'd be standing on the street with a placard, 'Friends needed', soon.

I took a bottle of wine out of the fridge. Ginny had always teased me about my rule of never drinking alone. In fact, she'd teased me about loads of things, but not in a way that made me feel stupid. Unlike now, when I felt like the thickest person on the planet. She'd told me over and over again how she was sure I'd help Victor through his grief, that our home would be the best place for him. Not because of my brilliance though. Because his dad was there.

A dad who I needed to inform pretty snap-snap that the secret had climbed out of its hole and would probably be common knowledge in the village by tomorrow. I sat in the dark, rehearsing how I was going to start the conversation. In the end, I gave up trying to find anything approaching the perfect words. I'd just have to be honest and hope I'd have a marriage left at the end of it.

My whole body was rigid as the phone rang out. I'd always been suspicious that these training workshops he talked about were an excuse for a big booze-up till the early hours, but there was a gratifying fumble and a sleepy 'Jo? Are you all right?' on the other end.

'Sorry. I had to call. It's all got out of hand.'

I filled him in, long past presenting myself in a good light. I imagined him propping two pillows behind him, sipping the water I knew would be by his bed.

'You did what? Why would you do that?'

I stammered, trying to remember why I had shouted out to Faye that Victor was Phoebe's brother. 'I think it was so much on my mind that it just came out. I'm sorry, I shouldn't have done it.'

'Didn't you think about what effect it might have on Victor, on Phoebe, even?'

And like a spark finding an elusive fuse, I lost it in a torrent of abuse that leaves not only the recipient but also the deliverer battered and bruised. The sort of words that might not end a marriage but would certainly put a severe dent in its carapace. 'I love that you take the moral high ground when if it wasn't for you, dithering between two best friends, trying them both out like someone at a buffet, none – I repeat none – of this, would have happened.'

Patrick tried to defend himself by pointing out that it was precisely because he'd been with Ginny that he'd realised that his heart lay with me and he'd come straight home.

There was nothing he could have said, nothing that would have appeased me. I didn't want to entertain the possibility that it was all just a convergence of circumstance, that everyone played their part. I wanted someone to blame, to rage at.

And like that evening when I'd blurted out the truth to Faye, the words that had been buzzing round my mind, so close to the surface that a mere scratch could release them into the atmosphere,

I hissed, 'You need to make your mind up whether you want to stay in this marriage. Because right now, it feels like our whole lives are dictated by another woman's child.'

And without allowing him to answer, I stabbed the call-end button, switched my phone off and sat crying in the dark until I'd finished the whole bottle of wine. I stumbled up the stairs, hoping to conk out into a dreamless sleep but instead had to doze sitting up to stop the room spinning.

When I next opened my eyes, Patrick was in the room.

'When did you come back?' As I peered out of sandpapery eyes with the stink of alcohol leaking out of me, I had a fleeting thought that my threat of ending our marriage might be a relief to him.

'I've just got in. I waited until five a.m. to be sober enough to drive – I'd had a few glasses of wine at the dinner, but nothing major.'

I lifted my head off the pillow, then lay back down again.

He gave a little half-smile. 'Shall I bring you a cup of tea?'

I nodded. 'Can you open the window?'

I pulled the duvet around me, wondering if I was up to this, whether I could find the energy to gather all the pieces of our lives and sew them back together, if not in a coherent form, at least in a way that we all had half a chance of being happy. Ginny would have scoffed at my lack of ambition – 'Half a chance of being happy! Such dizzying heights! Go wild!'

I still wished she was here to talk to about the very problem she'd caused. My heart was reluctant to relinquish the love I felt for her.

Patrick came back and placed a cup of tea on the bedside table. He also had a carrier bag with him. He raised his eyebrows at me. 'Did you try and find the answer in Sauvignon Blanc?'

'I did, but it didn't come up with anything.' I tried to make a joke, but my eyes filled.

He sat on the bed.

Through half-open lips, I said, 'Don't come too close. I haven't cleaned my teeth.'

He sighed. 'Trust you to worry about that. Why don't you go and clean them so we can talk without you sounding like a ventriloquist's dummy?'

I swung my legs out of bed, my stomach heaving as I moved, self-conscious about my utilitarian pyjamas, as though I should have been floating about in something silky as an advert for 'what you will be missing if we don't sort this shit out.'

Since Ginny died, life seemed to be one long run of resolving crises. It was hard to remember when we'd had any conversations resembling fun chit-chats. Of late, everything had revolved around firefighting discussions over how to manage Phoebe's behaviour or support Victor. Was this what marriage was about? Not giving up? Just gritting your teeth and buggering on? I'd hoped for more than that out of life.

I cleaned my teeth and got back into bed.

Patrick looked so forlorn, it was tempting to brush everything under the carpet and tell him that I'd had too much to drink and didn't mean anything I said.

'For what it's worth, I'm so sorry. I wish I'd done it all differently.' He paused. 'But I can't be sad that I'm getting a chance to know my son. I do understand how difficult that is for you. And if anyone has to pay the price for this mess, it must be me, not Victor. He really didn't do anything wrong.'

And there it was, the little heart snag that Patrick was offering himself in Victor's place. Like all good dads, I supposed. I veered between respecting him for it and a sick jealousy over that fundamental dad/son bond that obliterated any union manufactured by marriage.

'Can you run me through exactly what happened last night, starting with Faye?' He smoothed the duvet, his eyes cast down as though he didn't want to look at me, but whether that was to avoid my pain, I didn't know.

I filled him in.

'So Georgia is here? In Phoebe's room, I hope?'

Despite considering throwing caution to the wind last night, I still felt irrationally annoyed at Patrick's question. 'Yes. I managed to ensure no one got pregnant on my watch, all on my own.'

Patrick's face tightened. 'So the big question is what do we do about telling Victor the truth? It has to be today. There are too many people who know now. It's just a matter of time before someone blurts it out.'

'Are you interested in how your daughter feels about it all?'

Patrick's shoulders sagged. 'I *am* interested. I was just coming to that. This isn't a favouritism thing, Jo. It's a practicalities thing. You've already put Phoebe in the picture. I don't think it's so unreasonable to expect the same for Victor, given that it directly concerns him.' His voice cracked. 'He's only eighteen, for God's sake.'

I struggled to formulate a sensible strategy against the backdrop of hammering in my head. 'I think the best thing is for you to take Victor out on your own.'

'I'd rather you were there. I don't want this to be an "I'm your dad" issue, I'd like us to present it as a family thing.'

I breathed out. 'But it's not, is it, really?'

Patrick folded his arms. 'I can't see how it can work if it isn't. I hope you can find a way to accept it, that eventually you can see that no one, not me, not Ginny, set out to hurt you. At the time, it just didn't seem important.'

I put my head in my hands. 'Let me have a shower. Perhaps you can take Georgia home when they get up. I can't face Faye today.'

Patrick turned to go downstairs. 'By the way, I popped into see Ginny's dad just before dinner last night. He's moving into a home in a couple of weeks. He gave me a few knick-knacks for Victor. I promised we'd take him down to visit soon.' He looked at me. 'Well, I'll drive him if you don't want to come.' He reached into the bag at his feet. 'Her dad also sent this. He wanted you to have it. He wrote a note for you as well.'

I held my hand out. Ginny's favourite poetry book. Maya Angelou. I pressed the book to my face. In another life, Ginny could have been an actress. She'd been so good at reading out loud, preferring poetry to novels. I could see her now, balancing on a stool in our kitchen, her long legs tucked under her, flicking through a poetry book and reading lines out to us. 'Poets get emotion. They're intense about it. And so clever. Summing up life in so few words. I love the directness of poetry.' I wish I'd listened properly, instead of both envying her sophistication and dismissing her eccentricity.

'I didn't know you were planning to visit Tayo?'

Patrick met my eye with a glimmer of defiance. 'I wanted to talk to someone who loved Victor. And I know he hasn't got long left.'

'So you wanted to promise him that Victor would be okay?' The words grazed against my throat. 'Had Ginny told him?' I knew admitting that truth would have cost her. Her parents were so disappointed that she hadn't married well and her best friend's husband would be an extra notch up the displeasure scale.

'I didn't ask him directly but he didn't look very surprised when I brought it up. Sort of nodded in a "that all makes sense" kind of way.'

'Was he delighted to have you as a son-in-law by proxy?' Despite myself, I didn't want that proud old man to suffer any more pain than he had already. No father should outlive his daughter.

'He was very happy that Victor has a stable home. He spent most of his time impressing on me the importance of encouraging Victor to become a doctor or a lawyer. His face lit up when I told him how well he was doing in school.'

'If you leave out the fact that everyone thinks he's running a drugs ring.'

Patrick screwed up his face. 'I'm just going to rise above that. There are arseholes everywhere.' I tried not to notice that 'We' had become 'I'. 'Anyway, I'll leave you to shower. Have a think about how you want to approach speaking to Victor.'

Patrick's tone had a definite 'in or out' ultimatum about it. It underlined the shift in a matter of months from an understanding that if Victor put too much of a strain on our family life, we'd find a different solution for him, to the sense that I, not he, would be packing my bags. The unspoken words, 'Don't make me choose' hung in the air long after Patrick had left.

I sat in bed, hoping to alight on the one emotion that could herd all the others into order. I stroked the cover of the poetry book. *And Still I Rise*. The memory of Ginny reciting that poem strutting around our sitting room – the very image of sassiness – was so vivid I could feel her energy around me.

I studied the envelope from her dad, trying to marry up the fierce patriarch to whom Ginny had introduced me on several occasions when we lived together in London with the shaky, uncertain writing before me. I hesitated to open it, picking at the flap, frightened to read unmerited words of gratitude. With a sigh, I pulled out the flimsy bit of paper.

Dear Jo – Ginika wanted me to give you this 'when the time was right'. It was one of the last things she said to me. She repeated over and over again, when the time was right, when I knew about Victor. She didn't seem to be able to answer when that would be. I was afraid I would die before I understood. I understand now, but I don't know why this book. I hope it means something to you. I wish I'd been able to give it to you in person, but please do come and see me if you want to. Bring Victor. God bless you for looking after my grandson in these unusual circumstances. She was very lucky to have a friend like you. Yours sincerely, Tayo Yaro.

I stared at the letter, then at the book. He wasn't joking about the 'unusual circumstances'. Was the poetry supposed to comfort me? To let me know that she was still 'around' in some way? To remind me of the happy times in our flat? All I could think of now was whether she'd secretly been in love with Patrick the whole time. And if he'd been in love with her.

I flopped back on to the bed, my brain aching. A wave of nausea threatened and I wished again that I'd gone to bed with a mint tea. I opened the front cover of the book, wondering if there was an inscription. Nothing. If there was some kind of message here, I was way too hungover to figure it out. I got ready and went downstairs, pausing before I walked into the kitchen. I wasn't sure how much longer I'd be able to live like this, feeling as though I was entering enemy territory every time I went into a room.

Georgia was sitting with Phoebe and Victor, looking thin, pale and vulnerable. And ill. Not at all like the robust fresh-faced girl considered an automatic shoe-in for Oxford.

'Have you been in touch with your mum this morning? She'll be worried about you.'

Georgia mumbled, 'No.'

I glanced over to Patrick, who was making tea, looking strained and old. I didn't think Ginny had envisaged an atmosphere leaden with accusation when she'd begged me to take in her boy. She'd be disappointed. But I was disappointed in her. Lose-lose.

I forced my attention back to Georgia. I said, 'You don't look well, love.' Even though I was a fine one to talk as just leaning forward made my head feel like it was going to cleave in two.

She burst into tears.

I ran over to her. 'Oh what's the matter, my lovely? Are you worried about going home? All mums get cross sometimes, but I'm sure she'll get over it.'

Patrick wandered out, muttering, 'I don't think I'm going to be much use here.' I was glad, because I didn't want him weighing every word, judging whether or not I was handling a situation well.

Phoebe beckoned me into the hallway. I left Georgia crying on Victor and followed her out.

'Georgia's addicted to drugs, Mum.'

'What? What sort of drugs? That MDMA stuff?' It was a sign of how quickly the goalposts shifted with teenagers that I hoped it was MDMA and that she wasn't shooting up with something far more frightening.

'Adderall.'

I stared at her, combing through my drug knowledge, which appeared to fit perfectly on a drawing pin. 'Adderall? I don't think I know what that is?'

'You know, they use it to treat ADHD.'

'Georgia hasn't been diagnosed with that, has she?'

I knew it was serious because Phoebe didn't flounce off shouting, 'It doesn't matter!' when I failed to grasp what she was saying straight away.

'No, it's so she can study for long periods and really really concentrate.' She paused. 'You know, so she can get into Oxford.'

'Who is she getting that from?'

Phoebe's confidence in me didn't extend that far. She shrugged. 'It's really easy to get. Some people fake it and get prescriptions.'

'She can't be addicted to it, though. Otherwise everyone who was being treated for ADHD would have a problem.'

Phoebe was battling not to get impatient. 'She's been taking much more than, you know, what's recommended.' Phoebe stared at the floor. 'She says she can't study without it any more, but I think it makes her depressed. Then she takes Molly – MDMA – to lift her up. I'm really worried she'll kill herself, Mum. Victor's been trying to get her to see the doctor, but she's frightened the police will get involved.'

It was incredible that a teenager who thought I was so stupid most of the time could suddenly do an about-turn and have an inflated idea of my ability to solve problems, which was nearly as terrifying.

I put my arms out to her and she stepped into them. 'Thank you for telling me.' I kissed the top of her head, managing not to

scream, 'And now I have no idea what to do with that knowledge.'
'Has she talked to her mum about it, do you know?'

And that was when Phoebe pulled back, reverting to the 'doh, are you stupid?' face. 'Can you imagine what Faye would say? You can't tell her, Mum. You know she's always, "Well, Georgia's doing extra essays, Georgia's so ambitious, Georgia is aiming for the best."'

'Right, right. Okay, this is something I'm going to need to think about.' I didn't like to say that without telling Faye, my mind was completely empty of any possible solutions. 'Leave it with me, darling. I'll talk to Dad.'

Phoebe reiterated that we weren't to tell Georgia's parents anything, then went back into the kitchen, where Victor was talking in low, comforting tones.

I intercepted Patrick in the hallway who'd come out to investigate what was going on. I filled him in quickly. 'Jesus. Like we haven't got enough of our own troubles to deal with.' His response fell into the ungenerous category, but I really understood where he was coming from. 'I'm taking her home. We can't deal with Georgia until we've sorted out Victor. And we can't solve Georgia's problems overnight.'

Before I could respond, he marched into the kitchen, delivered the 'We're leaving in ten minutes' message, strode back out and whispered, 'And when I come back, we're both going to sit down with Victor.'

I stood upstairs watching them all drift out to the car. Georgia looked so wan. Victor was a man mountain next to her tiny frame. I was touched to see Phoebe pull up the collar on her coat for her.

I slumped back onto the bed, talking myself out of grabbing a suitcase and decamping to Mum's while Patrick did the whole 'And here's a dad I made earlier' reveal. I couldn't bear it if Victor was sorry for me, the consolation prize Patrick had picked up after being rejected by his own mum. Would he think like that? In reality, he'd probably wish that I was the one who died.

And round and round I went, watching the minutes tick away before they'd be back and I'd have to jump one way or the other. I couldn't imagine walking out on Patrick. It seemed unthinkable that this little cottage might have to be sold, the place where I'd taken it for granted that Patrick and I would weather life, woven together by all the many intangible things that make up a marriage. All the kindnesses – switching on the outside light in the winter so I didn't have to fumble with my key, fetching my Kindle from upstairs when I'd finished clearing away dinner, giving me a lift home from the station so I didn't have to walk back in the dark – stacked up into a tightly threaded safety net.

Or at least I thought they had. What was frightening now was how flimsy that looked. Could I spend the rest of my life trying – and maybe failing – to embrace his child? Would I start off with energy and a determination to be generous, vowing to see Victor as an unexpected but welcome addition, yet find myself cursing Ginny's duplicity every time our family had to shuffle round to accommodate his needs? And would I observe Patrick fulfilling a demand from Victor and endlessly monitor the scales to see where Phoebe featured? Where I featured?

I jumped up, jittery with the pressure to make a decision, to present a united happy family to Victor or to declare my exit. As I straightened the duvet, Ginny's Maya Angelou poetry book fell to the floor and a sheet of paper dropped out.

My heart constricted. Ginny's flamboyant handwriting with its curves and bold tails. I scanned the page.

Dear Jo,

I wish I could have this conversation with you, but, as you know, God had other plans.

I've left it to chance as to whether you ever find this letter because I couldn't make up my mind if it was even a good idea to write it. I feel that the universe owes me a small recalibra-

tion of destiny, at the very least. And you know I was always a great believer in fate. (Remember the Ouija board? Maybe you should give it another go and I'll try and commune with you!)

If you're reading this at all, it's because Dad has followed my instruction to give you this poetry book if he ever found out who Victor's father is. And if he knows and has handed over my beloved Maya Angelou, then I'm assuming (posthumously from my wine bar in the sky) that you know about Patrick too. In the end, I was too tired, too bloody ill and too nervous of Dad's reaction to tell him myself. I didn't want to use my last precious weeks locked in a circle of recriminations. So I took the coward's way out, but I'm hoping everyone will understand that I used up all my bravery on not letting Victor see how frightened I was of leaving him. Of leaving all of you.

So, assuming Dad was paying attention and this isn't a bolt from the blue, I'd like to clarify a few things. And, dear Jo, whatever you think of me now, please know that I never, ever meant to hurt you. I feel nervous now about what I'm going to put into words. But I really do feel the need to write it down, for there to be one true record of what happened and my feelings about it, even if I can't control how you – or anyone – react to it.

I've no doubt that you are sitting there in an emotional volcano – and who wouldn't be? Friend sleeps with best friend's future husband and doesn't mention it, then, hey presto, eighteen years later, friend asks best friend to take in husband's son… without breathing a word.

So. Let's get the worst bit out of the way. The whole sex thing with Patrick. Argh. You're never going to want to think about that. But just for one moment, remind yourself of how, two decades ago, we (well, perhaps just me) were on a mission to get women to stop apologising for enjoying sex and relish the opportunity when it presented itself. And because Patrick and I were friends, and we'd always done that stupid joking thing about hooking up with each other when we were thirty if we weren't settled down by then, it wasn't so outlandish that on a New Year's Eve when we'd hit the mojitos pretty comprehensively that we tried it out.

In my defence, I had no idea that he was already in love with you. I don't suppose you did either because you were obsessed with that bloke who never wore underpants under his trousers. Disgusting! (Can't remember his name – chemo memory fog or maybe brain dying before the rest of me.)

I paused. I'd been so busy resenting Ginny, I'd forgotten how she used to joke about dying, how funny she was. Her great warmth that wrapped itself around you when she walked into the room. I felt a weak flare of hope in my heart that her having my husband's baby wouldn't be the only thing I'd remember about her forever.

With hindsight, it was crystal clear the next morning though. We agreed that we didn't want to make it awkward for you and Cory, so we'd just chalk it up to too many cocktails and agreed never to mention it again. Although I tried to laugh it off, Patrick was straight onto Air Canada to get his flight changed so he could get back to London as soon as possible. At the time, I was mortified and pretty pissed off with him because he was acting as though he couldn't wait to get away from me. I mean, I knew it wasn't the start of any great love affair but his haste to disappear back to Britain wasn't the biggest compliment I'd ever had. It was only much later that I understood our dalliance had served to make him realise what he really wanted: you.

Anyway, if you remember – and it is so hard to remember – we didn't own computers or have ready access to email. (Can't believe that era ever existed now. Imagine being that old!) So by the time we got to speak to each other, I was four months pregnant and you were in love with Patrick.

You sounded so happy. So so happy. I didn't have the heart to wade in and throw a spanner in the works. I made the snap decision to tell you about my promotion instead. And once I hadn't told you the first time, it became impossible to say, 'Oh by the way, I should have mentioned this earlier, but your future husband is the father of my baby.'

Knowing you as I do, you'll immediately assume you were Patrick's second choice. That's just not the case. I saw how much he loved you over the years and actually it made it easier not to tell Victor who his father was because I figured that Victor didn't seem bothered about it, whereas I was frightened it would cause an earthquake in your lives.

I'm not sure whether you'll believe me. I hope you do, but I know there was a part of you that never felt good enough in any area of your life. Which I wish I'd been able to change over the years, but I don't think I ever did, no matter how often I told you how brilliant you were.

One arena where you were absolutely amazing and about which I am totally qualified to speak was in being my best friend. Even if Patrick hadn't been Victor's dad, I would have wanted you two to have him – although, to be fair, there weren't too many other suitable offers either… I mean, Cory? Come on!

I've no idea whether you'll ever read this letter. It will depend on my dad not dying before all is revealed, which will only happen if Cory has opened the first letter. Which means that one of you – my money is on Patrick – has had second thoughts about looking after Victor. I couldn't let that happen. He belongs with you (don't make me turn in my grave for eternity!), which is why I had to make arrangements for you to find out the truth.

Guilt engulfed me. Ginny had believed the very best of me and I'd let her down. Ironically, Patrick had been her boy's champion, not me.

Anyway, like I said, it's all down to chance, a last toss of the coin from me. Heads or tails from beyond the grave. It comforts me that one day you might just stumble across a last little bit of love waiting there from me to you, tucked next to 'And Still I Rise' for old times' sake. Still hoping to dance with those diamonds up in the sky with some gorgeous bloke who keeled over in his prime.

Seriously though, in some ways, I hope you don't ever get to see either letter and trolley on in blissful ignorance forever. In the end, I had to make a judgement call. Victor was so young to lose me and I decided that even with your ability to hold a grudge, you'd eventually get over it.

So, my darling, if you're raging about feeling betrayed by me, pleeeease don't let it taint your memory of our friendship. Initially I did what I thought was best in order not to ruin your happiness before you'd been together with Patrick long enough to weather it and then, well, I bloody went and died before I ever found a way to explain.

Please live your life, Jo, and try and find it within your heart to forgive me and love my boy. Especially love my boy.

Hard as it is to believe, this is my last letter to you. Thank you. Thank you for everything. For the good times. The quiet and comfortable times. The wild times. All the times. I love you. And I'll save you a place on my cloud if you hug my boy close and focus on what matters now, not what happened then.

Ginika xx

PS I challenge you to read 'And Still I Rise' and not feel as though you could take on the world. You've always been so much stronger than you gave yourself credit for. On the other hand, on re-reading that poem, if I wasn't hooked up to a drip right now, I'd have a shot at climbing Everest myself…

I stared at that letter, allowing it to both entertain and soothe me, just as her words had when she was alive. Now though there was an added dimension that brought the most incredible grief. My whole body burned with the injustice that someone who was loved as much as Ginny had to die. I was quite sure there were plenty of despicable people out there whom no one would miss and whose demise would do the world a favour.

I kept returning to that phrase, 'focus on what matters now, not what happened then.' So easy to say for her, so difficult for my heart to hold onto. My eyes alighted on 'You've always been so much stronger than you gave yourself credit for.' It was a great compliment but it felt a bit misplaced: I really wasn't certain I could get through this with my family intact.

I sighed. Ginny would have loved the opportunity to be in my shoes, with another chance to see the tulips push their little noses through the earth. To have the privilege of embracing the seasons rolling round inexorably, immune to human frailty or error. To hug her boy, again, without ration, without the second hand marking an urgent drumbeat. But she wasn't the one facing the logistics of blending this most bizarre of families, fronting out the twitterings and snickering of the whole village, wrestling with bitterness and hurt.

With a jolt, I realised time was ticking on. I looked at my watch. They'd been gone well over three-quarters of an hour. I had a sudden rush of insecurity that Faye would be listing all my faults to Patrick and he'd be nodding in agreement. If ever there was a good time to read 'And Still I Rise' and fine-tune my world domination skills, it was now.

As Patrick's tyres crunched on the gravel, I read the first verse and prepared to make my own definitive mark on my much smaller, but significant world.

CHAPTER TWENTY-FIVE

Patrick came in with a determined look on his face. Phoebe was glaring a 'right now, tell him right now' at me. I acknowledged her, wondering how she'd react if I couldn't bring myself to toe the family line. And all the while, Victor, glorious, laidback Victor, was humming to himself, wandering in as though the only thing he had to concern himself with was how to step over his trainers in the hallway for the tenth time without feeling the need to pick them up.

Patrick raised his eyebrows at me. 'I can see why you've fallen out with Faye. Bloody nightmare, she is. Tried to give her the heads-up about the Adderall and she just got really nasty, saying "Georgia is naturally clever and doesn't need drugs to enhance her performance," like she was a flipping Olympic sprinter or something. No wonder Georgia's falling apart under the pressure – I doubt that she's ever had a say in the steam train of Faye's ambition.'

'I know. Poor girl.' I found it comforting that Patrick had been on the receiving end of Faye's perfect mother/perfect daughter diatribes because he always seemed to assume that I'd taken everything the wrong way. But I also knew this mini-rant was just delaying the inevitable.

Patrick looked to me for reassurance. He mouthed 'Now?'

I was backing away from the moment that I'd see my husband bond with his son in a way that felt closed off to me. We couldn't dodge it any longer, however.

Patrick turned to Victor, 'Got a minute? Jo and I have got something to talk to you about. Phoebe, I think you should come into the kitchen too.'

Phoebe's lips kept twitching, as though she was having to stop her excitement from bursting out. Despite everything, I felt a rush of relief that Phoebe was approaching our family set-up with obvious joy. One fewer tripwire to negotiate at least.

Victor sat at the kitchen table with no more curiosity than as if he was waiting to be given a choice between fish and chips or curry for dinner.

I bustled about, making tea. I wondered briefly what people of other nationalities did when they were postponing their own moments of drama.

'Jo, come and sit down.'

I set the mugs on the table.

Patrick swallowed. Victor suddenly took on the alertness of a dog who'd scented a deer on the wind.

'Victor, I'm not quite sure how to say this.' And then Patrick started trembling and choked on his words. This man who never buckled, who marched forward through life scoffing at sentimental 'frippery' as he called it. Who carried great kindness in his heart but also great detachment. 'The thing is…' But no one could hear what the thing was because Patrick's words seemed to stick before dissolving into sobs.

Victor looked both mortified and terrified and Phoebe rushed over to Patrick and put her arm round his shoulder, 'Dad! Dad! It's all right. Mum, you tell him.'

And I had to. Right there and then. I thought about Ginny's letter, the confidence she'd shown in me and forced myself to take control. Somehow the words came to me, gracious and warm as though I'd finally given into the fact that families are complicated, complex entities and all we can do is cling on and hope that a couple of the stitches hold and something damaged and decrepit but still in one piece gets off at the other end of the ride. I reached over to Victor and held his hand. 'This might be a shock to you, love, but before Patrick married me, he had a relationship with your mum and you're actually his son.'

I decided to stick with the 'relationship' stretching of the truth and justify it as post-projecting a good example. It just sounded way too shabby to say, 'Your dad had a one-night stand with your mum.' I figured a bit of poetic licence was allowed.

And saying out loud those words, which had been sitting like a sore in my heart, refusing to respond to the antibiotic of reason, seemed to alleviate my own hurt. Despite everything, I registered a flash of pleasure at delivering news that might help Victor find a steady footing in the world again.

Victor sat there for a second, his eyes flicking from side-to-side as though it was some elaborate joke. He glanced at Patrick, then at Phoebe, who, bless her, looked as though she was going to implode with delight.

Victor blinked for a few seconds. 'Wow.' He pointed to himself. 'Blue eyes.' As though that fact alone should have flagged up his parentage long ago.

I forced myself on. 'It's a lot to take in. You're probably only just about beginning to process losing your mum. And now you've discovered a new dad.'

Phoebe burst in, 'And a sister!' and my heart rushed out a protective plea that Victor would embrace that idea out loud and in a way that would make Phoebe included in this new family dimension. She backtracked. 'Half-sister.'

He looked dazed but managed to say, 'That's cool. Really cool. A sister.' I loved him for not reiterating the half-sister, for emphasising the uniting rather than the dividing factor. And the accompanying look of pride on Phoebe's face.

Victor pinched the bridge of his nose. Patrick's mannerisms to a T, the slow measured response to life-changing information. I couldn't help thinking that if Ginny's DNA had been in charge of this particular aspect of his personality, there would have been a livelier soundtrack, probably The Gipsy Kings, or Freddie Mercury singing 'Bohemian Rhapsody', a leap onto the table for a bit of Scaramouche strutting.

I reached over to Patrick who was flapping his hand in front of his face, saying, 'Sorry, mate. Sorry, can't get my words out.'

Suddenly though, Victor's face broke into a smile so radiant, so like Ginny, that it was like one of those weird films where the actors are revived and recast years after their deaths.

At this, Patrick gathered himself, stood up and, just like they'd been doing it forever, they moved into an unashamed from-my-heart-to-yours hug. And then we were all cuddling and crying and Patrick was saying, 'I love my family, love it. I'm a lucky, lucky man,' as though we'd all been successfully excavated from the foundations of a building flattened by a tornado.

And in that glorious melee of disbelief from Victor, ownership from Phoebe – 'The rugby boys will have to invite me to their parties now' – and a maelstrom of gratitude from Patrick – 'Thanks, Jo, thank you. You're just so brilliant, I couldn't do this without you' – I felt a surge of love and compassion for this brave boy. The clanging bell of jealousy calling my attention to all the possible reasons to be insecure had withered down to a tinkling ring of concern, covered – but not yet smothered – by optimism.

Patrick raised his mug of tea. 'To Victor. To Phoebe. To Jo.'

I swallowed and lifted my mug. 'To Ginny. Thank you for our bonus son.'

CHAPTER TWENTY-SIX

Three months later, at the start of spring, we decided it was a fitting time to have a party to welcome Victor into the family officially. We were still finding our way, often falling down unexpected rabbit holes but there was at least a sense that we were all *trying*. Contrary to my expectations, Phoebe had kept up with her rugby and it had become the thing that she and Victor bonded over. And bless that boy for his generosity, he was free with his praise and advice and each time I saw my prickly daughter unfurl a little more. We were yet to be bowled over by a stratospheric surge in her grades but neither did I dread the phone ringing during the school day any more or feel the urge to riffle through her bedroom checking for a secret stash of drugs. After such a turbulent year, just like the snowdrops pushing through the soil, Phoebe was showing green shoots of maturity. She still flew off the handle, often shouted about us thinking the worst of her but calmed down more quickly and even apologised occasionally for being out of order. Victor had found a decent group of lads to hang out with, who seemed to accept Phoebe as part of the package whenever they bundled into our sitting room to watch sport. Being banished to the kitchen was a small price to pay for hearing their easy laughter bouncing around our home. From what Jasmine told me, Phoebe's camaraderie with this in-crowd had given her a boost among her peers and she certainly seemed more settled at school.

Phoebe, in turn, was helping Victor shape his slot in our family. Just occasionally he'd join in with her when she was teasing me and that little show of solidarity and confidence from him made my heart squeeze. And miss Ginny. I wished I could tell her that she didn't need to worry.

With everything starting to come into bloom in the village, it felt like the right time for the beginning of a new chapter. Despite my determination to look forwards, I still didn't want to invite Faye and Lee and Patrick agreed, saying, 'They can stay at home and watch re-runs of *The Black and White Minstrel Show*. Arseholes.'

Either I was more like Ginny than I realised or I'd somehow absorbed her attitudes through the ether. I'd always considered myself a non-faller-outer with people, limping along in unhealthy relationships, smoothing and straightening to avoid the embarrassment of facing facts: that the people I associated with weren't very nice – or were only nice if I accepted their behaviour without question. Ginny had always been a 'three strikes and you're out' sort of woman. She wasn't given to stand up rows but could also face down anyone who'd wronged her with 'I'm not sure that's something a real friend would do' without fidgeting or doing that pretend-forgive laugh I always did, which allowed someone to get away with being a shit. Late in life, as she was always urging me to do, I was becoming quite comfortable with stating a fact and letting the other person fiddle-fart around, trying to excuse themselves. And how liberating it was. Gloriously, arm-flingingly, bra-discardingly liberating.

So after a long half-term of Faye suddenly seeming to find something hilarious the second I was within earshot or shouting, 'Let's catch up very soon!' across the school car park to every random mother, caretaker and netball court spider, it was a surprise when she walked up to me and said, 'Can I have a word?'

'Sure.'

'I actually need to thank Patrick for telling me about Georgia's addiction to Adderall, among other things.' She looked at the ground. 'We've got her some help, you know, a counsellor.'

'I'm really pleased to hear that. I hope it helps her.' Friendly, warm with absolutely no interest in catching the olive branch.

Faye tried again, leaning forwards in an almost conspiratorial whisper. 'I gather it's common knowledge now that Victor is Patrick's son.'

'Is it?' And right there was my inner Ginny. That fantastically neutral tone of voice that ping-ponged back to the speaker the intent of their words.

'Well, I mean, lots of people seem to know about it.'

'Good. That's the way it should be.'

I was having to keep my nerve, not default to former Jo, the fixer of all social interaction. I was just weakening in my resolve when she said, 'He's actually quite a nice boy. He's been very kind to Georgia.'

I leaned in. 'She's really lucky to have him. He's gorgeous, generous-spirited and non-judgemental. *Actually* quite nice. Anyway, I must go.'

And I walked away, leaving her guppying in the car park, a small tinge of nostalgia for the good times we'd had together but mostly a strong rush of satisfaction that I had, as Ginny would say, discovered, before I wasted another ten years of my life, that she wasn't worth expending any energy on, *actually*.

Yet two days before we did our 'family extension' party at the local pub, Victor sidled into the kitchen. 'Jo, can I ask something?'

I stopped stirring my pasta sauce. 'Yep. Fire away,' I said, sending up a brief prayer for a 'Where are my rugby boots?' rather than an unforeseen drama. Though since the news filtered out that Patrick was Victor's dad, there'd been a flurry of people in the village making an obvious effort to distance themselves from any suggestion that they'd ever thought Victor had anything to do with drugs. I'd got much better at looking them in the eye and saying, 'Some people are so small-minded, aren't they? So depressing in this day and age.'

Phoebe was even more forthright, saying, 'That sounds racist' not just to my mum, but anyone she came across. She also put her stubbornness to good use by not feeling the need to nod understandingly when they blustered out an explanation. And one of the things I'd worried about so much – that she didn't care what anyone thought of her – had become a source of huge pride.

I put my wooden spoon down and smiled at Victor who was fidgeting about. He looked so like Ginny used to when she was trying to persuade me to go out when I was already in my pyjamas. 'Could you invite Georgia's parents to the party?'

'Faye and Lee?' We both knew I was buying myself time.

'It's just that I think they kind of realise they were a bit harsh on me and most of the village is coming. It's difficult for Georgia if we leave them out.'

'That would be a hugely generous gesture on your part.' It never ceased to amaze me how kind Victor was, when he could have been forgiven for lashing out at the world.

He smiled. 'Following your example, Jo.' He made a heart with his index fingers and thumbs. 'You've given me back a family.'

That was the thing with teenagers. I went through life thinking they had the emotional savvy of a walnut and then they had a little burst of brilliance that looked shockingly like wisdom. Or maturity at least.

For the first time since the funeral, I hugged him. Not the same as hugging Phoebe because I was acutely aware of body part positioning and of rounding my back so I didn't accidentally press my boobs into his chest. But there was comfort and warmth in the gesture and I found myself wanting to load him up with love, to fill in the crevasses of grief. In that brief embrace sat the knowledge I'd so often overlooked in my life: if I just stopped, put aside my big fat opinions about how a child should look/behave/speak, it was possible to learn so much from them, governed by instinct as they were.

'I'll talk to Patrick.' From being the bloke who'd usually taken the path of least resistance, I loved him for the ferocious way he'd defended our family, me included. What we'd lost in acquaintances who'd dared to comment unfavourably on our unusual circumstances, we'd gained in faith in each other. I'd even heard him describe me as the 'lynchpin that kept it all together', which seemed a bit excessive as I mainly felt I was blundering through, crossing my fingers for the best.

As I suspected, the tables had turned and Patrick, usually way more forgiving than me, shook his head. 'Jog on. Racist cow. I'm not watching Faye trough down sausage rolls I've paid for.'

I giggled. 'Would it make you feel better if I pay for her sausage rolls?'

He pulled me into his arms. 'Now you're going to tell me that we need to be the grown-ups?'

I leaned my head back so I could look at him. 'He doesn't often ask for much.' It was odd how Patrick not leaping to give his son what he wanted seemed to energise me to fight Victor's corner. Though to be fair, there hadn't been that many occasions when I'd felt he was favouring Victor over Phoebe. Even then, when I'd got off my high horse, I'd often had to accept that Patrick's focus on Victor was more around shared interests – which weights they lifted in the gym and high body count films – than specifically about a particular child.

He kissed me gently on the lips and murmured, 'As long as I don't have to speak to her. Or Lee.'

'Just a hello so we have the high moral ground. Otherwise we'll spend the whole evening knowing exactly where they are in the room and have to make the effort to ignore them. I don't want our special occasion to be taken up with thinking about them at all.'

Patrick stroked my cheek. 'When did you get to be so wise, Mrs Clark? Go on then. Tell Victor we'll open our doors to the enemy.'

CHAPTER TWENTY-SEVEN

Jasmine came to help me check the set-up in the pub. She'd brought armfuls of daffodils and tulips and a box of mismatched jugs. 'Daffs are from my garden. Bit early for the tulips, so Morrisons had to help out with those.'

'You must let me pay for them.'

Jasmine turned her head on one side. 'I bought them because you're my friend. So I will be hugely offended if you start scrabbling about for your pound coins. Thanks all the same.' Her big gappy grin brought spring sunshine into the room.

'Thank you.'

'Now, I've got Kai on board and some of the younger ones – I mean, no point in having a tribe if you don't put them to work. I don't want you worrying about which platter is the gluten-free and which one hasn't got I don't know what in it. I'll get my brood offering everything round so you can just enjoy yourself.'

Big parties where I was in the spotlight, albeit a joint spotlight, didn't usually have 'enjoy' as a subtitle, but Patrick had been very clear. 'We're not skulking about, hanging our heads and hoping people stop talking about the "Ooh, that boy was Patrick's son. Wonder what she thought of that. Fly on the wall…" What we're doing is celebrating, loud and proud, the addition to our family. Nothing will stop them all muttering behind their hands more quickly than us getting it right out there.'

I was glad I had Jasmine with me. Ninety per cent of me was polishing the fuck off finger for what everyone else thought, with a residual ten per cent of politician's wife mortification standing by her man after he'd been caught on a bondage website.

Jasmine laughed when I told her how I felt. 'Honestly, anyone who matters will be in awe of what you've done: managed to keep your little family together, hold down a job, deal with your best friend dying, take in her son, survive the hoo-ha about him being Patrick's, get Phoebe back on track – she did brilliantly in that rugby tournament last weekend. You've juggled it all and barely broken a sweat.'

'Um, that's a very positive picture you're painting there. Not quite the reality, but thank you.'

'No one's reality is perfect, despite what some of the people round here would have you believe.' She paused. 'You've kept your marriage together, which is a lot more than most.'

I did allow myself a little flash of pride at that. And I was also starting to make headway on accepting that Ginny had kept Victor a secret not to wound me but to *avoid* hurting me. Betrayal was no longer my default option when I thought of her. Missing her was, though.

Jasmine lined up some vases on the windowsill. 'You're so hard on yourself. When everyone gets here tonight, every time you doubt yourself, just have a look round the room and ask, which of the couples in this pub would be improved by being under a million times more stress than normal? Faye and Lee? Andrea and Rod? And look at me – just having children at all finished us off.' And she dipped her head as though she'd made her point. Which she had.

Her optimism reminded me of Ginny's mantra: 'Haters gonna hate. Our job is to love, love, love and look so happy while we're doing it, the hater will hate themselves.' I'd never be able to replace Ginny but Jasmine's friendship and view of the world did wonders for my confidence.

Patrick arrived with Phoebe and Victor, who were struggling to disguise their glee at a night of free drinks. I watched them together, Phoebe bossing Victor about, sorting the cuffs on his shirt, leaning up to whisper in his ear. And Victor, gentle with my daughter. Taking the mickey out of her, but in a way that built her up. I often heard him tease her, but there was always an underlying kindness with him, none of the stuff that passed for 'banter' that I heard her shrug off with her friends but carried a little shift of uncertainty in her voice signifying another hit to her fragile shell. Like Jasmine for me, Victor had shored up her self-esteem, lessening her need to draw attention to herself. She was still pinching tiny folds of skin on her stomach and folding over into an 'I'm so fat' before parties, but at least those occasions were interspersed with 'I think I look quite good in this.' She sometimes even badgered Victor to go for a run with her, which led to less time on her phone and, as far as I could see, a lot less agonising over who was doing what when.

Mum came in with Eileen from the post office. 'Ooh, new dress, Jo? Very colourful. You look a picture.'

I chose to channel Jasmine's positivity and assume that Mum was thinking of Monet's *Waterlilies* rather than Edvard Munch's *The Scream*, because red was well out of my comfort zone, but Phoebe had informed me that tonight of all nights I couldn't be a shrinking violet. 'We've got this, Mum. We're going to show everyone that we are proud of who we are and we can't do that if you're in some woolly grey sack.'

Even if Mum had been handing me a barbed compliment, I forgave her immediately when, later on, I overheard Eileen say, 'Strange that Jo's Patrick fancied a black woman. I wouldn't have thought he was the type.'

My mum seemed to double in size like a peacock spreading its tail. Phoebe had done an excellent job of picking her up on any un-PC comments over the last few months but I hadn't appreciated that she'd actually taken any notice. 'What type, Eileen, would he need to be for that? Look at that boy over there and tell me that his mother is any less—' She paused, waving her mozzarella and tomato on a stick while she looked for the right words, then burst out with, 'Any less anything than anyone, white, yellow, brown or bloody purple than anyone in this room!'

Eileen looked like she might choke on her celery. 'I was just saying—'

'Well, don't just say.'

I watched them sit in huffy silence for a few moments, before Mum said, 'Would you like a piece of pizza? If that's not too foreign for you?'

At which point, they both started to giggle and I had a reprieve from having to go to the next town to post my mum's parcels.

Whether everyone was here to support us or to rubberneck first-hand was immaterial. All that mattered was that we were a little warrior band, sometimes turning on each other but mainly battling forward united against the outside world.

I turned at the sound of my name. 'Cory! You made it.' I hadn't seen him since the fiasco of our last meeting but he'd phoned me several times since and had now adopted the irritating habit of announcing 'Family Liaison Services calling...' Because it was Cory, he got away with it. Goodness knows why.

He enveloped me in a huge hug. 'Get you in the red!' He gestured to his girlfriend. 'You remember Lulu?'

'Of course! How are you?'

'It's so lovely to see you again. You all look so happy.'

'We are.' As I said those words, I realised it was true, not just a façade I presented in public.

Lulu was so much warmer than I remembered, so enthusiastic. And so right for Cory, almost as though over time she'd conquered the necessary magic formula of kindness blended with not putting up with any of his stupid nonsense.

Cory was fizzing with that energy I recognised from the days when we'd all be slumped on the sofa after work and he'd roll in later than all of us, clutching a bottle of tequila, and somehow galvanise us all into doing shots and having a karaoke sing-off.

As soon as Lulu went to hang her coat up, I raised an eyebrow. 'What's the story?'

He grabbed my hand. 'I don't want to hijack your evening.'

'Hat time?'

'I love her. So yes.' He did a little embarrassed smile, as though it was alien to him to admit to any real feelings.

'Have you asked her?'

'Not yet. I'm nervous.'

I squeezed his hand. 'She won't be able to resist you. Who could turn down a bloke who has a signature dish of toad-in-the-hole and knows how to make the best gin and tonic?'

'She has seen me behave like a total dickhead, though.'

'Everyone has seen you behave like a dickhead, Cory. But we all still love you. Just keep the percentages on your side.'

He took a step back and said, 'You know what decided me, Jo?'

'What?'

'I've seen what shit you've gone through, what a struggle things have been and how you – and Patrick – but mainly you, let's be honest, have kept it together and been there for both kids. You didn't just throw your toys out of the pram, you hung in there. And I know I've always taken the piss out of you both for being square and steady, but I envy you.'

Cory. This man who historically defaulted to football and where he was going golfing whenever an uncomfortable emotion threatened to surface.

'You envy us? With, and I think I'm quoting, "our parochial little lives"?' I asked.

He nudged me. 'That's not fair. That's out of context. You were having a go at me for not settling down, telling me that in old age all I'd have to keep me company was the clap and Jim Beam.'

Lulu was approaching. Out of the corner of my mouth, I said, 'Let me know when I need to start growing a pineapple for my hat.' A great burst of joy spread through me. 'Delighted for you.'

He whispered. 'Can you believe that I actually want kids?'

I waved him away. 'In a minute, I'm going to call an ambulance. Catch you later.'

I beckoned to Patrick across the room. He came over and kissed me on the cheek. 'How are you doing?'

'I'm okay. Better than I thought.' I filled him in on what Cory had said about Lulu.

'Brave woman, that she is,' he said.

I could see he was delighted. 'Don't tell him I told you. He hasn't asked her yet.' I changed the subject, feeling a bit guilty for spoiling Cory's surprise. 'Phoebe and Victor seem quite the celebrities,' I said. They were holding court, surrounded by the rugby lads, Victor's friends from Cardiff, and girls clamouring for selfies with them. I was so glad his old friends had come, even if his granddad was too frail to travel. We'd agreed to visit him at Easter.

Patrick clinked his glass against mine. 'Thank you.'

Before we could have an extra little moment, the sort that in marriage you need to stop and admire like a butterfly on buddleia before something else needs your attention, Patrick nodded towards the door. 'Here come the Ku Klux Klan.' Faye and Lee with Andrea and Rod. Patrick grumbled. 'Amazing what a free glass of Blossom Hill can do to foster racial equality.'

'Victor wanted them here,' I said.

'It shouldn't be up to the eighteen-year-old to be the bigger person. Why does it fall to the boy with the least amount of life experience to set an example to the people with the most?'

'If we all followed that train of thought though, no one would ever learn anything from anyone.' I grabbed Patrick's hand and pulled him over towards them. A tiny jerk of resistance, then resignation. 'Evening, come in. Welcome to our family celebration. Grab a drink from one of our serving elves.'

Three of them bolted with relief towards Kai, who was passing with a tray of wine, but Rod hung back. 'Owe you an apology for the night of the accident. Got a bit heated without knowing the facts. All came out in the wash a bit later. Not my finest moment.'

Patrick looked like he was going to shake his hand, then changed his mind at the last minute. 'Thank you. Try not to be a racist idiot in the future.' And with that, he walked off, leaving me grimacing, watching the shock wash over Rod's face of receiving an insult rather than delivering one.

I stood there determined not to apologise for Patrick. Because he was right. It nearly killed me to suffocate my need to be liked. With a great surge of triumph, I managed to say, 'If someone had spoken to your son or daughter like that, you'd feel like Patrick too.'

Rod blinked in what – leaning on my new-found Jasmine-variety of optimism – I chose to see as agreement. Then I dashed to the loo before I let myself down by fawning around him apologetically to make up for speaking my mind.

When I got back, Patrick was dinging a spoon on a glass.

'Right, I'm going to keep this brief.' He paused and beckoned me over. He took my hand. 'So I know this party is a little unusual as not many people at our age get the incredible bonus of a new baby, especially one that sleeps through the night.'

I smiled at Phoebe and Victor, who had his arm round Georgia. They were all cringing but laughing in the way their age group did – perfectly happy to discuss the gories of who'd done what to whom at a party but anything vaguely connected to sex between their parents – such as a baby – and they practically needed smelling salts.

'But it's wonderful to be surprised in a good way at our age. We already had a daughter we simply could not be prouder of.'

Phoebe was doing an exaggerated 'Oh Dad' face but I could see she was pleased.

Patrick carried on. 'She's been brilliant at helping Victor adjust to living with our family and really generous-spirited. He, in turn, has been through such a difficult time but has amazed us all with his positive attitude and resilience. And who knew that he'd turn Phoebe into a demon on the rugby field! I'd like you to raise your glass to welcome Victor into our family, our lovely son.'

A murmur of 'Cheers' and 'Here's to Victor' went round the room. And right then, I understood Ginny completely – 'Focus on what matters now, not what happened then.'

I stepped forward. 'And I would like to make a toast to Ginny, Victor's mum. She was the best friend I could ever have wished for. She was a brilliant mum to Victor. I miss her.' I swallowed. 'Every day Victor reminds me of her and I am lucky to have the privilege of counting him as part of my family.'

I stopped, emotion clogging my chest. I raised my glass to unexpected applause and cheering. I caught Phoebe's eye and she blew me a kiss.

Patrick cleared his throat as though to release people to drinking and being merry, but my mother got to her feet. She was weaving about slightly, which didn't bode well. She'd obviously decided that the occasion merited a deviation from her 'one little brandy at Christmas' rule.

'When Jo said she was having her friend's boy come to live with them, I thought she was off her rocker. And I was just getting used to that idea when there was all that to-do about him being Patrick's son. But we've been so lucky to have him in our family, he's an absolute smasher. So if anyone here wants to gossip about us, well, please leave now before you drink any more wine that Patrick and Jo are paying for.' Mum waved her glass of sherry in the air.

Thankfully Patrick stepped forwards and guided her back into her seat before she started picking on specific guests to criticise. 'As always, I think the last, entirely accurate and diplomatic word has gone to my mother-in-law.'

And with that, all of Phoebe and Victor's friends erupted into a chorus of 'Simply The Best'.

Mum wasn't exactly in the running for community relations officer. But she had nailed my sentiments with startling accuracy and delivered them in the sort of style Ginny would have applauded. And yes, we were lucky.

A LETTER FROM KERRY

Dear Reader,

I want to say a huge thank you for choosing to read *Another Woman's Child*. If you did enjoy it, and want to keep up to date with all my latest releases, just sign up at the following link. Your email address will never be shared and you can unsubscribe at any time.

www.bookouture.com/kerry-fisher

One of the best things about being an author is that real life is always delivering little bursts of inspiration even in the most mundane of circumstances. The idea for this book has been whirling in and out for a long time, though I haven't been able to make a firm shape out of the elusive mist until now.

The first inkling arrived when we were writing our wills and considering guardianship of our (then) young children. It set me thinking about what an incredible upheaval it would be for anyone welcoming a bereaved child into their own family and how it was probable that, in a couple, there might be a difference of opinion and willingness. As always in my books, I love complex family dynamics so I looked at ways to make the stakes very high all round.

I don't know whether I led a very sheltered life or was lucky with the friends I had, but drugs never featured at parties when I was a teenager – unless I was so naïve I didn't notice. I wanted to explore the challenges of keeping children safe when their knowledge about the world outstrips – and outwits – that of their parents. I'm always interested in the challenges of being a parent and how some children seem to sail through their teenage years and others present all sorts of challenges. Parents often feel ill-equipped to deal with reckless and illegal behaviour – and become quite isolated as they try to help their child against a backdrop of other people's disapproval at a time when they most need support.

I also wanted to look at the natural tension that occurs as children start to lead independent lives and their peer group becomes all important. It's such a precarious and frustrating balance for parents: allowing children enough freedom to make their own mistakes while ensuring that they stay out of danger. Sometimes it feels as though every interaction is one long nagging session, impregnated with a sense of being completely irrelevant! I've frequently stood on the doorstep shouting, 'Drive safely/Stay with your friends/ Be sensible', hoping desperately that some words of wisdom have sunk in and that, when push comes to shove, they'll make good choices. However, I'm also fascinated by the wisdom of young people – time and again, I meet teenagers with such sound views about the world that I'm in awe of the fact that they've learnt so much in so few years.

Most of all, I wanted to write about casual racism, the sort that is so pervasive in daily life that people barely realise they're causing offence and feel attacked when challenged. Alongside that, I wanted to examine why people find it so hard to make a stand, the awkward trade-offs between social convenience and calling out prejudice.

I say this every time, but one of the biggest privileges of my job is receiving messages from people who've enjoyed my books. Sometimes, my novels have prompted readers to share their own very personal stories with me. The unflinching honesty of some of these messages that you entrust me with is humbling. Thank you.

I hope you loved *Another Woman's Child* and would be very grateful if you could write a review if you did. I'd love to hear what you think, and it makes a real difference to helping new readers to discover one of my books for the first time.

I love hearing from my readers – you can get in touch on my Facebook page, through Twitter, or my website. Whenever I hear from readers, I am reminded why I love my job – pure motivational gold!

Thank you so much for reading,
Kerry Fisher

kerryfisherauthor

@KerryFSwayne

www.kerryfisherauthor.com

ACKNOWLEDGEMENTS

I am very lucky in my professional life. My editor, Jenny Geras, is a joy to work with – I have complete faith in her judgement and know that my books are in the safest, most meticulous hands. And from the edits onwards, the whole Bookouture team is professional, detail-driven and enthusiastic – working their magic to make the books the best they can possibly be. And such kind people. Goodness knows, the world needs as much of that as possible. Special thanks to the publicity team – Kim, Noelle and Sarah – for working so hard to get our books to as many readers as possible. This is long overdue because I've worked with her a lot but a big shout out to Jade Craddock, my eagle-eyed copy editor – she does a brilliant job.

This is my eighth novel and ninth book overall. I first sat opposite my agent, Clare Wallace, in 2013, and heard the wonderful words 'I'd like to offer representation'. I was delighted, of course, but had no idea back then just how much the publishing gods had smiled upon me. I do now. It's been a real gift to have someone as smart, committed and thoroughly decent as Clare champion me. Thanks, too, to the rights team at Darley Anderson – Mary, Kristina, Georgia and Chloe – who are brilliant at getting my books out into the wider world.

It's been a very busy year workwise, and finishing the book while in lockdown presented a new set of challenges, so I'm grateful to my family for (mainly!) doing their best not to disturb me. In particular, I owe a huge thank you to my daughter, Michaela, for rescuing me from a technology meltdown more than once.

I'm very grateful to author Jacqui Rose for reading the manuscript from a race sensitivity point of view. Her observations have been invaluable. As well as the many articles I read to research casual racism, I also read *The Clapback* by Elijah Lawal, which helped me consider a lot of aspects that hadn't occurred to me. I'm still learning and trying to educate myself so thank you.

Also, I appreciate everyone on my author Facebook page who took the time to respond to my queries about how teenagers get hold of drugs and what happens when they shoplift. Your input was really helpful and terrifying! Thanks also to Jayne Puttman, who kindly contacted me about one of my other books and in the course of our discussion said that her dad had told her to meet each day 'with fierce determination'. Not only have I borrowed her dad's wisdom for this novel, but I try to live by it.

Finally – a huge thank you to the bloggers and readers who buy, review and recommend my books – and especially anyone who takes the time to contact me personally. Those messages make my day.

Made in the USA
Coppell, TX
03 February 2021

49578344R00162